"Me, model?" and handed him back his card. "Once I take this wrap off, you'll want this back."

Jason just stared at her for a moment. "You have *got* to be kidding," he murmured, totally taken aback and refusing the offered business card. "You never . . . I mean . . . you don't see . . ." He was at a loss and simply watched her take back the card and stare at it, as though not knowing where to shift her gaze.

"I don't doubt you're good, but I don't let people take pictures of me." She looked up, with a sad smile; then she turned away.

"I'm not a photog. I work in acrylic, oils, charcoal . . . and I'd love to do you—"

She turned around quickly, eyes wide.

"I mean, you know, on canvas . . . paint you. I didn't mean . . ." He started laughing. "Sister, no disrespect. That really didn't come out right." He held up his hands before his chest and was glad that she laughed.

"I was gonna say, dayum, bro," she said, chuckling hard.

"No, no, no, no, no, for real. I have a gallery down on South Street and work locally from my studio. I wasn't trying to be smart. You're gorgeous, and I'd love to capture you in some work I'm doing for the Rhythm and Blues Fest."

"I'll think about it," she said, with a smile, stepping up to finally get waited on. "But I don't have to get naked, or anything, right?"

Her voice was teasing, and he couldn't resist.

"Not unless you want to."

Books by Leslie Esdaile

The Series:

Betrayal of the Trust
Blind Trust
Shattered Trust
No Trust

And . . .

Keepin' It Real
Take Me There
Better Than

Published by Kensington Publishing Corporation

Better Than

Leslie Esdaile

Kensington Publishing Corp.

http://www.kensingtonbooks.com

DAFINA BOOKS are published by

Kensington Publishing Corp.
850 Third Avenue
New York, NY 10022

All Kensington Titles, Imprints, and Distributed Lines are available at special quantity discounts for bulk purchases for sales promotions, premiums, fund-raising, and educational or institutional use. Special book excerpts or customized printings can also be created to fit specific needs. For details, write or phone the office of the Kensington special sales manager: Kensington Publishing Corp., 850 Third Avenue, New York, NY 10022, attn: Special Sales Department, Phone: 1-800-221-2647.

Dafina and the Dafina logo Reg. U.S. Pat. & TM Off.

ISBN-13: 978-0-7582-1330-3
ISBN-10: 0-7582-1330-1

First mass market printing: June 2008

10 9 8 7 6 5 4 3 2 1

Printed in the United States of America

This book is dedicated to my daughter, Helena.
May she always know that she deserves Better Than.

Acknowledgments

Special thanks go to my agent, Manie Barron, who is "better than" them all (BIG SMILE), and to the Kensington family, who was there at the beginning, encouraging me to get better all along the way. But I have to give my most serious recognition to the readers who stuck by me all those years, the people who love each and every romance, hung through my chills and spills thrillers, and even tried to go down the scary path of paranormals with me. You folks are indeed the best! THANK YOU for supporting me while I stretch, grow, try different things, and create. You are <u>better than!</u>

Chapter 1

She was looking for a man who was better than . . . better than what she'd had before, better than all the nonsense she'd dealt with up till now. Oh, hell yeah, she needed a better than man!

Deborah Lee Jackson stood at her small stereo, with paperwork in one hand and her third glass of wine in the other, and pushed the REPEAT button so that Terrell Carter's soft, crooning ballad "Better Than" could make it all right, over and over again. She sniffed back the tears that had already started streaming as she walked back to the sofa to flop down on it.

"Preach!" she shouted at the song's crescendo, waving her divorce papers and then throwing them on the coffee table. They had the nerve to come right after Christmas, just like a water department shutoff notice might. She took a deep sip of her wine and closed her eyes, feeling every chord in the music reach down into her soul. "That's right. Treat her better than, brother," she murmured out loud to no one in particular. "Every woman deserves that."

As silent tears filled her eyes, a quiet prayer entered her heart: Lord, let somebody come into her life and treat her better than her ex-husband had.

Only married for two short years, and the man was in the streets with another woman, drinking and who knew what else, before the ink had dried on the marriage license. Maybe her ex had never even left the streets or the women he was running around with. This couldn't be all there was to life, could it? She was twenty-five, she barely made ends meet in a tiny little apartment, and she worked for the water revenue department, sending shutoff notices to people who were no different than her.

One thing was for sure: this was definitely no way to spend New Year's Eve . . . alone, drinking wine, playing sad love songs, crying. Deborah leaned forward and wiped her face with both hands, sloshing her wine. She should have listened to her girls and gone with them to the club. But after a long, protracted battle over the tiny town house that had been her marital home, it had taken everything in her and every dime she had to move into the apartment she was in now.

Admittedly, she had been on a mission to start anew before January rolled around. So, she'd pushed like a madwoman to get settled between Christmas and New Year's, and had taken a place all the way across town, leaving Germantown behind. She figured being in University City, close to a lot of colleges, would put her that much closer to her goal of going back to school, finishing her degree, and getting herself together. But what she hadn't figured on was the fact that all the students would be going home for the holidays, so it would be dead in Philly, where she lived. Desolate, empty, lonely, not what she'd expected. She'd been hoping that the neighborhood liveliness would stave off the blues. Stupid on her part.

Feeling another pang of regret, she stood and went to the stereo to release the CD and move forward to the next cut, just like she had to. The same song was getting on her nerves. "Thick Girls" came on next, and she cringed inwardly. Yeah, she was a thick girl. That was something else that had to go on her New Year's resolution list—and another reason why she wasn't trying to go to the club.

This New Year's she didn't want to feel like an Amazon as she stood next to her petite girlfriends. She was five feet eight in her stocking feet, and when you added heels and factored in her D cup breasts and wide behind, and her not exactly flat stomach, it meant she'd just be the third wheel, holding their purses while they danced. She'd been there, seen it, and dealt with it for years. Not this year. She was going to change everything.

She went over to the mirror that hung above the dinette set. Once she got her finances together, she would buy some nails, and until then, she would do her own eyebrows and feet. Maybe she'd do a private beauty makeover tonight to help herself feel better. But she needed to do something with her style that was dramatic. Dye her hair blond? Naaaah. Too extreme.

Well, maybe she wouldn't cut her hair herself, either—even though she was feeling radical tonight. It was the only good thing she had gotten from the family gene pool, as far as she was concerned. Long, thick, nearly jet-black hair, which hung just below her shoulders, and smooth walnut skin. Her black-Cherokee grandmother from North Carolina had given her hair that rivaled a weave. Deborah chuckled sadly and set down her wine. She had to make a change, though. Twists? Locks? Braids? Something!

But why couldn't she have gotten her momma's small feet and petite frame, rather than her father's athletic build? Then again, why would her mother be expected to give any more than she'd already given, after dying trying to have her? God rest her mother's soul in peace. No wonder her career military father

was always on her case; as far as he was concerned—
even though he'd never actually come out and said
it—she was the reason he'd lost the love of his life.

She was the cause of his unhappiness and therefore
the recipient of his lifelong criticism, which he hurled
her way. Too chunky, not good enough in school,
undisciplined, too fast, too this or that. No matter
how hard she'd tried, and she'd tried *so hard* to please
him, he just didn't know. He never had to say it; the
vibes were thick in the air and always had been.
Moving from Philly to Jersey, to North Carolina, to
Virginia, and then finally coming back to live with her
grandmother, she'd been on a roller coaster of unset-
tling moves all her life. Nana had been the only one
to save her from that, and now she was gone, too. So
where was home?

Deborah looked away from the mirror and down at
her left hand, which no longer sported the tiny eighth
of a karat diamond chip, which had once told the
world someone wanted her. At least Momma didn't
have to witness her divorce or be there when she'd
lost the baby. The only thing keeping her together
was the hope that her mother was in heaven, taking
care of her unborn child.

Blinking up at the ceiling to fight what was about to
become a terrible solo pity party, Deborah sucked in a
deep breath and began sorting bills out of the junk mail
before the walls closed in on her. *Do something construc-
tive,* she told herself. The bright flyer from the University Arts Center made her sit down at the table. This was
a good place to begin her self-improvement campaign.

Their new season brochure had all kinds of great
stuff for a person on a budget and for someone like
her, who just wanted to try things out before really
committing. The best part of all was that they were
right down the block—between Forty-second and
Forty-third streets—so the winter hawk wouldn't be

too much of a factor, nor would snow. Maybe she could take one of their evening classes right after work. She could just get off the 42 bus at their corner; SEPTA would practically drop her at their front door.

Kickboxing, yoga, ballroom dancing, salsa, aikido, ceramics, painting, sculpting, ballet . . . whew! Where to begin? This was the same problem she'd had in college: so many choices, so many things she liked to do. But then she'd met her husband, and somehow, she never got to find herself.

For a moment she thought of what her father had said when she'd entered Temple University. He might as well have been barking at one of his privates on a military base when he'd said, "Do something sensible, Deb. Take business so you can get a job when you get out. College is too expensive to be playing." She looked at the brochure. But he was in Arlington, Virginia; she was grown; and she didn't feel like doing something sensible right now.

Sensible had plunged her into a marriage with a military man . . . just because she'd gotten pregnant before she was ready and then developed gestational hypertension. She'd faked it, being strong on the outside even though she was fragile as glass on the inside. Sensible had had her dropping out of college to take a dead-end job so she could move around with him, going wherever he was stationed. Sensible had made her try to turn a blind eye to indignities in order to save the marriage, which had failed before it had even got started. Supersister. She was hanging up the cape and turning in her superhero spandex. New year, new day. As soon as that arts center opened, she'd be on a self-improvement mission.

Yoga. She would take yoga. Very illogical for a sister who wanted to drop half a ton. So? The brochure said it helped you find serenity. Oh yeah, that was a necessary thing right through here. Okay, she could try to bend herself into a pretzel for inner peace. And, yeah, maybe an art class, to find her inner child.

She started laughing. She had to be tipsy. Then again, she could possibly take a holistic cooking class as a part of their all-natural weight management program . . . uh-huh, to help a sister find her inner diva the natural way. Deborah checked off another box. Uh-huh, and this aikido was an opportunity to learn how to whup somebody's behind who was messing with her . . . yeah . . . to let out her inner warrior woman and work out her frustrations. Or maybe she should try kickboxing, Tae Bo. Yep. This was a complete self-help overhaul, major reconstruction.

Deborah pushed her chair away from the table, stood, weaved, walked to the sofa, and flopped down to watch the ball drop.

His best friend was the bane of his existence. He loved Wil like a brother, but Wil got on his last nerve. And yet, somehow, he could never say no to Wil's crazy ideas.

"I'm an artist, man. I don't do teaching classes and all that conformity crap. You know me. I roll solo," Jason said, as he wiped his hands on his paint-splattered jeans.

"Aw . . . c'mon, dude," Wil whined, leaning against the door frame, with a thud, and making his topknot of dreadlocks spill every which way. "This could be me big break on the jazz tour. London, dude? Be serious. But I have to have a way to pay my rent when I come home. You'll be kicking me to the curb and out of your third-floor apartment if I don't have me ends together. If I blow off the University Arts Center, then they'll give me post to someone else for the season, then maybe forever, if they think I'm shaky."

"You *are* shaky, man," Jason said, smiling despite his resolve to remain peeved. He turned back to the painting he'd been working on. Wil was not going to do that raggedy London cockney on him and get him to budge. Wil always did that, changed voices, trying to make him laugh. This time, it wasn't gonna work!

"Don't be like that, man. It's only six weeks."

"You're disturbing my peace and have invaded my no-fly zone, bringing drama into my studio. *Plus*, let me get this right. I'm supposed to work for *you*, do *your* job, which covers *your* rent, mind you, rent you're supposed to pay *me*? Tell me. What's wrong with this picture?" Jason shook his head.

"Dude . . . six little weeks. All you gotta do is teach Art 101 and maybe an aikido class, and you keep the money. I just need you to hold my position open for me so nobody else can jack it while I'm gone."

"Wait," Jason said, putting down his brushes. "You said art. Now it's aikido, too?"

"Aw, mon, no worries. You can work it. Six feet three, got da body the ladies would die for, with that Hershey's chocolate look they love, and serving that deep, mysterious artist vibe . . . Even your ornery ass might get *lucky*."

"Man, stop playin', okay. I'm not feeling teaching aikido on top of everything else." Jason frowned when his friend started laughing. Now Wil was working on him in a thick Jamaican accent. He needed to stop. Jason pressed on. "And for the record, I don't need to get *lucky*. Not over there, with a bunch of professors' bored wives and too-young and too-silly freshmen coeds who are out trying to experience 'the hood'," he added, making exaggerated quotation marks in the air with his fingers.

"Hey, I figured after your self-imposed dry spell for the love of art, you might be appreciative. A brother could get paid and laid—"

"You ain't selling this class very well, man. One art class. That's it."

Wil groaned. "C'mon, dude. You choose. All you gotta do is say you'll teach some form of martial arts . . . something you've been practicing for years and have reached instructor's level in. Or, like yoga. Whatever, dude. I know it's no issue, 'cause you're built Ford tough, you can handle a beginner class, and me and you have been going to the dojo for years. Twice a week. The art is like two nights, and uh—"

"Hold it. That's almost like a full-time job!" Aghast at the concept, Jason walked away from his easel. "You're killing me, brother. Aw, hell naw! You know how long I worked to be able to be *free?*"

"No, no, no, man, it's not like a real nine-to-five . . . It's an hour and a half—"

"Four nights a week!" Jason raked his Afro, accidentally getting paint in it.

Wil smiled and looked up at Jason's now multicolored hair. "So you gonna do it, brother?"

"Yeah," Jason muttered.

"Thanks, dude!" Wil pushed off the wall by the door, which he'd been leaning against, and hugged Jason hard.

"Get off me. You ain't right, man, and you know it."

"I love you, too, man. Ciao!"

Disgusted, Jason watched his friend walk away, smiling. "Holla at me when you get to London," he called after his too-jubilant friend.

The predicament Wil had put him in was messed up. How was he gonna be a real friend to somebody who'd been his boy since high school and not hook him up? Wil knew that. Damn! But it irked him to no end. Getting free of his deceased parents' bourgeois notions of success had been a long and arduous process. Having three very successful siblings, by their definition, didn't help. This just wasn't right, and to drop this bomb on him on the way out the door on New Year's Eve was too wrong. Now his January solitude and part of his February underground mode, when he should have been hunkered down, working, would be interrupted.

Worse yet, he had to keep this stint for Wil on the DL. If his family found out he was working a gig like this, they'd make assumptions and try to get into his business. They'd start the whole, "Why don't you teach at the university or go back for your doctorate so you can get tenured?" crap. He didn't wanna hear it. He was an artist, not a professor.

In their minds, he was their parents' oops baby, his mother's menopause child, the one who couldn't get it together. But just because his brother and sisters had practically raised him, with his grandmother, didn't give them the license to tell him how to run his life. What did they know? Their health sucked, just like his parents' health had—which was why they'd died young. Heath was the foundation of life, not acquiring material crap. His brother and sisters had about as much self-discipline as he had in his little finger; ate whatever they wanted, whenever, poisoning their bodies with toxins; and had no serious regimen of exercise, like his martial arts. But they wanted to tell him how to live? Never.

Jason stared at the vacancy in the doorway his friend had left. Wil was seriously dancing on the edge of their friendship with this request. Walking through the studio slowly, he began picking up stray brushes. So what if his forty-seven-year-old brother was an attorney; his next eldest sibling, his snooty, forty-five-year-old sister, had settled into a comfortable life and was a head nurse at the Hospital of the University of Pennsylvania; and his other sister was blowing up New York at forty-three, as an advertising exec?

All the drama, too, over Grandma giving him the house at Thirty-fifth and Baring was bunk. He'd taken what they didn't want back in the day—a house in the badlands that had been fortuitously regentrified and was now worth a mint. They'd turned their noses up at what was then considered part of Mantua, but was now dubbed Powellton Village, and he couldn't have sand-blasted them out of their parents' old neighborhood in West Mount Airy. It wasn't his fault that he was the only one who had spent significant time with Nana, that they hadn't had time or interest. He was not getting sucked into the job rat race. Just like he wasn't ready to commit to teaching at one of the area universities, he didn't want to teach at a local rec center—or whatever the hell it was that Wil had gotten him trapped in!

Jason grabbed a rag and wiped damp paint from his hands, watching the colors run together on the fabric. His brother and sisters all had at least a decade on him. He was thirty and self-employed. Making it from his rents, gallery exhibitions, and private clients was no small feat in his profession. He just hated that no one took his work as seriously as the more traditional career paths, not even his friend Wil, who, as an artist himself, should know better. Just because he worked from home, in his studio, didn't mean he had free time to burn. It took discipline, self-discipline, to do this.

He had to let it go. Jason strode across his studio, a slow-burning anger taking hold. Getting coerced into a semi-job was not his idea of how to begin the New Year. Bad karma.

Walking over to the large double sink, he began rinsing out his brushes. His concentration was shot for the evening. This was just what he didn't need, something messing with his mind and renting space in his head. For this same reason, he'd sworn off women—a professional distraction. He tried to think of the positives; he'd stay in shape by teaching. Then again, no, he wouldn't. These would be beginners classes!

Chapter 2

January in Philly was always gray. Gunmetal gray. Depressing, if one let it be . . . especially when the holiday fell on a Monday, thrusting one back to work on a Tuesday. She hadn't been ready to go back, but then again, admittedly, if the Monday holiday had been six months long, she still wouldn't have been ready to go back. She was just glad that she'd made it through the first four days of the New Year and could claim Saturday as her own once again.

Overwhelmed with a spectrum of new choices, Deborah stood in the rear of Campus Herbals, clutching her instruction sheet from her naturopathic cooking class, which would meet one evening per week, starting next week. Chickweed for burning fat, Vitamin C, recommended as a supplement . . . What the heck was Bragg Liquid Aminos?

The small, brightly lit store was crowded. It seemed as though everyone was on the same mission. New Year's resolutions abounded. Everybody was trying to kick bad habits, reaffirm good ones that had gone by the by, clean up, and clean out. She sighed. The folks behind the counter moved in the very calm, unhurried pace of the enlightened, but a sister had a schedule of errands to keep. If this is what yoga did to you, then she was going to reconsider her class choice!

Trying to stay in a harmonious frame of mind, in keeping with the sign on the window, which read, CHECK YOUR BAD VIBES AT THE DOOR, Deborah summoned patience. The one thing that her military dad didn't allow was patience with inefficiency.

Why did they have to have these long ass conversations about world politics and religion while pulling bottles of herbs and supplements off the shelf? Was she the only one in the joint that had something else to do today? she wondered as she watched patrons swathed in tie-dyed and natural fabrics leisurely banter with the store staff—all of whom seemed in no particular hurry. When the eldest staff member behind the counter started touching a woman's face, then neck, while doing funny things in the air with the fingers of his other hand, Deborah just gaped, hang-jawed.

Cold air repeatedly nipped her as customers came and left. She just hugged her burnt orange mohair wrap around her tighter, staring.

"What the heck . . . ?" she finally murmured as the eldest staff member began pulling different herbs off the shelf.

"Kinesiology," a deep voice behind her said, the register so low and sensual that it made her stomach do flip-flops.

She turned, opened her mouth, and then shut it, looking up into the face of a six-foot plus, Afro-wearing black king in a paint-splattered, olive-hued army fatigue jacket, with a wide, fluorescent white smile. He was chewing on a stick. *Lawdy have mercy!*

"Huh?" It was the first thing that her mind could get to her vocal cords, and it came out before her intellect could filter it.

"You've never seen an herbal diagnosis?" the unnamed vision of fine said, smiling wider. "That's why everybody hangs out and waits. Takes a while, but they don't let you walk out of here with a bunch of junk you don't need." He motioned toward the shelves with his handsome square jaw. "You can spend a mint in here, and most places, the whole herbal thing is a racket, but not here. The brothers and sisters in here are righteous and only sell you what you need . . . so folks wait." He shrugged and allowed his eyes to hunt the shelves.

"Oh," she said quietly. "It's my first time . . . I didn't know."

Jason just nodded. He had to. He hadn't meant to start a whole long dialogue with the sister in the store, but she looked so much like a brown version of Phyllis Hyman that he'd gotten stupid and had taken a risk. He kept his eyes roving the shelves, half forgetting what he'd come in to get. Damn his older siblings for making him appreciate what they called the classics. He'd fallen in love with Phyllis as an adolescent. One show's worth of her voluptuous, Amazon build; deep, sensual, sultry voice; and full features, thicket of dark hair, and smoky eyes had turned him on. Then the poor woman had died. Now what could have been her twin sister was standing in one of his favorite haunts, with that same husky register in her voice.

"It's all good," he said after a moment, trying to endure the store's traditional, leisurely pattern of service. He had to stop talking to this sister, even though that was what people came to the store to do—commune, chat, hang out, and wait for Doc to evaluate their needs. Still, he was trying to stay focused. The last relationship he was in had messed up his head and jacked up his inner vision, and with a major project in front of him for the Rhythm and Blues Fest headquarters, he couldn't even consider something like that right now.

"Can I ask a dumb question?" she said, her voice flowing over his senses like liquid silk.

"Yeah, sis, no problem," he said in a deeper octave than he'd intended. *Damn,* she was fine.

She smiled, and it made him swallow hard. She had the

mouth of a goddess . . . lush, full, just like her breasts . . . The burnt orange mohair draped around her was the perfect color for her flawless dark walnut skin, and the little cap of the same heavy yarn didn't hide a thicket of natural hair, which hung in two huge braids down to her shoulders. But it was her dark, expressive, almond-shaped eyes and the smile that reached them as she searched his face that really did him in.

He waited expectantly as she shyly glanced away. He had to remember to breathe. She smelled like cocoa butter and a musky perfume. He had to paint this woman, put her down on canvas the way she'd just etched herself into his mind.

"You're gonna think I'm a complete idiot, but what's kin-uh-something . . . the word you said before?"

Her question pulled him out of his trance. "Kinesi-ology?"

She nodded, with a wide grin. "Yeah, that."

He found himself leaning against the counter. Suddenly, the army fatigue jacket and heavy cable-knit sweater he was wearing felt too warm as he stared at her. "It's a metaphysical practice or method of determining if something is positive or negative for you. Anybody can do it."

She gazed up at him with the most serene and open look he'd ever witnessed. "For real? Like . . . I could do it?" She glanced away and looked at the herbalist, who was working behind the counter on the next customer. "Is that what he's doing?"

For a moment his voice got lodged in his throat. Two years of celibacy were uncoiling in his groin at the most inopportune time, and when she'd withdrawn her gaze, it had felt like as sharp a loss as when the door opened, letting in the hawk. "Yeah."

"Oh, that's deep!" she said in a quiet rush that ran all through him. "So, the guy behind the counter hands the customer a bottle to hold, touches her, does that thing with his fingers, and then either accepts it or puts it back on the shelf?"

Jason only nodded, the very unexpected erection making it hard to think. "Uh-huh," he said quietly. "He's making a circuit with his fingers. If the answer is positive, it's hard to separate one's fingers, if it's negative, then they break apart easy."

"Show me how to do it," she said, laughing and taking off her gloves and abandoning them with her papers on the counter. She turned her palms up to him, with a bright smile.

Almost afraid to touch her graceful hands, he studied her long, slender fingers as her warm palms coated his. "Wow . . ." He hadn't meant to say it, but it had slipped out. "They're so soft." His mind instantly flexed to places it didn't need to go; he was wondering if her hands were this soft, what the other very delectable parts of her might feel like. He was just glad his jacket hit mid-thigh.

She looked away, seeming embarrassed. "Excuse my raggedy nails. I didn't have time to—"

"I like a sister with natural nails. I hate acrylic." He wanted to kick himself. What was he saying! This sister didn't ask him all of that. Besides, he was supposed to be showing her kinesiology, not vibing on how her hands would feel running across his body. "It's better for the whole attunement to the natural," he said, making up some BS to cover for the out-of-line comment.

"Oh . . . ," she said.

He'd watched the way her kissable lips had made a small circle when she'd said, "Oh," and he began subtly sipping air through his mouth. "Okay, here's how you do it. Very simple." He turned her hands over, wanting to caress them longer, but couldn't come up with a way to legitimately do that. "Make two circles, thumb to first finger. Loop them together, the right inside the left. You are right-handed?"

She nodded, with a wide grin, doing as he'd asked, excitement making her face glow.

"Okay, then . . . Ask a yes-or-no question."

"Like what?" she said, with a slight giggle.

He stared at her. What he was about to do was so bogus, but he couldn't help it. "What's your name?" He had to pull it together. He'd practically breathed out the question.

"Deborah," she said, looking up.

"Deborah," he repeated, unable to take his eyes from hers for a second. "All right, pretty Deborah. Ask yourself if your name is Sue, and try to pull your fingers apart."

She cocked an eyebrow. "Okay. Am I Sue?" She let him gently guide her wrists and then looked up at him again when her fingers quickly slipped apart and became unlocked, breaking the small circle she'd made with her left hand.

"Okay," he said, letting her wrists go. "Now ask yourself your real name."

"Am I Deborah?" She tugged gently and then let out a little squeal. "Oh, look. They didn't come apart!"

"Yup," he said, nodding. "This is how you can speak to your own inner voice, make decisions, and get knowledge about directions to take without having to ask other people. Your own inner self already knows what's best."

"Okay," she said, holding up her hands. "That is deep. Like, I just pray, leave it with God, and go on about my business."

"Yeah, well, like my grandmother used to say, the Lord helps those who help themselves." He almost walked out of the store. He could not believe his rap was so old and dusty, or that he wanted to get with this sister so badly that he was pulling out grandma parables just to keep the woman talking to him! But as her expression melted right before his eyes, he knew he wasn't above rapping metaphysics, the church, art, old folk wisdom, whatever he had to in order to keep pretty Deborah talking to him.

"Wow . . . ," she whispered. "My nana used to say that, too." She looked down and began playing with her fingers, making little circles and he could tell, asking quiet, internal questions, and then laughing as her fingers either remained locked or broke apart. "This is amazing . . . Thank you. What's your name, in case we bump into each other in here again?"

"Jason." He fished in his jacket pocket, hoping she'd take his information, really praying she would. He gave her his studio card. "Have you ever sat for an artist, ever modeled?" Now he *knew* it was time to go—that was the oldest line in the book—and this sister deserved so much more than a corny line.

"You have *got* to be kidding!" she said, laughing.

He wanted to die. "Naw . . . it's just something I sorta do, so . . ." He shrugged and looked away, wondering why the store's staff was so damned slow!

"No, I mean, me, model?" Deborah shook her head and handed him his card. "Once I take this wrap off, you'll want this back."

Jason just stared at her for a moment. "You have *got* to be kidding," he murmured, totally taken aback and refusing the offered business card. "You never . . . I mean . . . you don't see . . ." He was at a loss and simply watched her take back the card and stare at it, as though not knowing where to shift her gaze.

"I don't doubt you're good, but I don't let people take pictures of me." She looked up, with a sad smile; then she turned away.

"I'm not a photog. I work in acrylic, oils, charcoal . . . and I'd love to do you—"

She turned around quickly, eyes wide.

"I mean, you know, on canvas . . . paint you. I didn't mean . . ." He started laughing. "Sister, no disrespect. That really didn't come out right." He held up his hands before his chest and was glad that she laughed.

"I was gonna say, dayum, bro," she said, chuckling hard.

"No, no, no, no, no, for real. I have a gallery down on South Street and work locally from my studio. I wasn't trying to be smart. You're gorgeous, and I'd love to capture you in some work I'm doing for the Rhythm and Blues Fest."

"I'll think about it," she said, with a smile, stepping up to finally get waited on. "But I don't have to get naked, or anything right?"

Her voice was teasing, and he couldn't resist.

"Not unless you want to."

She slid the card into her large mesh satchel. "Uh-huh . . . okay, Jason the artist. I'll have to do my fingers and see how I feel when I'm done." She covered her mouth quickly. "No! That didn't come out right. You know what I mean!"

"Uh-huh," he said, laughing and rubbing his chin. "But a brother could process that in *so* many ways."

Jason stood back and watched her as a rosy hue splashed her cheeks. It was like watching the pink palette of dawn lift the darker hue of night. She continued to laugh to herself as she was waited on, thoroughly captivating the store owner behind the counter. Pretty Deborah, with a behind that was making him act stupid. Gorgeous Deborah, with legs probably longer than his. Damn, the sister was built. Standing behind her in line was a fantastic disadvantage that was worsening his condition. *Pretty Deborah, give a brother a break and call. Sis, please call.* He should have put his cell phone on the back of his card, but to ask for it back now would really seem desperate. Doc needed to hurry up so he could step outside for a blast of cold air.

She made her purchase, waved, and said a quick good-bye. She then slipped out of the store and hurried down the street in the cold gray slush. He watched her from the window, in a trance. She was color against the muted tones of winter, a bright splash of orange and warm brown sugar spilling on gray halftones, blues, and charcoal.

"I can dig it," Doc said, chuckling. "You remember why you came in here, bro?"

Jason smiled, still staring out the plate-glass window. "To tell you the truth, man, no."

As she hurried down the street, out of eyeshot of the store, she was just glad that she hadn't fallen in front of the store with her klutzy self. Ohmigod, the man was fine! He'd called her pretty Deborah. And that voice—whooo! The voice of an intellectual, of one who knew about stuff she couldn't even fathom. His touch had run up her arms, tightened her nipples, and imploded in her belly. Those eyes.

But was she crazy? It was winter, after Christmas. Everybody who broke up during the holidays was on the prowl for winter, hunker-down booty. Every guy who had ditched his woman to keep from doing the holiday commitment thing was looking for a big-butt, good-cookin' sister to hunker down with until spring, just like hibernating black bears. But come spring, they'd ditch the good cook with wide hips to go find the chick who could wear short shorts in the park or a bikini on the beach.

Deborah stopped rushing and allowed her sobering thoughts to catch up with her pace. Jason the artist, with the strong, warm hands and intense bedroom eyes, would not want her come spring. He had the lines and was definitely a playa. Probably had a whole bunch of women getting naked and sprawled out for him on his studio floor. Not to mention, artists, from what she'd heard and what her father had always told her, were irresponsible and crazy. None of 'em—musicians, writers, poets, sculptors—were the kinda guys who had a nine-to-five or medical and dental. Yeah, what she needed right now was to get caught up trying to support some artist when she couldn't halfway support herself.

Totally depressed that the high of sudden possibility had faded in the cold gray of reality so quickly, she dug into her satchel and ditched the card in the next trash can that she saw. She didn't need the temptation in her midst. It had been so long since she'd made love or had any male attention that she didn't trust herself. A booty call at no o'clock in the morning was so possible for the winter weakened. Correction. She wasn't weak; she was *broken down*. Starved to the max. She almost slowed down to go back and retrieve the card but remembered she did have some pride.

No. She would not go dig in the trash like a homeless woman, desperate to find a number to dial just to hear a man's voice.

The first thing he did when he walked in the door was go check his messages. Nothing. Okay. He needed to stop tripping. It had only been a couple of hours. He needed to work, get something to eat. Maybe head down to Fourteenth and South Street, to Govinda's, his favorite vegan joint. He had to stop thinking about those soft hands and beautiful eyes. Had to get raw sex off his mind. He'd been more disciplined than that for a couple of years. Didn't need the drama. The sister probably had kids and some other brother going through madness with her. Yeah, she might even be married or living with some man; he'd never asked if she was free. Stupid, stupid, stupid! He had never gotten the facts.

He couldn't let the little head do the thinking for the big head. He had to put away his groceries. Walk it off. If he relieved the problem in this state, he'd only spiral, turning a want into a burning need. Then he'd be on a mission. The icy, frigid weather was good medicine for that. Hell, maybe he'd walk from Thirty-fifth all the way to Fourteenth. Maybe by then it would go down. Damn!

Chapter 3

On Sunday, gospel music lifted her out of her funk. The minister was preaching, the choir was rocking, and her troubles were laid on the altar, and during the entire walk home, she had Yolanda Adams plugged into her ears. All day she made it her business to clean her one-bedroom apartment, put a few plants around, and keep inspirational music blasting.

After the fiasco at the herb store, she'd temporarily lost her mind and foolishly continued on to the sporting goods store, to buy a yoga mat—which, the course said, she didn't need, unless that was a personal preference—and to try to find some cutesy exercise gear. Why some fine brother, who she'd never see again, would inspire her to go shopping was beyond her. That was why today she'd keep the Lord real close, just a whisper away, when support was needed.

How she'd reacted to a complete stranger didn't make sense. Then she'd really got her feelings hurt when she went into the sporting goods store, all big and bad, only to find out that the women's sizes there stopped at a large, which was essentially a size fourteen. Her behind hadn't fit into a fourteen since high school. An eighteen was a necessary evil, and so she'd gone to Lane Bryant and Avenue, only to come out of the stores with too many bags, filled with gorgeous and expensive lace bra and panty sets, lingerie that was over the top, and, yes, some cute, form-smoothing exercise gear.

"And that's just why I'm standing here, cutting up my vegetables and packing my fruit today," Deborah said out loud, bopping to Kirk Franklin in the background.

Ziplock baggies filled with pretty colors were strewn across the sink: baby carrots, celery, broccoli, grape tomatoes, green grapes, red grapes, honeydew melon, cantaloupe, and papaya, which was pricey at that time of year. She would make a spinach salad with sliced zucchini and squash, tomatoes, and red onions and would pack a tiny plastic container of all-natural, fat-free balsamic vinaigrette dressing, along with chickpeas and raisins to add to the crunch. Fruit would be breakfast and dessert. Carrot sticks and unsalted sunflower seeds, premeasured, of course, would be her snack. Gone were the Snickers bars and sodas from the vending machine. Same dealio with coffee. Herbal tea would replace that. Deborah grabbed several green tea bags out of the box to stash in her purse, along with a small jar of honey.

Like the instruction sheets from her class said, everything was about being prepared. Having enough natural choices at one's fingertips; enough clean, bottled water available when thirsty; and the ability to pause and gauge one's hunger or thirst was the key. Waiting until you were about to keel over and then grabbing anything you could get your hands on were to be avoided, it said. That was definitely her. Deborah sighed as she ziplocked another baggie. Okay. She'd be positive and go along with the program; after all, she was the one who'd signed up for the class. She read the banner on the page: ALL-NATURAL LIVING MEANS ABANDONING UNHEALTHY,

TOXIC CHOICES AND ALIGNING YOURSELF WITH WHAT IS GOOD FOR YOU.

Deborah stared at her cabinets with chagrin. She'd spent a mint to change over her spices. Her hand reached to throw away her seasoning salt and replace it with Spike—an all-natural salt substitute—but she just wasn't ready to go that far. Natural sugar versus white sugar, okay . . . but she wasn't ready to go straight to honey. Spelt flour versus white, refined— yeah, all right. Using fresh herbs and spices, like rosemary, basil, garlic, and ginger, versus garlic salt or dried herbs in a bottle, was okay. As an excellent cook, she could deal with that. But she was really going to have to study the recipes and doctor them with flavoring alternatives to get with the total program. Tofu was *definitely* going to be a challenge.

But she felt proud of herself as the aromatic scent of broiled flounder, with just a dash of olive oil, lemon, grated fresh ginger, and chopped basil, wafted through her kitchen. She had half of a baked yam with only a small pat of yogurt butter waiting, lemon water, and steamed asparagus—a natural diuretic— which would be her dinner. An apple, thinly sliced, with raisins for sweetness, cinnamon, and a small dash of natural maple syrup, all heated until bubbly soft and poured over one scoop of all natural, frozen vanilla soy ice cream would be her dessert.

Checking and rechecking the lists, she studied her cabinets and refrigerator as she put away her prepped food and lunch. The cabinet shelves were mostly stocked with what the class had recommended. Unopened sodas and iced tea mix and coffee had been replaced by natural juice sip boxes, coconut water, caffeine-free herbal tea selections, and the foundation of life itself—water. Bottled water.

Old canned goods from the regular supermarket had been turned in today to the church's food ministry, and she'd replaced those cans and jars with all-natural beans and jarred goods that sported preservative-free labels. She had a good multivitamin, B complex, vitamin C, something crazy looking called spirulina, folic acid, a vitamin D and magnesium blend for strong bones and teeth—which came in a huge horse pill, vitamin E as an antioxidant, chickweed, kelp—because they said it had key iodine to regulate her thyroid, okaaaay, hmmm—and an echinacea-goldenseal blend to stave off the common cold. Had she lost her mind?

Her freezer had given up its pies and pork chops and was now barren of red meat. Free-range chicken, fish, and turkey bacon had replaced that. Fruits and vegetables made the refrigerator look like a colorful greenhouse below. Eggs were free range; her breads were all pita look-alikes. She had yogurt butter, soy milk, cardboard-type cereals, and a headache just from trying to keep it all straight. The food pyramid had been turned upside down. She'd spent a mint on what looked like grass and herbs and, yeah, mint tea! Her counter had a new appliance, a juicer, and she now owned a steam basket and tea balls.

Deborah stood in the middle of her kitchen floor and hugged herself. "Lord, so you really mean for me to be all by myself. Because no black man in America would go for this mess," she said aloud. How would she ever make macaroni and cheese again? Or lasagna or cobbler or any of the things her nana had taught her?

She walked out of the kitchen, distraught, and went to her bedroom calendar. Heavily invested and too far gone to turn back now, she met the exercise challenge with the kind of military determination that would have even made her father proud.

"All right. Monday, thirty minutes of activity in the morning. Thirty-five sit-ups, arm weights, after ten minutes on the bike. With art class after work," she said out loud as she wrote her goals into the large white blocks. "Tuesday, the same, but work the legs. Then yoga after work. Wednesday, you're gonna sit on that crazy exercise ball and work core abdominals and follow the DVD that came with it. Then learn how to cook, and ride the bike when you come home. Thursday, back to arms, if you can lift them, and aikido at night." Deborah nodded. "Saturday, you work out an hour, and you've got your one hundred and eighty minutes a week. Plus, you did all your classes."

Nodding to herself, she clicked the pen closed and tossed it back on her nightstand. She was too organized for her own self, but oddly, it felt good. Her life was taking on definition by her own terms. If she could be steadfast and stick to the regimen she'd just designed, sans girlfriend interventions, maybe she would feel and look better by spring. *This would mean no clubs,* she told herself, because alcohol in the form of mai tais and daiquiris, or anything fruity and frothy, had so many calories, and so did Buffalo wings, and she wasn't that strong yet.

If she wanted to dance, then she'd have to find a good line-dancing class somewhere, but a club was out. Her regimen would also mean having to curb some after-church social activities that revolved around soul food. All right, eight o'clock service it would be. Same deal with baby showers and card party fall-bys and, oh, the movies! She loved going to the movies to escape for a couple of hours, but there was nothing remotely natural behind those counters. Fine. Natural, air-popped popcorn, spritzed with yogurt butter and Spike, and maybe some Old Bay seasoning just to add zip; Martinelli's sparkling apple cider; and a Blockbuster selection.

The feeling of being overwhelmed was starting to set in again, but she reminded herself that she was worth it. When she went back to school, she'd have to be disciplined like this, too, to make it through. "This is just practice for something better to come," she told herself as she walked through her now immaculate apartment to turn off her fish.

She'd even rearranged her closets and bureau drawers, casting away old clothes that didn't fit and turning them in to the shelter. Giving away shoes that were too small but still cute had been heartbreaking, but she'd done it. Gone were the old linens from when she was married, replaced by new sheets for a new bed, since her ex had claimed the old one. Good riddance. Now she had the pretty, feminine canopied one she'd always wanted. For once she was glad that her father didn't pry when she'd explained that she needed just a little help to get on her feet and into a new place. She would most assuredly pay back the small loan.

Deborah set the single portion of fish on the stove top to cool a bit before fixing her solo plate. Everything she'd ever known had been razed to the ground: clothes, shoes, underwear, spices, cabinets, refrigerator, routine . . . husband . . . sex . . . living quarters. Soon that sea change might even include her job—when she went back to school—if she could get a job on campus to help cut the cost of going to school. She dished her meal onto one of her mother's fine pieces of china after a contemplative moment and headed toward the dinette table.

"Lord," she said quietly, hesitating between words. "What are you preparing me for?"

He was supposed to be painting, but he had been on a mission since he'd left the herb store. His body required physical motion, due to an adrenaline rush, and walking from Thirty-fifth and Baring to Fourteenth and South hadn't been enough. The dojo had then called his name; he'd worked out there till they closed and he dropped. Sore muscles notwithstanding, he still had way too much energy, a nervous, unbalancing kind of energy that messed with his Zen.

Somehow during the course of the night, he wound up, of all things, cleaning like a madman. Nothing was in its right place. He reordered his living room, pulling the long, amber, leather sectional sofa to a new place, beside wide, fan-backed carved chairs he'd scored in Ghana; got books back up on the shelves; then decided that the way the stereo currently sat didn't maximize sound. It was time for a new CD shelving schematic, a plasma screen HD unit to save space. Wait a minute. He didn't watch TV. But he was on a mission . . . The place needed something else. *Color.*

All previous energy had to go. It was toxic. A depressing, artistic expression of grief. Sticky remnants of takeout and honey from fallen teaspoons pocked the hardwood floors. It was a wonder sunlight got through the floor-to-ceiling windows, given the layers of grime. Dust bunnies had practically become tumbleweeds and had to go. It was time for a new vibe, new feng shui. He had to get out of the deep funk that had consumed him. The fireplace sat idle. Layers of dust covered beautifully sculpted pieces from the motherland. The massive dining room had somehow become a way station. Crates and books and papers and sketches filled it. And the huge galley kitchen hosted a pet mouse and its tribe. *Aw, hell no!*

Everything was getting on his nerves. There just wasn't enough color. It all looked too drab, and that was siphoning his vibrations. He needed orange in that space. For some odd reason, that color was bouncing off the walls of his mind, screaming for attention. Tiles, hand painted. He'd fire up the kiln in the basement, maybe. *Nah. Whatever.*

He could feel himself about to take a sledgehammer to it all, to gut it and start anew. The broken futon frame was going in the trash. It was time for a platform. He'd build it. He needed something to do with the excess energy, which was wearing him out, for some unknown reason. The only rooms that didn't need a complete refacing were the two large bathrooms—although the department of health would definitely cite them—and his studio, the untouchable place of creation.

Home Depot, open all night, saw him about 1:00 AM. By 2:00 AM, he had hues of the sun in the trunk of his midnight blue Karmann Ghia and the car's interior was overloaded with bathroom and kitchen fixtures, shelving anchors, varnishes, track lights, and tiles. But he was forced to leave a crazy order for a delivery of wood and custom blinds; it seemed as though he'd be building a whole house, not just doing a little remodeling. By 3:00 AM it looked like he'd lost his mind: he was creating murals on the ceiling, drilling into plaster to install canister and track lights.

India.Arie was wearing him out, her testimony too deep, too profound, and too reminiscent of what he'd been through. He couldn't do Seal; this was not the night to be metaphysically mellow. Smooth jazz would take his mind where it didn't need to go.

No. There was still resident rage from being cold burned, burned by a fly sister who had wanted the bling. It had not been that he didn't have it; it had been a matter of priorities. He had been building a business, a home, a foundation for them, and had got straight played. It had been his own damned fault; he should have seen it going in. Jason swung a sledgehammer at the wall. He hadn't really thought about it hard until now. She'd wanted to hit the clubs, rock da ice, wear out the mall, and make every concert in the city, while he had been trying to make them independently wealthy. It was time to put on something ridiculous to work with. Luda. Yeah. He had shit to do. Set the CD changer up with Luda, Pitbull, Lil John & The East Side Boyz, Daddy Yankee, Fat Joe, 50 Cent, DMX, Dre, Shabba, Nelly, Yung Joc, T.I., and crank the volume to ten. Screw the neighbors.

Jason kept working as his mind replayed the past. The thing that had messed him up so badly was that she'd come off as an intellectual, not an around-the-way girl. Had been to the best schools, had a rap that wouldn't quit, could sit up till the wee hours of the night and get philosophical, appreciated art from around the globe, had a certain cultural je ne sais quoi, but had the face of an angel and the mouth of a . . .

He took a deep breath and closed his eyes, rolling his shoulders. Even in his mind, he didn't wanna call her what she was. His grandmother would do cartwheels in her grave. Yeah, he'd been suckered. This schemer was a digger and had had the looks to lay a trap, not to mention an overly exposed, tiny body, which she had used very, very well. What had been on his mind? He released the hammer. He'd been done with the species for a little over two years, with cause.

The wall between the living room and dining room came down with a loud thud. He looked up to be sure he hadn't accidentally taken out the center support beam. Cool.

Her having a baby by some knucklehead driving a BMW that he couldn't afford, while they were still dealing and in what was supposed to be a committed relationship, had been beyond foul. Then the fool didn't even marry her. Left her hanging, and she'd tried to take *him* down with a paternity claim? Thank God for DNA tests. *Fuck it*. He'd put glass block between the two rooms to give the space more light.

Yeah, when the pumpkin orange walls dried, he'd go along the lower section of the crown molding with burnt sienna, then in between with a fine brush in gold, and set it off with a border of Adinkra symbols spray painted through burlap. Uh-huh, had a damned baby on him. He *still* could not believe it. But that was cool.

New life, new shelves. New bed, for definite. The old one went in the dumpster. Everything that was a food product in the kitchen was gone in sixty seconds, courtesy of the contractors' bags. Everything except Wil's half-gone six-pack of Corona. There was radical, and then there was insane. He was just in a radical frame of mind. Jason flipped the cap off a bottle of Corona and downed most of it. But the fact remained, the freakin' cabinets probably needed to be sandblasted inside and out owing to the bachelor life.

The sun came up and caught him on a ladder. Squinting at the Sunday morning light and the crazy conditions that surrounded him, he felt fatigue setting in.

Oh yeah, he'd lost his mind. Two hours on the sofa, and he'd get up and keep going. He was a one-man wrecking ball, a master of disaster and demolition. He would just keep going until he passed out, and then he would eat, drink another brewski, and keep going some more. It didn't take but maybe a day or two to paint; a day to really clean; a day, maybe, to put up some shelves and lights, and change out fixtures, to give the space a new look. He would throw some huge elephant grass jawns around to put life and oxygen back up in the tip. Oh yeah, he was definitely tired and still pissed off. The mess had taken him back to the vernacular.

Regardless, on the normal-sized windows, he'd throw up wooden mini-blinds. For the odd-shaped ones, he'd call his boy who did stained glass, do a barter, and hang glass instead of drapes. He would honor his grandmother's cast-iron ware and hang it from the ceiling. He would redo her old, battered linoleum top and tile it . . . That he would take his time with. That was a place of sanctuary. It was maybe time to go down to the basement and bring up her old cherry-mahogany dining-room set and take the sheet off it.

Jason slowly came down off the ladder, beginning to feel every ache and muscle in his body, annoyed with himself. Burnt orange was making him act stupid. He turned off the stereo. Maybe he should have put on some gospel, like Nana did on Sunday mornings to find her balance. One thing was for sure: he needed to stop thinking about some chick that was never gonna call.

Deborah found a seat toward the back of the small studio class. She double checked her supply of brushes, her small canvas, her sketch pad, and her beginner's palette. Her arms were sore from her first morning attempt at exercise. She'd gotten a little carried away but told herself that was okay. Hopefully, the results would start to show soon.

She glanced around at the others, who seemed more comfortable than her. The ten students seemed to know each other and chatted amiably. They were mostly older women who had that very staid, very aristocratic intellectual look, which she was sure she'd never own. A few of the younger women, each sporting no-frills hairstyles, talked to each other like they were old friends or neighbors, discussing husbands and children, and politics on campus. There were only a couple of women her age, and they seemed excited and familiar in the way roommates might. She felt like the only oddball.

They all had on comfortable "save the environment" T-shirts or campus logo shirts that showed paint splatters. They wore beat-up jeans or paint-marred yoga stretch pants and old sneakers. Deborah groaned inwardly. They'd done this before. She hadn't. Like a dummy, she had on a brand-new, crisply starched, over-sized, sienna-hued button-down shirt and a pair of chocolate-colored, good wool slacks and leather flats that matched. She even wore jewelry—her favorite gold charm bracelet and her gold and diamond stud earrings, for chrissakes. But how could she have known! She'd always been taught to dress up for school or when meeting new people. Leaving a decent impression had been the foundation of her upbringing. *Don't let them think you're poor and ignorant. Look the part.*

Conversely, her classmates had come to the center doing comfort grunge and prepared to work on their easels. Deborah began packing her things away in her too-formal art case. Everyone else had a beat-up backpack. Vastly out of place, she needed to go home and change. No, she needed to drop the class. This wasn't for her at all. She was so stupid. Hopeless. These educated people here clearly knew so much more than her. If she couldn't even get the dress code right, then they'd probably snicker behind her back and laugh her out of class when she finally made her little stick figures on a canvas.

Deborah kept her eyes averted, hoping the members of the small class would be so engrossed in their conversations that they wouldn't see her. She could sneak away, ask for a partial refund, and take all the junk she'd bought back to the art supply store for a refund, too. But just as she was getting her brushes stowed, a deep voice filled with good nature made her look up and freeze.

"Hey, everybody. Good evening. I'm Jason. Wil had to go to London. Tough deal, being forced to travel overseas for a great gig. I feel oh so sorry for him, and I got to stay in Philly. So, I'm your sub," Jason said, with a smile, glancing around the room.

He hesitated for a second. She hesitated for a second. *It was him.* He had on a pair of paint-splattered

brown Tims; dark olive cargo pants, also badly splattered with paint; and an old Unity Day Festival T-shirt
that left no question about his fantastic build. White
cotton and blue letters stretched over what she could
only mentally describe as an ebony work of art. The
T-shirt was like blank canvas, and each movement of
sinew in his wide shoulders, lanky, athletic arms, and
his fantastically carved chest and stomach kept her
breath inside her lungs. *Breathe.*

The class instructor cocked his head to the side, his
jaw shadowed by new beard growth, which only made
him seem sexier and more ruggedly handsome than
he'd been before. His intensely brown eyes looked
past the rows before her and singled her out in a way
that made her face warm. His mass of hair was stuffed
beneath a floppy, crocheted red, black, and green
Rasta cap. The shock of color against the dark edges
of his hidden hair led her eyes to his smooth eyebrows
and curly lashes. Tupac came to mind as she offered
him a slight nod and smile of recognition.

He had to say something. Eleven eager students were
looking at him, and he had to quickly remember that
there was more than one student in the room. Fatigue
and preoccupation with his home rebuilding project
had had a stranglehold on him. Up until this moment,
he'd been cursing Wil, but now . . . damn . . .

"Okay. I see some folks have been here before," he
said, dragging his gaze to his class list. "But I like to in-
struct from a philosophical standpoint prior to jumping into the paint." He sat on the edge of the long
wooden desk. "It helps me to coach you if I know what
your goals are . . . why you chose this class." He kept his
gaze roving to be sure to evenly distribute it. "Some of
you may be looking for technical direction or to refine
skills you already own. Some may be coming to discover what's within. Others, still, may be here to simply
relax and allow their inner child to play. It may be all

of the above." He pushed back far enough to sit cross-legged. "So, it wouldn't make sense for me to stand over you, trying to hammer the basics, if you are interested in just flowing, or to tell you to flow when you need more technical guidance. Make sense, people?"

Heads nodded.

"That is soooo cool," a younger student in the front said, beaming at him, her blond lashes dusting her cheeks. "I mean, that's an awesome approach."

Deborah fought not to gag.

He gave the student a warm smile. "Why don't we go around the room? Give your names, say why you're here, and tell a little about your art experience, if any, and I'll do the same. Then we'll get started."

Deborah followed the curve of his mouth with her eyes and looked away, wishing that sexy smile had been reserved for her. It was silly to feel like that, but she couldn't help it. She banished the thought, wishing she'd gotten away while she'd had a chance.

Chapter 4

Deborah watched, sizing Jason up, looking for any inkling of a character flaw, as he went around the room. Scrutinizing him without mercy, she coolly noticed how his gaze remained attentive and respectful of each student. Rather than seeing a wolf on the prowl, which she'd expected, she witnessed a caring human being that seemed to make each person sit up a little taller in their chair, giving validation where needed without so much as a hint of impropriety. This was a different reality than she was used to, and the entire experience had a surreal quality.

As she'd thought, Keri, the blonde, was a coed and had come with her freckle-faced roommate, Tracey. Both were Penn students and admitted they were looking for an off-campus experience that would be fun and that wasn't a bar. The young Asian girl sitting with them was Nikki, a student at University of the Sciences, who needed something to de-stress her because of the heavy quantitative courses she was taking this semester. After hearing their brief reasons, Deborah began to relax. Yes, they were different from her, but then again, not. This was their New Year's oasis away from whatever was making them feel stuck. She could relate.

The older women in the group intrigued her, too. Ellen and Martha had a level of untold mirth in their expressions, like they'd figured out the secret of life, and it was funny. It was that same droll look that she'd seen in her grandmother's eyes. With no make-up, crinkles around their eyes from the many laughs and tears that life had obviously brought them, no hair dye—gray to the max, it was what it was—and no bras, these ladies were clearly comfortable in their own skins. One of them had a husband who was retired and making her crazy by being home all day, the other was widowed, but neither woman seemed to dwell on her misfortunes. Best friends, they'd come to class to escape. But they also were fairly skilled in a very low-key kind of way: they knew art, could paint, and had seen the better part of the world.

Deborah smiled. She might not have given these otherwise nondescript old ladies a second thought if she'd passed them in the supermarket. But she liked them right off. They were a hoot, like Thelma and Louise. Maybe, if she was blessed to live that long and that well, she and her girls might get to be like them, carefree, one day.

When Beth, short for Elizabeth, and Liz, short for Elizabeth, began to speak, Deborah's attention was riveted on what brought married women with children in their midthirties to such a class. Like Linda, Joanne, and Susan, both Liz and Beth spoke of breaking out of ruts, finding time for themselves, needing a change, wanting to hone gifts that might be hidden.

A couple of the ladies were in varying stages of a divorce; another had a clingy female live-in lover and needed a place to express her inner self. One just had her third child and needed space. Deborah listened to their stories, rapt. They weren't so different. The education and ethnic backgrounds were different, probably the economics, too, but what wasn't different was the motivations. The realization was profound.

"And, so, Miss Deborah, that leaves you."

Startled from her musing, she looked up at Jason, who bore the most mellow, sexy smile she could have imagined. She'd heard him hesitate, as though about to insert what he'd called her before, "pretty Deborah," into the sentence, then almost seemed to be searching his mind for a word other than "pretty" and replaced it with "Miss."

All eyes were on her, and she could tell from the curious gazes of the others in the class that she was probably as new to them as they were to her.

"I . . . well, I guess I came here for a change," she said, beginning to unconsciously twist the ends of her long shirttails in her lap. "My reasons are really . . . I don't know." She offered the group a self-deprecating laugh, feeling like a total nutcase as she glanced at the other women. She was waiting for Jason to let her off the hook and move on, but instead, he leaned forward, his gaze gentle but persistent.

"It's okay," he said quietly. "Art is about emotion. Change evokes that. Yes?" He looked around, and nods and murmurs of agreement filled the room. "So, what spurred your need for a change?"

She wanted to disappear where she sat—poof. She *hated* talking about herself. But unfortunately, there was no fairy godmother in the house. Jason clearly wasn't going to let it go, so she let out a sigh and spoke quickly, without punctuation.

"Okay," Deborah said, trying to sound casual and upbeat to hide her discomfort. "I feel like I should be standing up, saying, 'My name is Deborah Lee Jackson, and I am a rut. Not in a rut, I am one.'"

Hearty laughter filled the room, but Jason only

smiled, as though seeing right through her facade, which made her work harder to fortify it.

Deborah pressed on. "Here's the deal. I don't like my job at the water department, which stresses me out—you know how working in so-called civil service can be—so I wanted to come somewhere after work to unwind in a positive way . . . and since I just got divorced and just moved into the neighborhood right after Christmas, and since it was New Year's Eve, and the wine was good, I sat down and checked off a box for every day of the week, almost, to start the year right." She threw up her hands and gave the group a comedic scowl. "I lost my receipt, I can't take my art supplies back, and a sister can't afford to let 'em go to waste, so do what you can with me, Professor. Just don't expect Michelangelo. By the way, anybody got a job hookup at one of the universities? A sister is also trying to go back to school during this 'you do you' phase."

The class erupted in raucous laughter. However, Jason's smile became private, and he simply offered her a calm nod as he slid off the desk in one lithe move, which almost made Deborah slide out of her chair.

"*Ohmigod,*" Keri said, capturing Deborah's attention. "I wasn't going to say it but—"

"We just broke up with our boyfriends after Christmas," Tracey chimed in, cutting her girlfriend Keri off. "I know that it's, like, not as intense as a whole husband thing, but we came to find ourselves, too. The frat house was out as an alternative. Been there, done that."

Both coeds looked at each other at the same time and spoke in one voice. "Losers!" Then they laughed.

A couple of the older women nodded.

"Good for you, kiddo," Linda said, leaning over to touch Deborah's shoulder in support.

"Way to go, lady," Susan agreed. "And I do know of

some openings at Drexel, if you're interested. We should exchange cards after class."

"I won't speak ill of the dead," Martha said, with a wry grin, "but you're young and pretty, so count your blessings. I had to wait fifty years to find myself." She and her friend Ellen chuckled knowingly.

Deborah wanted to die. It wasn't because of the support. Had there been any other instructor in the room, it would have been okay, but with Jason standing there, it felt like she was on complete public display. Her and her big mouth! Why did she have to make jokes? Couldn't she just have said, "I'm here for a new experience?" Gawd.

He was glad that the room had erupted in sidebar commentary, or else he would have been at a complete loss. Deborah's spirit was *so cool*... Damn, he hadn't expected all that in the same package. Now *he* had to be cool and teach a subject matter that he had no clue how to convey— with her watching, pretty, no, gorgeous Deborah, with the flawless skin, set off by her burnt sienna shirt, her laughter warm and rich and deep, like the color she wore, and bottoming out in his groin. He'd kill Wil at the same time he genuflected when his buddy came home. Conflict ate at him. Now what? The icebreaker was something he remembered from his classes, but where to start? He hadn't prepared—he had been preoccupied with his home improvement mission—and he damned sure wished he would have cleaned up a little better.

Jason allowed his gaze to rove over the room. Sure, he'd taken all the formal courses necessary to give him a degree and had a portfolio that was ridiculous, but his talent came from an indefinable place within. No one had ever asked him to demonstrate how he did it. How the heck did he know? All right, for class one, he was gonna have to baffle 'em with bullshit.

"So, everyone here," he said, taking back command

of the room, "is here for change." Jason nodded, pacing himself, and mindful that a half hour had passed, so he only needed to get through another hour. He began walking a meandering path around the room, like he'd seen his old professors from yesteryear do, remembering how that had held his attention and built anticipation at the same time. "Change is good. Change is emotion. Change, like art, challenges the artist to go deep within. Change can either be embraced or rejected, but change will happen nonetheless."

He placed his hands behind his back as he walked, realizing that he sounded more like his sensei from the dojo than an art instructor. But as he watched Deborah watching him, he had to keep moving, needed motion.

"Just as background, since we're sharing," Jason said casually but very carefully, "I'll tell you a little about me before we get started." He didn't want to come off as arrogant; he just wanted to put the class at ease about his knowing a bit on the subject. He briefly let his gaze settle on Deborah before making it wander to the rest of the class again. He wondered if she knew what her thick-lashed, smoky, almond-shaped eyes did to a man. Whoever her husband had been, the man must have been out of his mind. He wondered if they'd been together long enough to have kids.

"I did my undergraduate work at the University of the Arts and then did a year in Paris, at the Sorbonne. Knocked around a bit in the gallery scene in San Francisco, then tried SoHo, but had to get out of New York before the city crushed my muse. From there, I headed down to Mexico and kept going through Central and South America, picking up influences, especially in beloved Brazil, and looped through the motherland, where I just got my mind blown artistically." He paused. "Then, *just* as I was about to defect and go live in Cuba, my family did an intervention," he added, chuckling at the memory and drawing laughter from the group. "So, I wound up at Temple University's Tyler School of Art, where I earned my master's. My specialty is watercolor, but I dabble in other mediums . . . not too shabby in sculpting and ceramics, either. I have a small gallery down on South. That's me."

Deborah had to purse her lips to keep the word "wow" from accidentally escaping. She'd been watching him lope around the room in his easy manner, moving with almost feline grace, and then he'd stopped and leaned against the desk, with a dashing smile that made her need to look away to regain her composure. *This* was the guy who'd asked *her* for *her* number? And she'd chucked it? She almost shook her head but stopped herself. She couldn't blame Keri, Tracey, and Nikki for gazing up at the teacher, eyes wide and lips dry. At this point, she couldn't even be mad at 'em. This man's body, easy manner, and resume as a combination just oughta be against the law!

"So, rather than start you off doing a bunch of still lifes, we're going to flow with emotion this first class." He glanced around. "Who would rather start there . . . show of hands, or have me go find some plastic fruit and set it in a bowl for you to paint?"

Again, his easy manner inspired laughter and whispers among the ladies, who agreed that this class was going to be fun. "Refreshing," one said.

"This is such a wonderfully different approach," Ellen murmured to Martha. "I am *so* glad we took this class."

"Good. I'm glad you all did, too, because I'm going to try some different approaches to keep it interesting. We'll experiment, make it up on the fly," Jason remarked, laughing deeply. "I want this to be free form, interactive, with your participation, yet individualized. So, if you need special attention, tell me. If I'm not hitting the mark for you, and you'd like to see more technique, holla. If I'm getting too narrow, also let me know. I paint in broad strokes, and I'm not big on details, but I promise you, you'll have fun. Deal?"

"Deal!" the class shouted almost in unison.

Deborah found herself absently nodding as she looked at the reactions Jason Hastings inspired. His rich laughter and the way she could have taken any of his statements made her belly do tiny flutters. Then she glimpsed him from the corner of her eye, catching a quick and scorching glance, one that had been aimed at her.

He quickly pushed off the desk, as though checking himself and stopping some inappropriate inner thought. He went to the board and began scribbling a color chart. Just watching him coolly battle with his composure was breath stopping. But she had to shake the thought. She was trippin'.

The man had given her his card the other day only because he was the real McCoy, a *real* artist, and not because he was trying to talk to her. He was probably looking at her like that only because he was annoyed that she hadn't called. Maybe he thought her unprofessional. He'd said he needed a model, and this might have even been what he needed one for—a class! Why pay a real, pretty cover model type when you just needed a chick off the street to sit her fat ass on a stool so folks could sketch or paint a regular body? Therefore, what she'd seen in his eyes wasn't a scorching look. That was some crazy notion inside her head. It was a justified scowl. Deborah let her breath out and stifled the sad sigh that was trying to escape with it. This educated guy had been around the world with exotic beauties . . . What would he ever want with her?

"All right," Jason said, pointing to the board. "Here

we have our primary colors on the left, and I've written down what the mixes and combinations in the center column turn into on the right. But as you look at each color, I want you to play with lightening and deepening it. Then, as you pick a color and make it, think of what emotion it inspires. Cool?"

"Like blues and greens feel cool and calming," Liz said. "And pinks are peaceful. If you paint a baby's room in that, it's supposed to make them very mellow."

Jason nodded, with a smile. "Exactly. When you see red, what do you see? For some, that might mean anger, because of the associated phrase 'seeing red.' But for others, it might mean passion or represent horrifying violence."

"I'd never thought about it this way," Beth said quietly, glancing around at everyone.

Jason shrugged. "It's all in one's perspective. Heavy, dark, bold colors inspire what in you, the artists? There's no right and wrong, because it's your inner palette. So, I want you to talk to your palette, just with color strokes, for the remainder of the class this evening. Everybody get up, stretch, go get some water in those baby-food jars at the sink, and set up your canvases. Next time we'll get into form and balance, the use of shapes, and some brushstroke techniques. But tonight, you're not trying to paint anything in particular. You're releasing emotion through color . . . so there's no pressure. Once the paint dries, in our next class, we'll discuss what you released as the class views each others' work."

Mortified that she'd have to show her work to the entire class, Deborah protested silently before her mind could sanction her voice. "Wait, wait, wait," she said, eyes wide, but with a smile. "You mean, we have to let people see what mess we put on the canvas? I thought all artists refused to let you see their stuff until it was finished, like in the movies." She tried to laugh, hoping he'd relent. Instead, his smile dipped from engaging to sensual as his voice dropped an octave.

"Being an artist," he said, staring at her so intensely that she swallowed hard, "makes you vulnerable. Whenever you put something on a canvas, a mural, on a wall, in any medium, if you're honest to your craft, there's a piece of you there . . . and, yes, the public gets to scrutinize that."

As though catching himself, he tore his eyes away from Deborah and raked the rest of the class with his gaze. "Trust me, ladies, when you put your work up on auction or exhibit it at a gallery opening, there is nothing more stressful. It strips you naked and keeps you honest, if you haven't lied to yourself and to your work. This class will be safe. But, now, you have a mutual reason to bond. Fear of next week's class." He chuckled, went to the sink, and began filling water jars to pass out.

Deborah nearly fainted. Linda pinched her arm and spoke through her teeth, in a humorous whisper, as she filed toward the sink.

"Dear God," Linda hissed. "I'm going through the brochure and checking every class that Wil was supposed to teach."

"You're married," Susan said and laughed. "Happily."

"I know, I know, but eye candy and audio stim are not a felony," Linda replied, with a giggle, keeping her voice low.

"Is he having the same effect on you as he's having on me, ladies?" Ellen said, fanning her face. "Or am I having another personal summer? Gracious me."

"What else does he teach?" Keri whispered in a hiss, subtly glancing around at her friends. "Whew. Awesome."

This time Deborah nodded. But she remained mute as stone as she accepted a water jar and quickly went back to her desk, hoping he didn't notice her hand slightly trembling. Dang, this didn't make no sense.

After a few flustered minutes, though, she settled herself behind her easel, glad that she wasn't the only woman in the group to feel the raw sensuality oozing from this man. That was, in an odd way, comforting. At least it let her know she wasn't the only one tripping.

She stared up at the rough color chart Jason had created on the board, then down at her brushes and her blank mixing palette, and up at her eight-by-ten white canvas. Color. Where to begin? Her favorite colors had always been in the rust and orange family. Dipping her brush in the water, she dabbed red and yellow onto the board and began making a deep orange, allowing the brush to flow on the canvas, as he'd instructed. After a while, inhibition fled her. She was lost in the creative process.

The near red orange hue gave way to golds and rust tones, mixed with pinks and magentas. Then she added a blue splash of coolness, taking it to lavender. Sunrise colors flitted through her mind in waves; elongated shapes with feathered edges began to form in the layers of hue. She changed brushes, compelled to find a dark brown for contrast, and then her brush yearned for brilliant, primary yellow, which moved out in heat waves until it cooled at the edges of her canvas in pastel yellows and whites.

"Okay, people. Good job," said Jason. "Let's start washing out jars and brushes, and you can leave your work to dry on the ledge by the back blackboard."

Deborah's head jerked up. An hour had passed already? Deep. She froze as she watched him stop by each desk, nodding and making a comment, with a genuine smile. Women seemed to float off their stools and to the sink, each one patiently awaiting his approval. Admittedly, she was no different and had to remember to breathe.

When he came to her, she looked away, embarrassed, and tried to force a chuckle. "I told you not to expect Michelangelo. And now that you told us how much you travel, I'm pretty sure you've seen his work one-on-one."

"Wow . . . ," Jason murmured quietly. "Angels at dawn."

Deborah stared up at him. "Huh?"

The look he had on his face as he shifted his gaze away from the canvas almost made her fall off the stool.

"Can't you see them?" His voice was a gravelly whisper as he went back to the painting. "Wings here, parting the dawn. Slips of bodies, like silverfish, elusive, androgynous brown bodies. Wings almost indiscernible in the layers of changing dawn light, but there, feathered texture differentiating them." He looked her dead in the eye. It was a quick pivot. "Damn, you're good. Raw, but good. You see with an artist's eye. Imagination beyond what's on this plane, pushing the envelope."

She didn't know what to say. She knew she had to respond, but her voice was trapped in her throat as he looked down at her, warming her with his intense gaze. "Thanks," was all that came out in a near whisper.

"You were supposed to call me about a modeling job," he said, with a smile, and then quickly crossed the room, as though running from her. He grabbed several jars that students had yet to dump and began fastidiously straightening the classroom. "Make sure you get all the paint out of your brushes so they remain flexible and will do what you want, when you want, on the canvas."

Deborah stood on shaky legs. What could she say? She'd chucked his number. She made her way to the sink with several other students and waited her turn to wash out the brushes she'd used.

"Sorry about that . . . Uh, I had so many bags and receipts, I lost the card," she said quietly, knowing the comment sounded lame.

"No problem," he said in a jovial tone, way louder than she'd hoped he would. "Just give a brother the cold shoulder when he's trying to paint. No problem."

"I did lose it, for real," she said, now laughing as she got closer. She ignored the inquiring glimpses of her fellow classmates.

"It's cooool." He walked away and began putting stools up on the long table by the back wall and bidding students good-bye as they left.

"Aw . . . c'mon," Deborah said, laughing. "Would I be like that to a guy who taught me to do that thing with the fingers?"

Several students raised their eyebrows and hurried out of the room, with whispers and smiles.

"Deborah, you are going to have to remember the terminology, kinesiology, before folks start talking."

She glanced around and covered her mouth. "No, no, no, that's not what we're talking about!" She started laughing and dropped her brushes in the sink, suddenly realizing that she'd been splattered, had wiped her hands on her shirt, and had been smudged.

The sound of her voice ran all through him. "Well, at least you now look like you're gonna stay in my class and not bolt." He motioned toward her shirt as she pouted, watching her mouth in a way that he knew he shouldn't. "Sacrifice that one. Make it your painting shirt."

She closed her eyes and groaned. He almost followed suit for different reasons; her voice was decimating him.

"I'm glad you got one broken in during my class . . . I take it you didn't have one before?" He knew it was over the top but couldn't help it.

For a moment, she just stared at him, and her smile widened, increasing the throbbing in the erection she'd suddenly caused. "Did you really see angels at dawn in my painting, or—"

"Was it just a line?" He was so glad the other students had left. He folded his arms over his chest. "I don't do lines about a person's talent. Karma. Some things you don't play with. They're sacred. A person's belief in themselves is that. No. I saw angels."

"Oh," she said quietly and squeezed her very clean brushes with a paper towel. She tried to dab her shirt and stopped when he shook his head no.

"It'll smear, it will stay wet, and it is gonna ruin the inside of your good coat. Ask me how I know."

Again, she stared at him, now understanding the army fatigues and his paint-splattered look. The man was constantly working, creating, and the clothing thing was an afterthought.

"I thought, maybe, you'd done kinesiology to determine whether or not you should call," he said after a moment, trying to bring back the conversation's former levity while also trying to wrest his gaze away from her shirt. The vision playing in his mind was so raw, it made his stomach contract to keep anything lower from twitching. All he could think of was her standing in the middle of his studio, paint splattered, in that shirt, nude beneath it, with the shirt unbuttoned, hair out . . . He had to stop.

She glanced away shyly. "Would you give it to me again . . . that is, if you still want a model? I'm sorry."

Okay, okay, he had to be cool—had to be nonchalant—and had to try not to drop his wallet and wig.

"Yeah. I think I can do that," he said in his most controlled delivery and in a pure baritone, which had not been planned. It just came out that way when he was around her. "This, uh, number on the class list . . . Is it cool for me to call, or should I lose it?" He had to know.

Her eyes registered a level of shock he didn't expect. It was slightly disappointing, and it grounded him enough to enable him to slowly retrieve a card and hand it to her.

"No, that's a good number," she said quietly, her fingers grazing his as she accepted his card.

It felt like electricity was passing through his system. "Here," he said, fetching the card from her grasp. "Lemme put my cell on the back. That just rings at the studio or, when I forward my calls, at the house." He patted his pockets and then looked frantically around the room.

"I have a pen," she said in a near murmur and then walked over to where she'd been sitting, to dig in her purse.

He was trying to remember to breathe in through his nose and to let it out through his mouth as she bent over and found what she'd been searching for and then returned with a writing instrument. He made sure to accept the proffered pen with Zen cool and then carefully, legibly, wrote down his cell number.

"Do you have another card?" She gazed up at him, with a shy smile. "They don't give people in my position cards, but I can write my cell on the back of one of your cards . . . since you already have my home number and know I live down the street. I'll put my job number on there, too."

He nodded, hoping his racing heartbeat didn't crack a rib. "Yeah," he said as calmly as possible and handed her another card. He watched her nimble fingers write her numbers in a feminine script. Then, unable to stop himself, he pressed for more time. "Since you just moved into the neighborhood and it's right around the corner . . . you wanna go to the

Green Line? It's a coffee shop that's open late. Two blocks south of here, right on Forty-third."

She gave him a little smile and a tiny shrug. "Sure, why not. As long as it's close. I can't put my coat on, because of the wet paint, and was gonna run home, down the block, without it."

He hesitated, not wanting to seem desperate or like a stalker. But it had been so long since he'd had female company this close that every nerve ending he owned was wide open. His brain wasn't working. All the blood had drained from it and was otherwise occupied. He walked across the room more quickly than was probably cool and grabbed his fatigue jacket. As soon as he returned to stand before her, and not waiting for her to protest, he draped it over her shoulders. Then, just as suddenly, he wished he hadn't done that. The chivalrous act might have been romantic if he'd washed the sucker about two years ago.

She glanced down at her shoulders, swimming in the coat.

"My bad," he said, humiliated. "You don't want this old funky thing on you, but I figured it would beat pneumonia, and I didn't want you to mess up your nice work coat."

She stopped his words and covered his hand with her soft palm. "Thank you, Jason. That was so sweet. But you'll freeze in just a T-shirt out there. I can't let you get pneumonia, either. Now how would that look, Professor?"

For a moment, he was speechless. The burn her soft touch produced traveled through his hand, up his arm, hit his spinal column, and made him want to pull her into an embrace. That not being an option, yet, he just stood there, dumbfounded, for a second. The gentle timbre of her voice, the way her eyes looked up at him, the tilt of her head, perfect for a kiss, were making him irrational.

"I'll be fine," he said in a near rasp. "It's just a few blocks."

"My place is closer." She stared at him.

He didn't know how to process the comment. If it meant what he was hoping, he was gonna praise dance. But she didn't seem like the type. He arched an eyebrow, speech failing him, but he needed clarity, lest he make a real ass of himself.

"If we run down the street, I can run up to my apartment, grab a jacket, and give you back your jacket before you freeze to death, you can warm up for a sec, and then we can go get coffee." Her expectant smile almost did him in. "Oh no!"

"What?" He'd breathed the question out, mental faculties slipping fast.

"I don't drink coffee anymore. Just herbal tea . . . See, since it's just me, and I don't have to impose this on kids or any live-in, you know, I started the cooking class here and just did this whole cabinet purge thing. I'm trying to go all natural and move toward vegetarian, which is why you saw me at the herb store and whatnot. So, I can't have, like, coffee and stuff that's not on the lists they gave us to review for class." Her eyes held a frantic quality, with anticipation imploding in them. "Is that a problem?"

"They have herbal tea and vegan stuff there," he said, swallowing hard. She was going all natural, was in the midst of a lifestyle change, too . . . her first time going toward the natural life . . . was a virgin to the experience and excited about it . . . didn't have kids . . . man left her . . . lived down the street . . . fine as hell . . . had untapped creative potential . . . would let him see her place. *Breathe, man. Be cool and breathe.*

Chapter 5

A thick, heavy male scent wrapped around her body as they hustled out of the building, talking and laughing. His voice coated her ears while the scent of a man coated her insides, both sending her into sensory overload. Good Gawd, his shoulders had to be massive for the jacket to swallow her like it did. It weighed a ton, and oddly, for the first time in her life, she felt petite. It was the sexiest feeling in the world, this man taking long strides beside her, his conversation and focus solely on her as he sheltered her from the wind. Hot dang, he was walking on the outside of the curb, something, she'd been told, she was supposed to expect but that had never happened all her life.

As they approached her building, she suddenly understood why women became thieves of their lover's clothing: to be swallowed whole and consumed by a shirt, a basketball jersey, an old T-shirt, or sweat jacket. Oh . . . yeah . . . masculine scent was making her hyperventilate. She didn't want him to freeze but really didn't want to take his jacket off. No man had ever given her his jacket. She didn't even think they did that kind of thing anymore.

Even though it was twenty-eight degrees outside, he

didn't complain as she fumbled with her keys. He had a thin sheen of sweat on his brow, and the way his heavy-lidded eyes appraised her made her work harder at the task than maybe she should have. No doubt about it, there was a very thick vibe happening—but it was happening too quickly. She needed more information and wasn't trying to end up a class groupie.

But he was standing so close to her and leaning on the door frame at such an angle that they both practically fell through the door as she pushed it open. Their breaths were creating steam puffs as she managed the second door, and their conversation became strained, then went silent, the moment they crossed the threshold.

"I'm on the third floor," she said quietly.

He glanced at the stairs like he wanted to take them rather than wait for the old elevator. The expression on his face literally wet her drawers. She pressed the elevator button and looked down at her shoes.

"You like it here?" he finally said, obviously straining to make conversation.

She watched his Adam's apple move in his throat. "Yeah." She was straining to make conversation, too.

The elevator lumbered to a stop, and the doors opened. He peeled himself away from the wall he'd been leaning against and followed her inside. What was she doing! Suddenly, it dawned on her that every security risk she'd ever been warned about had been heightened. Trying not to freak out, she justified things in her mind. She knew where he worked, had telephone numbers. Surely, they wouldn't let a predator work at the center, around all those bigwigs' wives, would they?

New worry coiled around her and added to the trivial as they exited the elevator and walked down the hall, toward her door. She had a dinky little stereo, a teeny TV not worth squat. No cable. No art on the walls yet. Nothing decent to feed a man in the joint. Popcorn, maybe? Not even a Blockbuster movie in the place. Oh yeah, unless she was just gonna be straight hoeish, she had to get him in and out of her place with quickness. Any thoughts of sitting on the sofa and easing into a little kiss-and-touch session were out. She wasn't set up for dating, just healing! Deborah almost groaned audibly. Why, God, huh? Why was she so dumb?

She inserted her key into her door and turned it, then hesitated, looking up at him. "You're gonna have to forgive the condition of my place. I just moved here, recently, and it's not really together . . . but if you have a seat, I'll give you back your jacket and grab a sweat jacket or something, or I'll take off this top so I can wear my coat, and we can run down to the café you mentioned."

Compelled, he touched her cheek and simply couldn't pull back his fingers from the satiny smoothness of it. "Pretty Deborah, don't ever apologize to anyone for your home. It's your space; I'm the intruder. Thanks for trusting me enough to invite me up."

She smiled and opened the door before her knees gave out on her. All her suspicions had been confirmed: this man was cracking, wanted her, and she was not prepared. Although his attention still didn't answer the many questions she had about his overall intent—dang. If she could just shake her rigid upbringing for a second, tonight she wasn't sure that she'd care what his long-range goals might be.

Jason glanced around as Deborah handed him his jacket and left him, singsonging the words "I'll be out in a flash." If she'd stayed by that door a few seconds longer, he might have kissed her hard, his body and mind on autopilot, and pressed her against it. But that would have been a total violation of her trust. Wrestling with lust, he tried to busy his mind with other things as he slipped on his jacket to cover his feeling of being too exposed. At least now she couldn't see the wood she'd given him. He'd keep his jacket on at the Green Line, for sure. Then again, that was a problem, too. Her fantastic feminine scent was all in the fabric, making him heady.

Jason looked around, admonishing himself. The simple, clean, almost eat-off-the-floor quality of her space brought on an unexpected wave of nostalgia. In his travels and during his bad-boy bachelor times, he'd been to many women's places, spontaneously dropping by for sex, but he had never been invited into a place so pristine. Not that it mattered, really . . . but, then again, it did. Said something about how she lived, in an odd way. His grandmother had kept house like that, as had his mom. He'd thought that had gone by the by with the older women who'd left the planet.

It was clear from what he saw, this was a sister who wasn't into conspicuous consumption and who lived within her means, yet everything was tasteful and just so. His hands ached at the prospect of maybe filling her bare walls with something she'd like. Then again, maybe he was mistaking the ache in his hands for the need to touch her bare skin and sugar walls. He wasn't sure; his judgment and mind were both cloudy at this point.

"Okay. Now I'm ready," she said, walking toward her small brass coatrack.

Yeah, she was. It took a second for the thought to leave his groin, travel up to his brain, get processed, and then come out of his mouth. "You look great." The process had obviously hiccuped. He wasn't supposed to say that, to tell her the truth. But the T-shirt showed off her ample breasts—he could see her nipples pouting through the fabric—and the black jeans she'd slipped on just gave up her curves in a stunning, skin tight way.

"Thanks . . . I just wanted to get out of that ruined shirt."

He continued to stare at her, barely able to control his arousal. "The shirt's not ruined. It's your work shirt, now . . . and I'd love to paint you in it."

She laughed and put her hands on her hips. "Paint me in it?"

He nodded, no longer able to smile. "Yeah . . . just wearing the shirt."

Her smile faded as she stood across the room from him. "In just the shirt . . . like . . ."

"Like nude under it . . . yeah."

"You serious?" She swallowed hard. "Like, where could I even consider doing something like that? I mean . . ."

"At my studio," he said quietly. "It's up to you. But I'm working on a piece for the Rhythm and Blues Fest. Actually, it's a series for them for their twenty-fifth anniversary gala, and it'll hang at their head-quarters downtown. When I saw you that first time, I was like, *That's her.*" The longer she stared at him, with disbelief in her eyes, the harder he pressed, feeling like her deep well of brown liquid gaze was drowning him in a truth he hadn't even admitted to himself.

Hell yeah, he was rapping hard. It had been two years, and something about this woman had him wide open. His words came out with passion, just like he painted, just like he wanted to get next to her right now, but he knew that wouldn't be right. Deborah deserved respect, so he'd tell her in an old-school way, and she could process it however she liked.

"For Rhythm and Blues, a woman, voluptuous and sensual, is what I had in my mind, the kind of woman that makes men sing rhythm and blues, made Marvin holla, and the rest of the brothers croon. You feel me? Inspiration personified, pretty Deborah, that's you. There was a peace and emotion missing in what I was working on. It needed something, the way gumbo just ain't right if there's a missing spice. I didn't know what it was until I saw you, a sister with . . . curves, motion, just the right sass in her walk and in her attitude, but not too much. There needed to be balance . . . an understanding gentleness in her eyes. Yeah. Standing in a doorway, eyes closed, shirt askew, coming out of her lover's bedroom, obviously sated . . . or maybe resetting an old platter to hear their song again after making love. I'll do that one for the old love songs, which probably resulted in me and you being here on the planet. That's just one panel. I have others in my mind."

He turned away, having said too much, and looked around the room, trying to get his head together. "Nice place, really nice. What kinda tea do you like?"

She blinked twice and didn't speak for such a long time that he turned around and stared at her. She couldn't get her mouth to function; what he'd said had turned her brain to jelly. "You're working on something *that* important, and you, for real, want me to model?" She looked down at her body in disbelief. "Me?"

His brows knitted. He had a slight frown. "Yes, you, Deborah. I don't want some video hoochie momma for this piece. I want a real, honest-to-God woman, with all the curves, gorgeous face . . . thick, natural hair. Especially for the retrospective aspects. Women didn't start looking anorexic until recently. I should show you some of the masters' works."

She laughed softly shaking her head. "Me in *just* the shirt . . . I don't know, Jason. I'd have to think about that. Like, couldn't you do it with me wearing a bodysuit underneath?"

He smiled, dragging his gaze down her body with appreciation. "Yeah . . . I guess I could . . . but then I'd have to imagine the shading, the minute changes in shadows and hues as the light played against what was supposed to be skin." He returned his gaze to her eyes. "Let's go get some tea. You don't have to decide tonight. I'll be sketching from the visual I already have in my head . . . but I'd sure love it if you would sit for me."

The way he looked at her and the sound of his voice were melting more than her resolve. "I have to work during the week," she said, hedging. "Then, after that, I have all these classes I just signed up for."

"Weekends work for me," he said quickly. "And I'd pay you the going rate."

Taken aback, she went to go get her leather bomber, wishing she could still wear his fatigue jacket.

"I don't know if I'd feel right getting naked for some guy and letting him pay me." She smiled at him and tried to make a joke of it. "Hey, even if you are an artist, my momma ain't raise me like that."

It made her feel like a million bucks when she saw the startled expression on his face and he glanced away, with a sly smile. Obviously, his momma hadn't raised him like that, either.

"Strictly professional," he said, still grinning, and came over to help her on with her jacket. "Ask around, check with the people who do this kind of work, and they'll tell you, 'Naw, ain't heard that brother's name on the circuit. Not like that.'" He winked at her and stepped back. "Over tea, you can ask me any question you want to, if it'll make you feel more comfortable . . . because to be honest, Miss Pretty Deb, you look like you're about to bust."

She had to laugh to keep from crying. He had no idea. "Okay, I've got one question that won't even wait till we get to the tea place. Is there a wife, a girlfriend, a deranged lover, or any combination like that, or a baby's momma that will come at me with a butcher knife if she happens to roll up on me in your studio, wearing just a shirt? I have security issues, man, not that I doubt your resume."

They both laughed as he followed her to the door. "Valid question. Thoroughly legit. The answer is no." He watched her lock the door from the hallway, wishing they were both on the other side of it. "I have been drama free for two years."

She sucked her teeth and rolled her eyes, then began walking down the hall. "Puhlease. Now I'm gonna have to really do my homework. Two years?"

He held up his hands in front of his chest as she pushed the elevator button. "On my momma's grave. No kids, no wife, no live-in, no baby's momma. I've been a blessed man. I ain't trying to go out like that, and before you can ask, no, I'm not gay, bi, or any combination thereof. Period. I had a situation that got ridiculous about two years ago, I stepped, and I decided to live the quiet life. I've just been working."

Too many facts were hitting her already "shell-shocked from fine" mind. But the most important one surfaced. "All joking aside, J . . . when you said, 'On my Momma's grave,' were you just playing, or have you lost your momma? I lost mine, and that's nothing to joke about."

His expression became gentle and serious. "I'm the last of four kids in the Hastings clan. My eldest brother is seventeen years my senior, then I have a sister fifteen years older than me, and what they thought was the baby, she's thirteen years older than me. I was an oops baby. My mother and father are both gone, so my nana raised me . . . so I was raised old school, and even though I don't do church, like they used to make me, I know that saying something on one's momma's grave ain't nothing to joke about."

They fell quiet as the elevator came and they got in.

"I lost my momma before I knew her. She died having me, so my nana raised me . . . She's gone, too.

My dad, well . . ." Deborah looked up and offered him a sad smile. "They broke the mold. Old-school military. That's why I'm probably having trouble just saying okay. Ya know?"

The look on her face was a mixture of emotions that devastated him. The honesty in her eyes, the sadness, the joy from some funny memories that were obviously running through her mind, the wistful tone, and the underlying strength were twisting him into knots. If he could capture that look on canvas, it would be his best work ever. She had to sit for him. That was all there was to it.

"Yeah, I do know," he finally said in a gravelly voice. "Your parents and mine were really from a generation back before most of our peers." He shook his head. "It's a different aesthetic, but I know what you mean. You take your time deciding."

"Thank you for understanding," she said, wishing that he'd just push the button to go back upstairs.

This man, this fine-ass, talented, educated man, whom she'd almost taken for a wannabe street philosopher in a health food store, was awesome. His lingo and look, just like his wild Afro, belied what was deeper within. Just because he spoke Ebonics as an easy cover and wore paint-splattered clothes didn't mean his mind wasn't a razor. He'd studied in Paris? She couldn't wrap her brain around this jarring contrast of realities.

They stepped out of the elevator in virtual silence, and she was glad when they walked out into the frigid night. He'd said he hadn't dated in two years, or had she heard him wrong? That had to be a stone-cold lie . . . but he'd sworn on his mother's grave. Okay, maybe he didn't consider a booty call a date. Most men didn't. They differentiated between a booty call and a woman who had the right to make demands. Later she'd loop back around to learn more. But for now she was content just walking beside him on the way to get some tea. A significant part of her wished they were close enough for him to put his arm around her to block the hawk.

"I'm in a strange position, though," he said out of the blue.

She hugged herself tighter, bracing against the whipping wind, as they walked faster. "How's that?"

"I never mix business with my personal stuff, and now I've just met a really great model who I sorta wouldn't mind seeing if it got personal. So, that creates a double bind. Like, I'd want to put my arm around you because the hawk out here ain't no joke, but since you're my student, plus possibly my model, now all of that's *way* out of order."

"I won't be mad or take it any kinda way," she said, making her teeth chatter theatrically.

He laughed and put his arm around her as they hurried down the block. She fought not to let him see her eyes cross.

"Cool," he said, with a wide smile. "'Cause after the self-imposed drought, I'm not half sure what the rules of engagement are anymore."

"Tell the truth," she said, bounding up the three wide cement steps to the café. "You were in jail for two years for protesting or something. That's why, right?"

"No!" he said, becoming indignant, but having to laugh at her outrageous comment. "Why can't a brother make said decision?"

"I'm just saying." She chuckled and shrugged as they entered the bright little coffee shop, which had a near-capacity crowd. "Every man I've ever heard tell of this, who has been in a drought, not that I personally know all that many, has either had the choice made for him by the system, has medical reasons, has preference issues that do not involve women, or . . . hey . . . they're lying and are married."

"You are so wrong. That is so not right," he said, becoming peevish as they waited for the person in front of them to get a latte.

"Oh no, I missed a category. They're in church and claim it in the name of Jesus." She put her finger to her lips. "But, they lied."

They both looked at each other for a second and then burst out laughing.

He held up his hands. "I'm not gonna try to convince you of my straight and narrow path. I'm a black man in America and guilty before I'm even charged."

"Oh, now, see, don't go leaning on the crutch, brother. You're leaning on the race card."

"Crutch? Crutch!" He couldn't believe she'd said that and had to laugh.

"What will you have?" the server asked, looking dismayed by the politically incorrect banter.

"I'll have a white tea," Deborah said, chuckling as she batted her eyes at Jason.

"She wrong," Jason said, giving up straight Ebonics to make her laugh. "I'll take a jasmine. She hate me," he said, referencing a Spike Lee flick that he knew she had to have seen, leaning down in her face for a second to make her laugh even harder.

God, he loved the sound of her laughter, and the way she could be so bold and then pull back. That Philly humor, that home-girl, homebred vibe, which he hadn't been able to find anywhere else on the globe, had no doubt opened him right up.

"If I hated you like the way they was so-called hating in that flick, man, you'd be paying me child support. Go 'head and get your tea," she said.

Even though he was laughing, he complied. They'd gotten as close to an outright proposal to jump each other's bones as was advisable, and the concept was messing with his mind.

"Since I'm being interviewed for legitimacy," he said, not wanting to lose the exciting repartee that had evolved between them, "let Miss *Bossy* Deborah now decide where to sit."

"I'm not bossy. Like the song . . . I'm just asking a brother some questions so I don't get shot." She covered her mouth, laughing behind her fingers as a few very college-looking faces went ashen and Green-peace types turned briefly to stare. "See? You're caus-ing a scene."

He pulled a chair out for her. "No. Your questions are. Me, I'm just minding my business."

She sat and smiled up at him. "Well, there are crazy people out here in the world, Jason. I have to know if you're a serial killer, an axe murderer, a child moles-ter, a deadbeat dad. I have questions before I get naked under a shirt with you."

"Just put all my business in the streets," he said, laughing and sitting, with a thud, loving every minute of disturbing the peace. He leaned in. "I don't think they're ready for this conversation in here."

She blew on her tea and folded her hands under her chin, with a mischievous grin. "Although I have more questions, the primary ones you've answered."

"So?" He slurped his tea, realizing he should have waited; it was too hot.

"I'll think about it."

He swallowed another too-hot sip. "Good. 'Cause I really want you to, Deborah." That didn't come out right; it had too much bass in it, was way too close to begging the girl. But an image was locked in his head: her freed breasts swaying under a shirt, almost visi-ble nipples, but not. Deflecting his embarrassment, he pushed back in his chair. "But the question is, will anybody do a drive-by on *me?*"

She smirked. "All in my business . . . no." She sipped her tea.

He looked at her. "Women *lie* . . . fine as you are. Get outta here."

Her smile widened. "Nope. Lemme see. A coupla months before the separation. That told me something was wrong. No happenings, if you get my drift. Then, it takes two years in the state of Pennsylvania to unhitch, if the person has issues, like he or she wants to contest everything, down to the knife, fork, and spoon. Hmmm that brings us to the week before Christmas, and this is the week after January first." She sipped her tea. "I'm a no drama kinda woman, J. You won't get shot, not even by my dad."

"He's in the military. See? I listen."

"He's in Virginia," she countered and took a swig of too-hot tea.

"So, what are you saying?" he asked, rolling the tall paper cup between his palms, a nervous habit.

"I'm saying I'll think about it," she said, picking at the lip of the cup, her nerves shot.

"We talking about sitting for the painting . . . or . . ." He held his breath, wanting to kick himself. *Too fast.*

"About sitting for the painting, but I'm flattered about anything else." She looked up and caught his gaze. He let out his breath. "I didn't even put any honey in this. Lemme go do that. I'll be right back."

"Hey, I'm sorry," he said, hoping she wouldn't retreat and that he hadn't totally blown it.

"You don't have to be . . . I ain't gonna lie. Was thinking about it, too . . . but . . ."

"Honey's over there," he said, with a nod of his chin, needing her to go and give him space to pull himself together.

"You have to admit this is not the usual request and is a little strange."

He watched her slide out of her seat and allowed his gaze to caress her curvaceous, luscious behind. He was just glad he would have a full week to finish his home improvement project. Maybe he would be finished by the next class, if he could convince her to

stop by for a quick sitting. He knew there was a reason
he'd been compelled to give his entire joint a face-lift.
Just the change in energy alone had drawn this beautiful woman into his space, he was convinced. He
couldn't take his eyes off her as she drizzled honey
into her tea. He had a hard-on that was giving him a
headache by now. He wondered what her skin would
look like in amber light, translucent gels like the
honey, sienna . . . yeah . . .

The next time she saw him, he'd have his shit together. 'Fro shaped or clean cornrows glistening—like
Iverson's. Would be righteous. Would make sure the
refrigerator was stocked, merlot was in the house.
Damn, what did pretty Deborah like? White tea. Yeah,
he'd have that. Maybe see if she wanted to go to
dinner. There was this little place by the dojo, in Chinatown. She licked spilled honey off her forefinger.
He made a tent with his fingers and steepled them
over his cup, breathing in the aroma of his jasmine
tea, and finally just closed his eyes. He wanted this
woman so badly right now that the best thing to do was
to just not look at what he couldn't have immediately.

Chapter 6

She took her time adding honey to her tea, perhaps drizzling more into it than she should have. But one thing was for sure: she needed some time to catch her breath and to pull herself together. Who did one consult regarding matters of this nature? Certainly not her biased-to-the-wild-side girlfriends, and a therapist seemed like overkill. So, rather than make a sudden fool of herself, she tried to strongly remind her body that withdrawal from regular sex was probably like withdrawal from any addictive substance: It made you act *stupid*. Being that close to Jason Hastings, with his sexy, signifying self, just sucked the air out of the cafe and her lungs. Even now, halfway across the room and focused on her white-tea improvement, she was having difficulty breathing.

Didn't that brother know how crazy he was making her? Although her nana had raised her better, right now she was about two seconds away from throwing caution to the wind. And even though she had about a hundred questions of a personal nature to ask him, she lifted her chin, threw her shoulders back, and decided to keep to safe topics—like his career, what it was like to go to college, what it was like to have all those brothers and sisters. Yes. She could do this. She went back to the table, with a smile.

He had made up his mind while she'd given him space. He was leaving this alone, at least for tonight. It wasn't about mentally torturing himself in a public place. From this point forward, the conversation had to be strictly about general topics.

Although he had a hundred questions he wanted to ask her, probing too deep would be like hitting black gold: it would cause a rush through his system, he could tell. Everything so far about Miss Pretty Deborah had told him so. An old-fashioned girl, with a good heart, warm spirit. Funny and could joke around, had humility. Knew church. That was good, because even though he'd forgotten a lot, that was how he'd been raised. It also meant she had a moral compass, unlike the hoochies he'd dealt with before . . . though right now he wished her compass would point to him. Regardless. All her pushing back did was make him want her more. Didn't get a lot of that, a sister who stood her ground and had questions.

The problem was, however, trying to convey to her that he wasn't trying to dog her. The urgency had to do with two factors: one, she'd straight blown his mind with her fine self, and two, he'd once been in a regular, steady relationship. He almost closed his eyes just thinking about it. Three times a week, maybe four. Early on, every day. Then cold turkey. If she didn't believe anything else, he hoped she'd believe that.

But a self-imposed dry spell had seemed like the thing to do, especially after being scared to death. It didn't have a damned thing to do with religion; it had to do with survival, which in the end, yeah, maybe, had a spiritual twist to it that rang true, like fate.

A sister making a baby on him meant that for all the condoms he'd used, she hadn't. It also meant that whomever she'd slept with, essentially, he'd slept with, too. Jason gripped his tea more tightly than intended and took a deep swig of it. His ex had put him in a position of having to hope and pray and to bank on some other brother's sexual diligence, and given that the knucklehead had knocked her up, that wasn't likely. So he'd panicked for months, then got tested every other month until the doctor said to chill. Then he'd been blamed for making a baby he didn't make. Nah. Nobody had come along, until pretty Deborah, that made him even want to take a risk like that again.

"Okay. Now that my tea is straight, I'm good to go." Deborah slid into her chair and sipped her brew, with a smile, peering over the tall cup's rim.

All eloquence and good intentions fled him as he watched her eyes drink him in. "Tell me about your wanting to go to school," he said, deflecting the conversation to her. Right now he couldn't think, much less talk.

The cold air was a blessing, but his arm around her shoulders was breaking her down. *Be strong, sis,* she repeated over and over in her mind as they silently trudged along. She'd told this man things she'd only told her best friends, such as what it was like growing up as an only child. She'd been amazed to find out that even though he'd had siblings, he'd grown up like that, too. They both had practically been raised by their grandmothers; his had been an amazing woman and sounded so much like hers. Blunt speaking, hard loving, gospel thumping, house cleaning, and long living. His grandmother had outlived his mother and father, just like her nana had outlived her momma. That pain was a quiet one they'd shared as they sipped tea and the crowd thinned out.

It had been so long since she'd sat in an establishment until it had closed and she'd been literally put out. But to share Jason's company felt oh, so good. He seemed to hang on her every word, remembered what she'd said in the beginning of their conversation. He would loop back to it or remind her of a statement made days ago, which let her know he'd been listening then, too, when they'd only just met.

As they took their time going down the block, she wondered if his leisurely pace had anything to do with hers. She knew she was stalling, trying to let the cold air and cutting wind slap some sense into her. She wondered if he was thinking about how to angle his way in, or if she'd talked too much and maybe he'd changed his mind.

Anticipation and dread did a line dance in her belly; something like the Electric Slide was happening up and down her spine. The warmth of his arm over her shoulders, his body heat sheltering a part of her from the January blast were making her conscience go two steps forward, then two steps back, then hop, spin, dip, and go in a whole different direction.

It had been so interesting and thoroughly sexy to listen to him talk about his experiences in college and abroad. Yet he hadn't put her down for not having had those experiences yet, and he'd had great pointers concerning how to go back to school for her degree in business. He had even encouraged her to hook up with the lady from class who'd said she knew some people that might be able to help her get a university gig. He was willing to teach her how to network and had broken the silence on things she'd always known to be true but didn't know how to actually do. That was how he'd seized so many opportunities—hard work and networking.

Still, she didn't want to ruin it by saying yes tonight, and she didn't want to ruin it by saying no. Yet, she wanted him to keep looking at her with that hungry, "I really want some now" look . . . but she wasn't trying to tease him, either. It had just been so long since a quality guy had come along to offer her that knee-buckling expression.

Sure, plenty of dawgs and snaggletoothed old men had leered at her on public transportation. That wasn't validation of anything more than being female and owning certain equipment. Those were the types of men that wouldn't care if the equipment was attached to her body or not. In fact, down on Thirteenth Street, she was pretty sure they sold a vessel product that didn't have to be attached to anything but the user. Jason didn't make her feel like that when he looked at her and talked *with* her, not at her.

Deborah sighed, wishing she'd held it in. How could she explain to this really nice guy that she didn't want to be burned, and she wouldn't burn him, either, and not because someone had done him wrong, which, given all the indicators and round-about probing, it sounded like they had? Her mind was on fire, set ablaze by the conflict.

How could she just say, "Look, my husband was cheating, so I damned near had a heart attack, thinking he might have given me HIV. Then I got tested so many times, they asked me not to come back after I had ten negative test results, so I voluntarily took myself off the market, until I ran into someone who seemed like they were worth the risk. But I ain't trying to die, don't wanna come up coughing." How did a woman express that and at the same time let a man know she wanted to be with him more than he could imagine?

She pursed her lips to keep the truth from spilling out. The woman who had tossed Jason Hastings back into the streets was either crazy or out of her mind. Then again, it also begged the question, why? But she wasn't going to go there on this first outing, which she wouldn't call a date, because it had really just evolved out of class and wasn't a formal outing. But the turn-on from this man was gonna make her break down and do something she swore she could never do with a straight face—go downtown and buy something that needed batteries. He smelled so good, just natural, of some kind of musky oil. She wondered if there was a natural herb she could take to kill a case of horniness.

With her building in sight, he had a decision to make: press the sister and make her uncomfortable, and therefore make her bolt, or chill. It had been a very cool evening; she'd shared a lot and had garnered his respect. She had a level head on her shoulders, had an awesome family parallel to his. It felt like he could talk to her all night, but the place had shut down his rap and kicked them out. She felt so warm and soft under his arm that the natural thing to do would be to put his body around her in a full embrace and just lower his mouth to hers. That would set a full-court press in motion; he knew himself that well. If he kissed this beautiful woman, felt her body against his—if she rubbed against him and was in any way pliant—he was going for broke.

"I had a really good time," she said, breaking his trance and stopping in the street outside her apartment building.

Okay. Sho' she was right. He took that as his cue. "Yeah, I had a nice time, too. Maybe we can get some real dinner after the next class, or something?"

She gave him one of her Mona Lisa smiles and let her gaze slide away as her voice dropped. "I'd like that."

It was twenty-eight degrees outside, with a windchill factor of ten, but it might as well have been August. He couldn't move. That look, that tone. *Just say it again like that, baby.*

"If you're taking that cooking class, I could pick you up and take you down to Whole Foods on the parkway so you wouldn't have to haul your stuff on SEPTA. I mean, it's no trouble. I have to go down there to stock up, too." He hesitated, waiting, needing to hear that soft timbre brush over his senses again.

"You'd do that?" she murmured, staring up at him with wide eyes. "I couldn't ask you to go to all the trouble, really." Then she looked away.

He was so messed up, he took a step closer. *Just say something again, just like that, before I have to leave you.* "It's no problem. You have my cell number. I can show you some things to steer clear of, too, and sorta help you get started with this whole vegetarian change-over. There's a few good places to go down in Chinatown, too . . . They have shrimp that isn't shrimp but tastes like the real thing."

"Wow. For real?"

He almost closed his eyes. "Yeah." His breath was short.

"Maybe if I learn how to make something good, I'll pay you back by making you a dinner. Deal?"

He nodded, reduced to one-word responses. "Uh-huh."

"I should probably go upstairs . . . It's getting late, and I have to get up early in the morning for work."

"Cool."

"Good night. Thanks again for a great evening and the tea."

He just raised a hand and waved, unable to function on a verbal level.

Jason stood in the doorway to his house and glanced around at the chaos and plaster dust. Sleep? Forgetaboutit. Finish those walls and his platform bed? A must. Head to the barber in two days for a shaping, then over to the braiding salon on Forty-fifth to get his shit right. Take a black garbage bag of sweaters and cargo pants to the cleaners.

Dig in the closet and find his butter-soft black leather pants. Go to the damned shoe shine joint on Fortieth and put a military shine on everything. Hit the state store. Merlot was now an essential part of entertaining. He had to go find his old, mellow collection of CDs and bring them out of basement cold storage. He was running on adrenaline like his car was running on fumes. Go get gas. Pay the cable bill, and get it back on. Go to the supermarket after cleaning out the fridge.

How the hell had he allowed his life to get out of control like this?

Sit-ups. Do your routine, and *do not* call that man. Make sure your body is so tired, Deborah Lee Jackson, that when you hit the pillow, you go out like a light. Twenty-two. Get to thirty-five. He wants to see you naked under a big shirt. Don't even imagine what it will be like to get with him. That will make you rush, and you do *not* need to do that. Thirty. Oh, shit, the brother is fine. But, girl, you got things you are trying to accomplish, and you have things you need to know first. Don't jump headlong into some mess, from the frying pan into the fire, like Nana would say. Oh, Lord, he said he was gonna take you to the *supermarket* . . . like a husband?

Breathe, girl, just breathe. Don't go there. See, you're already irrational.

She could barely keep her eyes open on the bus, and by the time she got to her desk at work, herbal tea wasn't making it. Caffeine was calling her name, and the smell of everyone's coffee on their desks was making her evil. Her arms were sore from doing wall push-ups like a madwoman. Her belly hurt from crunches. Her thighs felt like heavy, immovable logs . . . and she was supposed to do yoga tonight? Yeah, right. But she had to stay on point, remain on task. If she was gonna get naked under a big shirt, she had to get a Janet Jackson stomach or quit.

"Rough night?" her coworker LaVern said, watching Deborah bring a shaky cup of herbal tea to her mouth.

Deborah smiled. "Yes and no." It felt good to finally have something juicy to think about. Maybe she would even share a little.

LaVern laughed. "Sounds like a man, girl."

"Maybe," Deborah said, hoping someone, anyone, would just ask her so she could revel in feeling the butterflies dance inside her.

"Tell all. Is he fine?"

Deborah briefly closed her eyes as LaVern leaned in close. "He is *all* that. An artist and—"

"Oh, girl, puhlease," LaVern said, laughing. "You know artists are broke. What's he drive?"

"Uh . . . I don't know," Deborah said, feeling her butterflies die one by one.

"Lord have mercy, girl. Did you run the financials? Like, what was he wearing? Did he have on a decent watch and an expensive pair of shoes?"

Deborah looked down at her keyboard and began keying in entries from her never-ending stack of work. She didn't want to mention Jason's beat-up, paint-splattered Timberlands or paint-smeared clothes to LaVern. The mood had shifted. "He didn't wear a watch . . . Like I said, he's an artist."

"The operative word is *starving artist*," LaVern shot back as she began keying in entries. "Chile, when you gonna set your sights higher, on some of these businessmen downtown, in the suits, who are rolling in dough? We keep trying to get you to come with us to happy hour, but you're always running home right after work, and that's why you're meeting that quality of man, girl." LaVern sighed. "Where'd you pick this stray up? While walking through campus or at the health food store?"

Deborah cringed. "No . . . he's not a student. I think he's a professor."

"Even worse, chile! God, Deb, what do you want with some broke Joe who can't get away from the college life? You know how many professors cheat on their wives with tight-butt little coeds? Right up in them dorms, I bet."

Tea was curdling in her stomach. "About as many as bankers, politicians, and downtown lawyers that play the hotel circuit with tight-behind secretaries, I imagine," Deborah said dryly. This was exactly why she wasn't going to say a mumblin' word to any of her other homegirls yet.

"True that," LaVern said, not the least bit fazed. "That's why if you're gonna play and be played, at least make it worth your while. Come out of the deal with some ice, a tennis bracelet, a trip to Jamaica, some damned something. Girl, act like you know."

She came into the rec center feeling so blue that she'd almost skipped her classes, but never being a quitter, she'd reminded herself that this was her New Year's resolution, and it had never been about Jason Hastings in the first place. It was her self-improvement project. Giving up in the first week would make her feel like a total failure. So she did what any self-respecting woman would do: she went into the ladies' room, blotted the tears away, changed into her exercise gear, and came out with her yoga mat, ready to go.

* * *

If it wasn't for this being his boy's job, he would have called in and told them to find another instructor to teach yoga tonight. His back was so tight from lying on scaffolding and doing the ceilings, and from lifting glass blocks, that all he wanted to do was remain stationary on the couch.

So what that he had paint in his hair and all over his face and arms. He'd put on a bandana and tell the class the truth: he was renovating his house. Everybody in the area was doing that as property values soared to half a mil. No shame in that game, and half the class of foreigners didn't use deodorant, so hey. He fit right in.

Rather than quit, he did what any self-respecting friend would do; namely, he took his ass over to the rec center to endure an hour-and-a-half interruption to his mission. He made himself okay with the concept, justifying it as a necessary thing. The stretches would loosen him up. The yoga and meditation would quiet his mind. Through focus and balance, maybe his libido would cool, and he could get some rest.

He parked haphazardly after circling the block four times to find a parking space. The area was becoming as tight on parking as Manhattan, with the regentrification that was consuming it. Gone was a sleepy urban section of Philly that had working-class families. New theaters had sprung up, along with ultramodern bowling alleys, posh restaurants, coffee shops, and dozens of yuppie mobiles.

Annoyed, Jason took the steps two at a time, harried from being five minutes late to class. But normally, people taking yoga were real cool, didn't stress about the small things, so in the grand scheme of karma, what was five minutes? Those who had been exposed would be sitting on their mats yogi style, eyes closed, breathing, which would put the new folks in the right frame of mind. It was all good, he told himself as he bounded up to the second floor, pulling off his jacket. Then he froze.

She was sitting there in a pair of black yoga tights, her thick thighs laid open, her lower belly slightly rounded in a way that made his palm ache to run over it. Her eyes were closed, and her lush lips slightly parted. Her hair was pulled up into a loose ponytail, and her white tank top left *nothing* to his imagination. It clung to her large breasts, revealing a deep cleavage, which made his mouth go dry. The chilly temperature in the room had made her nipples stand at attention beneath the Lycra fabric. Her palms faced up, wrists relaxed against her knees. And her feet . . . perfectly manicured pink and white toes, with designs on the big toe. This woman took care of her feet. Good God in heaven, this woman was gonna make him cancel class just to get with her. Didn't she know he was an artist, and that if she wanted them painted, he could do that, too?

Okay, he told himself firmly. *Take off your shoes, walk across the floor, sit down, meditate for a moment, and start this dag-gone class. You are the sensei. You are the yoga instructor. Your place of balance is within. Go deep. You have better sense than this, man. You can't sit here in front of twenty students with wood!*

"Good evening," he said, quietly bowing from where he sat once he'd composed himself. "I'm glad everyone has come to class, and those who've experienced yoga before have led the new people into silent meditation, which in the tradition is called *Dhyana.* Let's begin by talking about the basic ethical principles, or *Yama.* We'll then go over the rules of personal conduct, *Niyama.* In this class we will be practicing yoga postures, also known as asanas, and we'll focus on correct breathing, *Pranayama.* But in yoga, what we are dealing with is the concentration of the mind,

Dharana, for the ultimate absorption into the infinite,
Samadhi."

He smiled and calmly looked over his class, hoping
that his concentration and discipline would return.
"Once we have opened with a prayer of respect and
have become centered as a group, we'll go over the
foundation principles and start with a few basic poses,
like Tree Pose and Downward Facing Dog, to start the
energy flow. Namaste."

Having Deborah Lee Jackson in his class would turn
out to be his greatest challenge. He had to give each
student equal time, had to be sure each student posed
correctly, lest they twist their bodies in a way that could
cause injury. And the last thing he wanted was for Deborah to be hurt. But resting his hands on her hips to
position her shredded all the training he'd ever had in
life. Feeling her thick, supple curves move with his
gentle prodding evaporated his concentration. Every
time he guided her and then walked away to find a
new student, his palms burned, just like inappropriate
images of her burned in his mind. But out of respect,
he made sure that he kept his tone clinical, distant,
controlled, and focused on her asanas rather than her
other very lovely attributes.

From the moment he'd walked in the door, with
the stealth of a cat, and begun sharing his knowledge
in a language that she hadn't a clue about, she was
done. Admiration turned into intimidation as she
watched him master the universe of her mind. Never
in all her born days had she seen anything like it.

The principles he spoke about were no different,
really, than the ones she'd been brought up to believe: not wasting, not resorting to violence. All the
things he spoke of would make the world kinder and
gentler. He also didn't lie. All these years she'd been

alive, and she was breathing wrong? She had never known there was a right and wrong way to breathe, but immediately felt the difference as her lungs filled and her mind calmed—that is, until they began to do their poses.

What looked easy—namely, turning one's body into a V, with her hands on the floor, her feet firmly planted, and her butt stretched up toward the ceiling—demanded muscles inside of muscles that she didn't know she had. And it certainly didn't help her so-called calm breath control when he came over and placed one flat palm on her lower belly and the other on the small of her back and lifted her into the correct position so she could, as he said, "feel it."

Oh yeah, she felt it, and none of it had much to do with ethical principles, but it was indeed enlightening . . . damned near Nirvana. Heat swept off her Lycra-covered hips and turned her belly into a kiln, glazing every inappropriate place of her. She was just glad her pants were black. Each time his wondrously warm hands slid away from her, the cool air rushed in to spank her silly and to get her to snap out of it. And she had to snap out of it, big time and immediately.

Warrior poses that looked like the sort of deep lunges she used to have to do in gym class, but with much more precision and serious muscle burn, had her about to pass out. Him, nah. He was talking as though he was sitting on a sofa, while everybody in class was keeling over, limbs trembling, and losing their balance, and had a plea for mercy in their eyes.

Her only question was, why was she all sweaty, while he looked as cool as a cucumber? How could a person stand on one foot and talk, with their other foot pressed inside their thigh in some tree pose? Yeah, right, envision the roots of one's energy going down into the floor when everybody was falling, grabbing the wall, and dang sure couldn't get their leg up to mid-thigh, let alone their heel to kiss their crotch!

Deborah blotted her face with both hands after the cool-down meditation, and then Jason released the class. She knew God was merciful. She had needed to see this to make up her mind. Nope, she wasn't sleeping with the man, even if he was a saint. What, to get embarrassed? Aw, hell no. Uh-huh. Not her. The man could hold his body in positions that, as far as she was concerned, defied gravity. Naw. She had a few old moves, but they didn't include no danged downward-facing dog, or cobra, or anything that crazy. No . . . oh . . . no. God bless him, Jason Hastings could find a nimble ninja chick for the winter. She was out.

Chapter 7

He knew he had to go over who had what injury and stay and talk with those students that wanted to delve into Eastern philosophy after class, but Deborah was packing up and had only given him a sweet but civil greeting, and his concentration was fried.

"Yo, Deborah, hold up," he said, trying both to listen with full engagement and hurry the stragglers along.

"Oh, it's cool," she said, seeming to pack faster. "I'll catch you next week. I know you have people to talk to."

"Can you excuse me for a second?" he asked a group of eager yoga students and then slipped around their huddle. He tried to dampen the urgency in his voice when he addressed Deborah. "It'll only be a few. I thought maybe you might wanna go down the street for some tea."

He watched her struggle with the decision and then cave.

"All right, but I can't be out late, like I was last night."

"Cool."

Jason dashed back to the group and gave them his attention, but he made it clear that he was packing his gear to get out of the class. Then it dawned on him.

Damn, half the class would probably go over to the Green Line. The last thing he needed was a long walk over there, discussing technique, with Deborah made a third wheel by someone wanting to show off their yoga knowledge. A few diehards finally went to get their mats, and he made a break for it.

"Listen," he said under his breath. "I've gotta get out of the teacher access zone. Feel me?"

She didn't have a clue what he meant, but by the look in his eyes, she could tell he felt like a trapped man. "Okay."

"I know another place, if you don't mind a short drive."

She agreed but wasn't sure why. He had her by the elbow, and he kept walking and talking as he steered them both past pockets of people that would have waylaid them. When he stopped before a mint-condition, drop-top Karmann Ghia in midnight blue, she bit her lip. She'd never say a word to LaVern, but it made her feel better to know that her girlfriend had been so dead wrong about this, like everything else.

"Hop in," he said, laughing as he opened the door for her. "Gotta move fast before the technique junkies swarm."

When he slid in and turned on the motor, she couldn't help but comment. "Sorta like yoga groupies. Dang." She looked out the window. "But I could see why," she murmured.

He stepped on the clutch and shifted gears. Did she say what he thought she said? Nah. His mind had to still be processing what it wanted to hear. After seeing her raise her hips in the air, he'd been no good. He'd worked the class hard enough to bring back his own clarity, which was probably unfair . . . but, hey. Pretty Deborah's skin glistened still, with a sheen of perspiration, and her body was more flexible than she knew . . . Her body had responded to her own inner voice and to gentle guidance from his hands. She had no idea how badly he wanted to hold her now, with a firm grip, and feel her yield, but this was *not* the place.

Oh yeah, next week, in order to keep his focus, he was gonna really have to work on the class's core support and go four layers deep, to their transversus abdominis, to get at the six-packs hidden in their abs.

"So, where are we going?" she asked.

He came out of the daze. He'd been on autopilot and was halfway to his house. "Uh . . ."

She arched an eyebrow. His palms were moist.

"I, uh, was renovating the house and looked like crap, and I was sweating in yoga class. Thought maybe I could throw my duffle bag in the door, at least find something better than a bandana to wrap around my head and a clean T-shirt, if I got one, and then we'd head to a tea salon down on South."

"Oh." She nodded and glanced out the window. "I did that to you the other night," she said, with a smile. "But you never broke a sweat. I seriously need a shower, if you're gonna get all cleaned up."

"You don't need a shower, believe me," he said, wishing he hadn't. "What I mean is, I'm not getting cleaned up, per se . . . just presentable."

"But you don't have to go to all that trouble. I can't stay out late tonight, and I seriously think you look fine the way you are." She bit her lip. Why did she say that?

His concentration was definitely fried. "Uh, okay, well . . . I just didn't wanna offend you . . . I've been working pretty much nonstop, and, you know."

Now she had him babbling as he pulled up to his block. The place was a wreck still. It was a bad idea to show it to her half complete, but he didn't want to share her or himself with the outside world for a little while.

She watched him get out of the car and round it like she might run away. It was the strangest thing to observe a guy of his caliber so totally flustered. She didn't know what to make of it and wasn't sure exactly why he was nervous. It wasn't until he started talking a mile a minute and apologizing about his home that she realized just how nervous he was.

"I'll warn you, Deb," he said, fumbling with his keys. "I just came in here one night last week and lost my mind, took a sledgehammer to it. Actually, you should be careful as you walk through . . . but these old houses have a lot of potential. Problem is I'm a one-man crew, so, you know, I do some, rest some, teach some, gotta paint some, and I might have it finished in about a week. It's not demolition to the studs in all rooms. Just some paint, some moving around, but it'll—"

"Oh . . . my . . . God . . . ," she whispered, cutting him off. She simply stood in awe and looked up at the eighteen-foot ceilings and the beginnings of a mural of a goddess, her arms open in the foyer.

She didn't even ask him—she couldn't find the words—as she crept forward as though inside a temple, looking at the detail he'd put into the very borders of the crown molding. Then she looked at the hardwood floors and simply gasped.

"May I?" she finally asked, turning to him.

He nodded, breathing shallow breaths through his mouth. "Yeah."

"Look at what you've done to this dining room!" she said, her voice like thick, warm syrup that he could taste. "Glass blocks and exposed brick . . . Jesus, man . . . What would ever make you apologize?"

She ran her hand up the glossy wood banister, and he could feel it where he shouldn't have until he shuddered. She stroked the newel post and just shook her head. "You carved this yourself, didn't you?"

He nodded and pushed off the wall that had

caught him. "Lemme show you what I'm doing with the kitchen."

"Can my heart stand it?" she said as she smiled.

He smiled in return as he led her forward, hoping her heart couldn't. When they got there, he was rewarded by the way she clutched her chest.

"Just stop it, man. A galley kitchen in West Philadelphia?" She rushed over to the double sinks he'd put in years ago, just gawked at the stained-glass and portal windows, then spun to study the tiles. "These are hand painted!"

"Yeah." He looked away, feeling a rush of pride. "Down in the basement, I have some stained glass that I'm gonna hang in the living room, once I finish slinging paint and banging. Want some tea?"

"I would love some," she said, "as long as you don't stop the tour. I know I'm being nosy, but this is beautiful."

He should have gotten the merlot, taken a shower, fixed the platform. Shit, his timing was messed up. This was unplanned and crazy, spur of the moment. He should have been prepared. "Cool. I'll put the water on and show you the studio. That's where I usually work. The place on South Street is more like a collective. It's an old property that was in the family for years, when South Street was owned by us. Now it's where artists can show their work, and we take turns working down there to keep regular hours, but here's where I create."

He had to stop; he was babbling again. He filled the kettle with spring water and watched her press her face to his back windows. "The winter wreaks havoc on everything back there, but I try to keep the bonsai inside and do what I can out back . . . Lately, I've been remiss."

She spun on him again, this time folding her arms.

"Okay, I'm in your business. How come you're not married and not snatched up and still in circulation?"

The question came as such a direct shot that he could only laugh. "Been asking myself that about you, Deb. What's up?"

"You first, since you've shortened my name to a nickname and I asked you first."

"You called me J last night," he said, with a shrug, "and almost made me kiss you, so—"

"Did not," she said, looking away and walking back toward the kitchen door.

"Did, too," he said, following her after he'd turned on the teapot. "But let's call it a draw, and I'll show you the studio."

"Okay." Although her question still lingered, she was too overwhelmed to press him for answers right now. She had to practice every breathing technique he'd shown the class as she followed him up to the second floor. The way his muscles kneaded each other within his straight, proud back and wide, sinewy shoulders hitched her breath every few seconds. But that dip in his lower spine and the way his butt curved in his gray sweats made the wide hallway feel unbearably tight, just like everything on her had become.

He opened a set of French doors, and she thought she might pass out straight away. Stained-glass panels in soothing blues and greens, like a bejeweled ocean, glistened in floor-to-ceiling windows. A thick futon mattress draped in rumpled midnight blue linens lay discarded on the floor, beside evidence of work in progress on a huge platform frame with floating steps. A can of varnish awaited it. What looked to be a thick Oriental rug was rolled up and standing in the corner. Minimalist furniture, blonde oak like the floors and the bed platform, rimmed the room. An indoor garden of bonsai had stolen an entire windowed wall with a southern exposure. A closet had been torn out, down to the studs, but a large rice-paper screen covered up the damage.

"Like I said," he murmured, "I'm still working."

"I can see it . . . the vision of where you're going."

He studied her eyes for a moment. "Can you?"

She dragged her gaze from his. "I think so."

"Master bathroom is over there," he said, with a nod. "I took all the rooms on this floor and consolidated them into three—master bedroom, master bath, my studio—so I can roll out of bed and work. But, maybe, in the future, I'll hook up the basement for that. If I'm working in oil, fumes from that can be wicked."

"Can I see?"

He hesitated. "Sure."

Understanding his need to show her the studio last, somehow, she crossed the room and opened a set of recessed doors, which gave way to a stunning paradise adorned with blue and clear glass block.

"Oh. My. God."

"You are gonna have to stop saying that," he said quietly as he followed her in.

"I'm sorry. I'm sorry. I know you're not supposed to use the Lord's name in vain, but look at this shower all in glass block and a custom-built glass-block tub, brother. Tiles that are just ridiculous. I won't say the name of the Most High in vain again, but—"

"It's not the usage, but the tone of your voice . . . okay?" He looked at her.

She stared at him briefly and looked away, flustered. "Can I see the studio?"

"It's a mess. I've got works half completed, drop cloths all over the floors, it's worse than downstairs, and there's really not much to see. Looks like a war zone in there."

"If I'm gonna sit for you, I'd like to at least see

where you'd have me." She smiled and was devastated when he swallowed hard.

"You will?" His question was a whisper.

Her voice failed her, and she could only nod.

He pushed off from the door frame and didn't look back, but was acutely aware that she was following him. He opened another set of recessed doors, which slid into the walls.

"This is where I do my thing," he said quietly, walking forward and beginning to pick up things from the floor.

"Don't," she said, her voice so quiet and reverent it was almost like she was in church. "Jason . . . I've never in my life seen work this profoundly beautiful."

She stood in the middle of the room, her gaze tender as it swept from sketches tacked to the walls—paint creating an unintentional kaleidoscope on the floors, drop cloths, and ladders—to fifteen-foot canvases, suspended and anchored, that began to tell a story. She kept hugging herself, almost afraid to move, lest she bump some masterpiece in progress, destroy a one-of-a-kind, or simply step on his favorite brush.

"Like I said, this is a war zone. I come in here and really lose my mind," he said, leaving off with his attempt to clean up and going to stand by the door. "But if you're inclined, I can set up a comfortable seating situation, light you, do some sketches, then transfer one of them onto one of the panels I owe the client project I've been commissioned to complete."

It came out before she could censor it. "Oh . . . my . . . God . . ." But it wasn't until he closed his eyes and turned his face away like she'd slapped him that she really began to understand his point. Yet that did something extremely crazy to her psyche. Never in her life had a man reacted to her like that. "Tell me why you're in here by yourself, Jason. For real."

He looked at her without blinking. "Because no

one ever came in here and understood what this space means to me." He shook his head slowly, raking his fingers across his bandana, taking it off, and then running his palms down his face. "You walked in here, into this room, like it was a cathedral. This was her room, Nana's. I joined Nana's room and the one next to it, which was mine, to make this room. This was the place in which somebody believed in me . . . where they told me I had a gift . . . told me that I should pray on things. Told me so much wisdom, Deb, that I can't even explain it all now."

"Then, it's sacred space, like this whole house. I don't understand someone not appreciating this or what you do."

His intense gaze held her where she stood. "I've learned to cope with it. Artists are notoriously difficult people to deal with, they say. I guess that's true. I rent the third floor to my boy, Wil, and he's as much a pain in my ass as I am a pain in his."

She could feel him deflecting the question, retreating and evading, and something very crazy within made her need to know. "What happened?"

"She got pregnant by some other guy, tried to play it off as mine because I had a house. Took me to court, humiliated me in front of my family, who swore I did it and was trying to get out of it. Like I'd do that." He shrugged. "They never really knew me, my brother and sisters, so can I blame them? Thing is, I'd been trying for almost ten years to live holistically, and then I realized how one unfaithful slip of a partner could have cost me my life. I was done. I just kept working."

Deborah remained very quiet, watching the emotions implode within him, and she thought of several women she knew. "I take it you weren't flashy enough for her. Had to focus and didn't have time for the clubs." It wasn't a question; it was a statement. "She must have been out of her mind," she whispered, staring at him.

"What about you?" he said, with an edge to his voice, lifting his chin. "Isn't that what you all want?"

She shook her head. "No, J. Don't go there. We're not all like that, and you know it . . . or you wouldn't be holding out for one that isn't. Be honest."

He looked away. "Well, what do you want? You asked me about me, and I really don't know how we got on this subject. This was just supposed to be a tour."

"Tea kettle's whistling. If you make me a cup, I'll tell you."

He appraised her with unsure eyes, and then she marveled at how he made that question in his eyes retreat behind a wall of pure bravado. "Cool. I'll make you some tea."

This was not how this was supposed to go at all. He was supposed to wait, have his thing totally together, and then learn some more about Deborah—and *then* push up on her. If she backed off, then she wasn't the one. If she moved forward, once he showed her that he was serious, then, cool. He just had to stop slamming dishes around. For the life of him, he wasn't even sure why he was. Tension was giving him a headache. He really needed to soak in some Epsom salts and go to sleep. His life had been turned upside down since he'd bumped into this woman in the herb store!

"I'm not married anymore," she said, leaning against the refrigerator, "because my ex felt that it was his right to run the streets."

Jason stopped slamming mugs and set down the loose tea canister in his hand very slowly. "He really ran on you? I know you said . . . but . . ." He shut his mouth and raked his finger through his unruly Afro.

"For the same reasons an unfaithful partner scared

you to death, one scared me to death, and I pulled back from the whole dating scene. I was tired. Emotionally exhausted, ya know?"

He nodded and didn't say anything as he began filling a tea ball with jasmine leaves. Yeah, he knew *exactly* what she meant. Everything she said was registering in his gut as the plain, old-fashioned truth, creating a parallel existence he could identify with, the nexus of which had everything to do with how they were raised. So, he let her talk, needing to hear more, saying nothing.

"I had just lost a baby, and he was in the streets. That's why I don't have any kids. So, as much as it hurt, it was a blessing in disguise . . . because I would have been tied to him for life by way of my kid. And I never, ever, ever wanted that kind of drama in my life."

Deborah looked away. She had to. This man had told her so much that sounded like the truth . . . His nana was so much like hers, and she had proof, evidence, that he lived alone and was the artist he'd claimed to be, and the rest of what he'd told her before just felt right down to her core. Slowly awakening trust made her feel so suddenly vulnerable that she hugged herself. It was too soon to feel like this, too fast, too quick, she told herself, but she couldn't shake the heat that had crept between her thighs.

Jason paused and looked at her, his gaze destroyed. "Deborah, no woman deserves that shit. Baby, I hear you . . . man . . . That's foul. I don't understand some of our brothers. Really I don't."

"That's why I was asking you a lot of questions," she admitted quietly. "I wanted to tell you, but didn't have the words . . . Don't hurt me, and I won't hurt you."

He set down the tea ball and the kettle.

She continued. "I wanted to say, 'You know, Jason, it's been a really, really long time, and I want to so much that I can imagine what it feels like and my body reacts, but I don't wanna get sick, I don't wanna get played, I don't wanna have another piece of my soul scarred.'"

He crossed the room as she closed her eyes, his fingertips daring to trace her jawline. "I know where you're at with that," he murmured, allowing the pad of his thumb to follow the high, regal ridge of her cheekbone. "I wanted the real thing, not acrylic or weave or illusion, you know?"

She nodded and touched his mouth with trembling fingers. "I wanted somebody to call me pretty and really mean it, and not make me feel less than because my hips were more than . . . you know what I mean?"

"You're gorgeous," he said in a quiet rasp. "I haven't slept since I met you . . . That's what started the home improvement project. You should have seen it before."

He stepped nearer but not enough to crowd her if she didn't want that from him. She closed her eyes and turned her face away, making his truth spill out in a rush.

"I'm not lying, girl. It was a mess. Not a contractor's mess, but filthy. But after I met you and waited up all night for you to call . . . I was losing it. I needed to do something with my hands."

"Are you serious?" She stared up at him.

"Yeah," he said, swallowing a breath. "I can't explain it, but I did."

Her hand touched the center of his chest. "I stayed up half the night, exercising . . . because . . ." She looked down, but he lifted her chin with his finger.

"Because two years all of a sudden kicked my ass, just thinking about you."

His mouth found her lips already parted. The taste of his mouth and the feel of his body slowly pressing harder against hers pulled a moan up and out of her, which he quickly swallowed. Long, graceful, yet mas-

culine fingers became tangled in her hair, pulling out
the ponytail scrunchy, and for the first time in years,
her hands burned as they roamed across broad shoulders, up a muscular back, to rest for a moment against
shoulder blades that were covered in ropes of sinew.

Hard, pebbled nipples grazed hers just as a lean
torso rubbed against her belly. A tightly muscled
thigh parted hers, stealing her breath, and then his
hard length ground against her swollen mound. Soft
fabrics allowed her to feel every ridge till she cried
out. That whimper tightened his embrace, deepened
his kiss, and made his breaths more ragged. Soon her
flat palms were fists holding his shirt, her pelvis rocking to find that ridge along his shaft that gave rise to
his head. Knowing what she craved, he dipped low,
held her by her waist, his face searing her cheek as
her demanding thrusts turned his leisurely, slow
grind into a more urgent dance.

He'd found the spot, the place between her saturated thighs that needed tender loving care. The place
that she'd fought so hard not to touch or awaken since
the day she'd met him. They couldn't keep their
mouths joined as he pummeled that aching place
until her inhibitions peeled away and her hands covered his ass. The moment she grabbed him there, it
was as though he snapped. His head dropped back, his
grip went to her hips, and the refrigerator was
damned near rocking off its base with every thud that
inched her up it.

Tears wet her lashes. She was so close but so far, it
was absolute torture. Her hands slid down into his
sweatpants, needing to feel the smooth globes of his
muscles flexing and contracting under her palms.
The moment she touched his heated flesh, he released another deep moan, the vibration of which
almost made her climax.

"Oh, God, I need to but shouldn't," she gasped, with a near sob.

His tongue immediately fought with hers, one arm and hand now the anchor, the other freeing her tank top, lifting it so he could get to her waistband. As soon as he found it, he tore his mouth away from hers and bent, forcing her to hang on to his broad shoulders and arch her breasts toward his seeking mouth. His full lips captured a stinging nipple, and he suckled her with care. Her voice was a near shriek as her thrusts lost form, becoming erratic. His voice bottomed out, and he moaned.

"Oh, God, Deborah . . . ," he gasped, finding her other breast at the same moment his hand slid beneath her stretchy yoga pants and his forefinger found her bud.

His touch sent her hands into his hair and changed her thrusts into crazed wriggles as she sought a steady drone of contact, which he wouldn't allow. Then, just as she was about to beg him, hysteria taking her by storm, he clamped his thighs around one of hers, with a shudder, flicked a finger past her throbbing bud, and sent two long fingers sliding over her slick essence and deep into her haven.

She climaxed so hard that she couldn't breathe. Initially, no sound came out of her mouth; her body simply convulsed like she'd been struck by lightning. Then, like a delayed Doppler effect, her voice went through the kitchen in waves as she thrust her sopping mound against his touch, repeating his name until she slumped against him.

He'd stopped moving, but his breaths were so ragged, they made her look up. The agony that shone in his eyes reignited the inner fire deep within her valley. She took his mouth hard, and his returned kiss was frenzied as his hand slid out of her pants.

"You have anything in here?" she asked, gulping air.

He nodded. "Yeah, upstairs," he said between deep breaths, squeezing his eyes shut.

The expression on his face told her everything. She raked her fingers across his nipples and pulled them into her mouth through his shirt, making his body buckle.

"Baby, I gotta . . . oh, God," he murmured.

His stomach contracted so hard, and he kissed her till their teeth banged. She knew he'd never make it upstairs. Her hands slid deep into his sweats, and when she gripped him, he pumped against her so wildly that she could barely hold him.

"Go, 'head, baby . . . We've got all night," she whispered and watched relief spread across his face as he palmed the refrigerator, threw his head back, and convulsed, with an openmouthed holler.

Both slumped, damp from passion. She just held him, not moving, listening to him catch his breath, intermittent shudders coursing through them. Hot, wet, slick essence oozed through her fingers, and as she tried to draw her hands away, he squeezed his eyes shut tighter and just shook his head no, with a grunt. She understood, being so hypersensitive, that the slightest touch produced sweet agony, but that was a power she'd never owned. She'd never seen a lover react like that from her caress.

Without moving, she rained kisses on his shoulder and the side of his neck and face. He was still rock hard, wasn't going down between her palms, but he finally recovered enough to kiss her back and to slowly begin moving against her again.

"Deborah, I swear, I never expected it to get this far tonight," he said, taking deep breaths and letting them out slowly, while pumping. "I'm not gonna hurt you. I'm not playing you," he whispered, taking her mouth between words. "I need you to trust me enough to come upstairs with me and stay all night. If you go home now, I will lose my mind."

He pushed her tousled, wild hair away from her face, and the scent of her on his hands, the look of raw need on his face, and the promise in his eyes let her know she couldn't leave.

"Okay," she whispered and reluctantly let him go.

She dragged her hands up his lower belly and over the tight bricks of his abdomen, feeling burning skin and springy curls, which relaxed into a trail from the thicket at his base to feather up toward his navel. The sound he released made her need to feel his massive erection imbedded deeply within her.

"I'm not going anywhere," she suddenly promised him.

He ripped his shirt over his head and kissed her, wiping her hands off with the shirt. Then he dropped it without looking at it and picked her up by the waist. She shrieked.

"I've got you. Trust me. Let's go upstairs," he said.

"I'm too heavy," she argued, trying to regain her balance by grabbing the refrigerator.

He took her mouth. "Hold me instead. Go with my flow, and we won't fall. I've got balance like a cat."

Unsure, she locked her arms around his neck, her heart thudding from fear, not passion, this time. He paced through the rooms and took the stairs without even breathing hard. The farther up they went, the more she relaxed, until she wanted him so badly, she began hyperventilating.

He lowered her from his body at the foot of the futon, and she watched him in the semidarkness as he rooted through his drawers. When he came to her, he had a box in hand and just gracefully pulled her down onto the thick padding.

"I don't want you to start distrusting me. I can show you the receipt," he murmured against her neck. He then began to kiss a slow trail down her body. "I bought these on a hope and a prayer while making supply runs. I haven't been stocked like this in the house in years." He stopped the soft, damp, pelting caresses at the edge of her tank top and slowly raised it while staring at her.

"I believe you," she whispered, her body on fire for him. He was actually talking to her, looking at *her.* Oh, God, she was gonna lose her mind.

"Good," he breathed against her cleavage, allowing his cheek to nuzzle the sensitive tips of her breasts. "Because I want you to feel like you can be open, like you don't have to hold anything back . . . You have to have trust for that."

Kneeling between her legs, he slid her sports bra straps down and then gently lifted the center clasps, opening each hook until her breasts bounced free. He helped her lean forward and remove the undergarment, raw passion etched across his face. She watched the moonlight shimmer in his dark eyes until he briefly closed them, as though unable to bear looking at her naked breasts.

"You are *so* beautiful," he murmured, leaning down to softly take her mouth.

His thumbs stroked the tender undersides of her heavy lobes as he forged a gentle trail of kisses down her chest, which caused her to arch. The sensation of that slow swirl of his thumbs shortened her breath as she waited for his mouth to consume her. Each patient flutter of his tongue as it circled a nipple made her lift her hips and try to make contact with any hard surface of him that she could. But he held himself away from her, as though testing her resolve, dragging his hot hands down her sides as his tongue paid homage to her belly and his hands caressed her hips, then slid under her behind.

Multiple issues of trust tumbled against each other,

colliding with reason as he slid her pants and panties down in one fluid move. She wanted his tongue against her so badly that she was gripping the mattress, thighs parting without consulting her brain. What he was about to do was the height of one's word as a bond. It meant that he'd believed every word she'd said, that she'd been tested and hadn't been active since, and she, too, had to believe what he'd said with all her heart and soul. Fear of making a mistake almost put the word "stop" on her lips, but the way he rested his cheek on her throbbing thigh while stroking the other one caused her to moan instead.

He kissed the tortured skin of her inner thigh and looked up, his breathing labored. "You sure?" he murmured against the angry surfaces. "I'll stop if you want, but . . ."

Practically thrashing, she shook her head no. "Please . . ."

It had been so long since she'd felt what his gentle suckle between her thighs promised. Tears slid from the corners of her eyes. Skin against skin, there, with no sheath, was maddening. She stared up at the subtle relief of stars he'd painted on the ceiling and then closed her eyes tightly, still seeing their images branded inside her lids, as his tongue ran the length of her slit. She practically sat up; the wail was so deep and feral. The moment he opened her with an intense French kiss, he had to hold her hips steady, and yet there was no way she could hold back.

Her womb and canal contracted hard with each lick. She needed to be filled by him so badly that she simply reached for the box. Their eyes met as he looked up at her and then let his tongue unravel her mind. She was still clutching the box through the sobs and shudders when he slowly kissed his way up her stomach, to allow her to taste herself on his mouth, and then turned her over.

The way he blanketed her with a hot swath of warmth felt like the most natural thing in the world. His hands ran up her arms, stretching her out beneath him as he collected the box. She cried out as his thighs gated hers, his stomach clenched against her buttocks and then her spine while his eager breaths caressed her shoulders. The sound of tearing foil made her grind against him, and as he drew back from her, she followed his warmth, as though an invisible string joined them, from her backside to his pelvis. But a deep groan of frustration claimed her as he gently pressed her forearms down, and lifted her hips higher, his hand on her belly, just like he'd done in class, giving her cues with spine-long kisses.

She was so aroused that the crown of her head hit the mattress in defeat and a sob broke her voice in half. "Jason, please . . ."

Hearing her like that, with her gorgeous, high, round ass lifted and waiting for him, he needed to draw on all the discipline he had. His hands swept over the butter smooth surface, his urgent kiss landing on each cheek, making her buck. He held her steady, impaling her slowly so he could hold back, but the tight sheath that fit him and her husky gasp made him pull her against him hard, with a groan.

She hollered his name, and that made him move. It had been too long, and he needed her so badly. It was too much to be loved by name, have her sobbing for him. This voluptuous goddess, this destroyer of pasts and builder of futures slid down so slowly that she made him follow desperately just to stay in. Then, without warning, she pushed up and spread her legs, assuming the position she'd just learned. Her torso was raised, her pelvis and thighs flat against the futon, in the upward-facing dog asana, while he worked against her, losing all perspective. Each time she changed position, it broke his stride slightly, making him more insane. Then she did the unthinkable: she reached back and held his hip and murmured, "Stop."

Shuddering like he'd been shot, he tried to stop moving. She looked over her shoulder and slid off him, then turned over. His breathing restarted.

She kissed his chest. "I want to look at you."

His hand was shaking so badly when he caressed her cheek that he simply replaced the touch with a kiss. But when he tried to lower himself to her, she shook her head no and guided him onto his back.

Tears slid from the corners of his eyes as she mounted him. He arched so hard at the anticipated sensation that he sat up, with a groan. Just seeing her framed in stars, her pendulous breasts bouncing, her thick tresses all over her head, chin tipped to the ceiling, nails digging into his biceps, all of it, was blowing his mind. She smelled so good. Her juices running down his shaft, her lips punished plump by his, her breasts filling his hands, then his mouth, her cries driving him to the brink of endurance and beyond . . . The visual of her ecstasy was forever painted on his psyche, carved there.

"Oh, Deborah, God, baby, take it!" He was having a seizure, an out-of-body experience, coming so hard that he was speaking in tongues.

Her kisses pelted his face; her breasts were crushed against his chest; her voice reverberated off the walls till he shivered, the soundsation dredging his sac as much as her thrusts. Thick, satin smooth thighs clenched and released him till he pounded the futon. Cushioned hips, her weight a godsend with every thrust, almost lifted him up with each stroke. "Just get it, baby. Oh . . . right . . . there . . ."

When he dropped, she dropped, both wheezing and gulping air. He couldn't speak; he just held a fistful of her hair caveman style and slowly released it. She didn't say a word; she just kept smoothing his hair back away from his face, with her cheek pressed to his chest. They both reached for the edge of the condom at the same time, and that was when he understood where she was. Her legs tightened; he let go and stroked her thighs. She bent close to his ear, her words and breaths coming out in puffs.

"Don't . . . not yet."

He found her mouth, hungrily taking it at the same time the pad of his thumb found her bud again. One pass across it and she sent a wail into his mouth, then collapsed against him and started crying. His arms immediately embraced her, and the only thing he knew to do was rock her until she calmed down. He wondered if she believed in something as esoteric as soul mates, but he didn't want to go there. He was so wide open, it was ridiculous. She was absolutely incredible. Submissive and aggressive. Following and leading. Giving and demanding. Gentle and rough. He wanted to spoil her rotten, needed to do that, wanted to paint her, but also needed to temporarily pass out.

"Call out sick tomorrow," he murmured, drifting, finger painting long strokes up and down the satiny finish of her damp back, hips, and backside. "Let me cook for you, baby. We'll go to the supermarket, get some wine, come back here . . . with your fantastic burnt orange shirt. How about we hide from the world for a coupla days and create a new reality? Shit, we'll get a doctor's note and . . . my sister's a nurse . . . It's flu season. Just stay with me, Deborah, like this. I'm so tired of being alone."

Chapter 8

Despite the all-night lovemaking marathon, Deborah's eyes opened at 6:00 AM, and panic swept through her. She had to go to work! She was in a man's bed. She wasn't home. She recalled every bit of her strict military upbringing, the rules that had been ingrained in her, and like a soldier at reveille, she moved, got up, freaked out, and headed to where she might have dropped her purse. The kitchen.

She quickly pulled on her clothes, glancing back once at Jason, and then slipped out of the room, almost running down the hall, barefoot. The one thing she couldn't lose was her job; as bad as it might be, it represented independence. No matter what he'd said in bed, the thought of being dependent on a man she'd just met was making cold-sweat panic course through her.

When she spied her purse, she prayed her cell phone battery would hold up long enough for . . . for what? If she was gonna go to work, then why was she rushing to call in? Truthfully, even though it would be cold as hell, she had enough time to power walk from Thirty-fifth to Forty-third, get a shower, get dressed, and jump on mass transit . . . so . . .

Deborah walked over to the stove and turned on the kettle, watching the last of the dark gray of night lift through stained-glass portals. She closed her eyes and said an urgent, murmured prayer. "Everything is happening so fast. Please, God, don't let me be stupid. Don't let me lose my job, my mind, my self-respect . . . but I'm so tired. Just let this be real."

"I had the same prayer this morning," a deep and quiet voice said behind her. "When I reached over and you were gone."

Startled and embarrassed, she turned around quickly to look into a pair of serious eyes, which practically devoured her where she stood.

"Deborah, I'm scared, too."

She nodded, clutching her cell phone. "My job is all I got, and I've never depended on . . . If I screw that up, I ain't got nowhere to go." Suddenly, tears rose in her eyes. "If I get sick, won't nobody take care of me. My momma and grandma are gone, and my dad, he'd be so through, he wouldn't come to the rescue like no cavalry. Extended family isn't close like that. If I get pregnant, it would be me by myself. I can't play."

She felt her voice rising in hysteria, choking up as the panic became overwhelming, while he simply stared at her. "You don't know what it's like being out in the world all by yourself. I *have* to go to work!" She backhanded away tears, which were now streaming down her face. "I can't take risks! Just because my job isn't fancy and prestigious like yours and I don't have my degree doesn't mean my work isn't important. Mine *pays* my bills, keeps my lights on. It's my survival, Jason!"

"It's okay. It's okay," he said, coming to her, soothing her with his voice as he neared her, opened his arms, hugged her, and began rocking her. "I'll just take a quick shower, and then I'll drive you home, and I'll wait for you to change and I'll drive you to work, okay?" He kissed her temple. "I'll be so careful with your heart, Deborah. C'mon, baby. Lemme take you home . . . It's all right."

Just seeing her so afraid stabbed him. Shudders reverberated through her as he stroked her back and tried to comfort her. He knew what a man could do to a woman to inspire such heartache; his own brother had run through three wives and was working on a fourth half his age. His sisters had been through turmoil that he didn't even want to consider. In this very kitchen, he and his real sensei, Nana, had shared many a philosophical conversation

And yet, the fact that Deborah was determined to stand on her own, alone, without even thinking he might make her life easier when he could, reinforced what he already knew: she wasn't a gold digger, wasn't playing games. This hardworking, proud, beautiful woman, who was smarter than she gave herself credit for, had already stolen his heart before the first kiss. Now she held it for ransom, and he was the one who needed to be deathly afraid. Never in his life had he felt like this.

"Let me go grab some clothes and take a shower real fast," he said, not wanting to let her out of his embrace but needing to very soon. "Then I'll take you home, okay?"

She nodded, sucked in a quavering breath, and slumped against him in relief.

"Do you want me to wait down here?" he asked, not sure, as they pulled up to her building.

"No," she said in a quiet, faraway voice, not looking at him. "It's too cold . . . and we keep starting tea and never getting the water into the mugs."

He smiled as a shy smile peeked out on her forlorn

face. "You shower and get dressed for work, and I'll make the tea." He couldn't help touching her soft cheek. "You're gonna change my biorhythms and break me in to mornings . . . gonna make me start getting up before noon and going to bed early just to take you to work so I can see the early light on your skin." He shook his head and opened the car door and got out.

She watched Jason circle the car, wondering if God answered prayers that quickly, or if, like her minister said, she was rushing the hand of the Almighty with her own will, not His. But Lord have mercy . . . This all felt so right. She'd been married briefly before but had never had a husband who willingly got out of bed to drive her anywhere, much less to her job. Plus, this man said he would putter around her kitchen while *she* got ready to meet "the man." Unheard of.

Deborah closed her eyes. *Thank you, God.* This man had stayed in her life beyond a premature night of passion, had shown up in the morning, still at her side. She watched his long, weary strides and smiled with tears of appreciation in her eyes. Jason was clearly tired, haggard. His chin was awash in five o'clock shadow that hadn't been tended since the morning prior. His wild mane of hair was stuffed under a Jamaican Rasta cap, but he was as fine as he wanted to be and was there for *her.*

She swallowed hard as he came to open her door, something she simply had to get used to. This fatigue-wearing nonconformist was, surprisingly, a gentleman in every sense, and one that respected her job, her wishes, and her lot in life. Jason Hastings was a conflict of realities, was everything her father had always told her to be wary of, and yet was everything her nana had told her to hope for. The dichotomy put butterflies in her stomach as his hand enclosed hers to help her from the low-riding vehicle. His warmth coated her from her heart outward. How could she be falling in love with a man so quickly? It didn't make sense and frightened her nearly to death. She wasn't ready; there was still so much to do to prepare herself.

How could she find someone so perfect when her life was a mess? Deborah pondered it all as she dug out her keys and they made their way into her building. Every magazine and talk show said you had to have your act together in order to expect someone to walk into your life with all that, too. She needed to lose weight and get in shape. He was in shape in ways that made her stupid. She was just getting on her feet financially after all the trauma and drama. He clearly had it going on. From the way it sounded, he had a real family. Hers was broken and messed up. He had his education on point, all the way up to a secondary graduate degree, and she was just in the formative stages of figuring out how to get back to school.

Deborah looked down sadly as she inserted the key into the lock on her front door. The heat of Jason's body loomed behind her. She was definitely a work in progress, while he was a completed work of art. Beautiful, together, refined, educated, warm spirit . . . good soul. What did she have to offer this man, other than the obvious? And men didn't stay for booty. That was too easy to come by and very plentiful on the open market. Maybe Jason was just God's way of telling her, something like this was possible. Right now, all she wanted to do was curl up in a little ball and weep. If only Nana was here, she'd know the answer.

"Tea's in the kitchen," she said, fleeing from him as soon as she opened the door. She just needed space, distance, and a shower in the worst way, to wash the wondrous scent of him off her.

He watched Deborah race across the small expanse, his nerves standing on end so tensely that he had chill bumps running up his arms. Jason remained at the entrance of her apartment and briefly closed his eyes. It was as if the exchange they'd just had had unearthed something encoded in his DNA. Taking your wife to work, making tea, hearing her in the shower, the hubbub of a household coming alive in the morning. Dad, on the night shift, would be coming in; Mom, on the day shift, would be leaving. Family. Stability. Home.

"What measure of a man if he gained the whole world and yet lost his soul?" Jason thought of the Bible passage as he crossed the room and began hunting in the cabinets for tea without taking off his jacket. Old gospel was pounding in his head from Nana's ancient radio in the kitchen, a haunting that didn't inspire fear, just melancholy. What did he have to give this woman, really? His life was built on shifting sands, not permanent rock, like his siblings had. They had medical and dental. They had solid jobs; his salary fluctuated wildly, depending on the work commissioned in any given year. The only semi-steady income was from the gallery downtown, but that was split among the collective. Wil's rent was cool, but nothing to raise a family on. Taxes from this year's project would eat his ass alive, and a third of the cash would go up in smoke. His house was in shambles, and he hadn't even had enough discipline to wait to bring her there until it was fly.

He was a work in progress, and she was a goddess. Stable, nurturing, righteous, sensual, gorgeous, caring, her heart as deep as a wishing well . . . her body as lush as a secret garden. He didn't deserve her and had frightened her. Of course, she'd panicked. Why would she turn her life over to him? Why would she jeopardize her stability for his insanity, his lusts?

Jason shook his head as he filled the kettle. He was gonna get it together. Would paint the hell out of that project, would fix up the house, would go get himself organized, would go see an accountant, would get himself set up as an LLC business entity and stop living on the edge of artistic feast and famine.

The singing kettle broke into his thoughts, and he covered the green tea bags with hot water, remembering how she liked her tea sweetened with honey. He drizzled it from the jar, mesmerized as the translucent amber poured over the edge to become a long, gooey strand of pure sweetness . . . good God, just like she tasted . . . just like her skin felt after they were done. Sweet and sticky. He had to get his mind out of the gutter, had to take her to work to show good intent. Had to wrestle back his filleted discipline and remember that in some circles, he was considered a sensei.

Jason licked his thumb and closed the jar, glancing up as Deborah walked into the room and simply stared at him.

For a second, she couldn't move. Common sense told her to go around him, grab something for lunch out of the refrigerator, and make small talk while accepting the tea. But something primal in his expression made her know that was a bad idea, just as something totally irrational within her had begun to thrum as she'd watched him lick honey off his fingers. Her throat constricted, keeping small talk at bay.

"I have to go to work," she finally murmured.

"I know," he said, staring at her and then allowing his gaze to slide over her rust-hued silk shirt and black wool skirt, down her black hose–sheathed legs, to her high heels. "That's why I made you some tea."

"Thanks," she said quietly, but not moving as his eyes ran back up her body and washed over her spill of hair on her shoulders.

Desire coiled and uncoiled in the nest of her stomach as he appraised her, and she had to admit that she'd left her hair out just for him. The smoky eye shadow, which she rarely wore, was also for him, and so was the shimmer of sheer copper gloss she'd added to her lips, along with the light dusting of the same hue along her cheekbones. This morning, everything she'd put on was just for him, even though she had to leave him. She never wore thigh-high, lace-paneled stockings to work, or heels, or a black lace bra and thong beneath it all. She might, on occasion, spritz on some perfume, but not something as sensual as Bath & Body Works' warm vanilla sugar. But it was all wishful thinking for later, if he'd see her again tonight.

He slowly moved the tea across the counter, toward her, as though moving a chess piece or checker across an invisible board, but he didn't back away or advance. He held her gaze with his intense stare, not saying a word. She'd have to go near him to claim the tea, and she hesitated, not trusting him or herself. Stone serious, the muscle in his jaw pulsing, he lifted a mug to his mouth, blew on his tea calmly, staring over the rim, and took a long sip—watching her.

She set her purse down on the coffee table and neared him, steeling her nerves, and finally got close enough to pick up her mug. The thong was a bad idea. She was so wet, she'd have to go to the bathroom to blot before the January wind gave her frostbite. But she was going to work, regardless. She studied him over the rim of her mug as she blew on her tea, and she willed her hands not to tremble when his lids lowered to half mast and he inhaled deeply.

"You look really nice," he said quietly.

"Thanks," she murmured, sipping tea and feeling pure want radiate off him like heat waves.

"What time do you get off from work?" He set down his mug and absently caressed it on the counter.

"Five," she said, taking a slow sip. "But I have my holistic cooking class tonight, from six to nine."

"I can teach you to cook all natural," he said, without blinking, his voice bottoming out in a clipped murmur.

She smiled and took another sip of her tea, determined to stay on her personal improvement mission. "I already paid for the class."

"All right," he said, tracing her eyebrow with his thumb. "Then, maybe afterward . . . I can pick you up, and maybe we could make dinner at home together?"

She closed her eyes as his thumb lazily caressed her cheek and collarbone. Did the man say cook together *at home*? "I'd like that," she whispered.

"What do you want to eat?" he murmured, stepping closer. "I'll go to the market while you're at work."

She set down her tea and looked up at him. "Whatever you want," she said on a breath.

"That's not in the supermarket. It's right here, but you have to go to work."

"Yeah . . . I do," she whispered in a near pant.

His hands cradled her face so gently, it was as though they were barely touching her. Yet the heat rising from his palms was dizzying.

"I don't wanna mess up your makeup," he whispered. "Just one kiss before you go?" He tilted his head, his lids heavy. "It looks like honey on your mouth."

"Okay," she said so quietly that she could barely hear the words.

When he stepped in and slowly pressed his body to hers, she released a gasp. His heavy jacket, with its rough texture, grazed her breasts through her silk shirt, and the feel of his arms wrapping around her and consuming her made her deepen his light kiss.

It had begun as the most delicate slide of his tongue over her bottom lip and a gentle press of his full lips against hers, but soon she was backed up against the counter, and his tongue halfway down her throat.

But she couldn't blame the man; she'd started it with a moan, by deepening the kiss, and by clutching the back of his jacket. She'd literally watched his discipline peel away from him, layer by layer, until her clothes were a wrinkled mess and her skirt was hiking up her thigh.

As though talking to herself, she repeated her reality like a mantra. "I've gotta go to work."

He kept nodding like a madman and grinding against her harder. "I know. Uh-huh, I know. What time you have to be there?"

"By eight thirty," she panted, helping him take off his jacket.

"I can beat the traffic," he said into her hair, kissing her neck as he began to unbutton her blouse.

"Okay, but I really have to go in," she said, arching, listening to his jacket thud against the floor.

"Uh-huh, okay, I know, I know," he said, his voice tight as he freed her blouse and then stopped for a moment to stare at her lace bra. "Oh . . . God . . ."

She couldn't catch her breath as she watched him look at her in the full light of day. Pure passion caught fire in his eyes, and he simply shook his head in a slow wave of disbelief, unzipped her skirt, and let it pool at her feet, then stepped back an inch, closed his eyes, and dropped to his knees. *Never* in her life had she seen a man react to her like that, *ever.*

"I gotta call out," she said fast as his searing hands covered her hips and he French-kissed her navel. "Gotta leave my boss a voice mail that I have the flu."

"You wore black lace," he said against her panties, sweeping his hands up her silk hose. "Oh, God . . ."

"Jason, I have to get to the phone. . . ."

"Uh-huh, I know, yeah . . ."

Her gasp sliced through the kitchen. "Then you have to stop kissing me *there* so I can talk."

He rocked back on his heels and looked up. "I didn't bring anything over here, 'cause I thought . . ."

Panic lit her eyes. "Oh . . . shit . . ."

"Call in, and gimme your keys. Store's around the corner. Cool?"

He was on his feet, looking wild in the eyes, and then he swept up his jacket like the apartment was on fire. She'd given a man she had just met the keys to her place, and she was dialing her boss, practicing a cough so she could get laid. This was too insane, but what the hell. Jason was running down the hallway like he'd robbed a bank. Deborah pressed her face to her frigid window and watched Jason whip a parking ticket off his windshield, spin around like he was disoriented, and then run down the street to the CVS drugstore at Forty-third and Locust. She wrapped her arms around herself and waited for voice mail. He was rushing for her—*for her.* Damn! It didn't get any better than this.

As soon as the long voice mail ended, she made her voice sound as pitiful as she could. Gravelly and husky was easy, courtesy of Jason. She clicked off the phone and spun toward the door, listening to the locks turn. He was back that fast? Ohmigod!

He fell through the door, his shoulder to it like he'd break it down if he couldn't figure out the keys, bag in hand, breathing hard. She hugged herself, standing in the middle of the floor, in black lace and heels. She was about to walk toward him, but he shook his head no.

"Don't move," he said, his eyes drinking her in. Then his gaze went to the window and followed something she couldn't see.

"Jesus . . . I've gotta get to my studio real soon," he said, dropping the bag on the coffee table. He moved the coffee table away from the sofa and then stood back. "You should see what I see, the way there's a swath of light, a panel of it, coming down, bathing your skin, hitting your hair, picking up an iridescence in your askew bra . . . Lord, woman, dancing over your

belly, putting a sheen on your stockings." He shook
his head. "Where I kissed you is still glistening, and
your hair is wild. *The Morning After*—that's what that
one will be titled. Uh-huh. Yeah. Bedroom, muted
shades in the background, all blues. Goddess hugging
herself, pensive eyes, smoky, wondering if she shoulda
done what she did."

"Should I have?" she asked quietly, moving to the
sofa, needing to sit down before she fell down.

"Uh-huh." He slipped off his jacket and unlaced his
sneakers, stepping out of them as he took off his
cable-knit sweater and began unbuttoning his jeans.

She sat down slowly, unable to take her eyes off him
as his hat hit the floor and his mass of wild hair sprung
loose at nearly the same time he dropped his pants
and boxers. A physical masterpiece sauntered over to
her and placed both hands at either side of her head,
on the back of the sofa. He dipped low to capture her
mouth in a deep kiss. But as she felt his body, she
broke their kiss and pressed her lips to his chest and
then looked up. Slow awareness overtook his expression, shortening his breaths. She nodded, and his grip
on the furniture tightened—it was all in the visual in-
terpretation, his expression said—I trust you.

Leaning forward, she reached for the bag with one
hand, while stroking his naked hip with the other to
keep him before her, and watched him close his eyes.
Allowing her lips to press against his breastbone as
she dropped the bag by her feet, she straddled his
legs, her tongue following the ridge of each large
brick of his chest until she captured a raisin-hued
nipple. Just the sound of the moan he released made
her bolder. She could feel his arms trembling, not
from holding his weight, but from the repressed need
to lower himself to her. That made her splay her
hands across his stomach to hold him back, then find
each brick beneath her palms to pay homage to the

masterpiece of fine art with her tongue. Good Lord, this man was fine.

When she found his navel, he kissed the back of her head but dared not move beyond that, not sure how far she was going to go. The box of condoms was on the floor, by her feet. What he hoped she'd be bold enough to do required ultimate trust, and he wasn't sure he'd inspired that in her yet. It was already enough that she had allowed him to have her and had taken a day off from work for him. His body had already betrayed him, too. From his member to the floor, a thick drizzle of his need for her made a clear thread, which told on him.

Her warm, soft hands swept up the burning insides of his thighs as she tongue-kissed his navel, making his groin contract and his shaft jump with each pass. He was just waiting for her to touch him where it throbbed hard enough to hurt. When she cupped his sac, the sensation alone made his knees buckle and forced her name out on a whispered rush of breath. "Oh, Deborah."

He began to lean in to her and bend to take her, needing to make contact in the worst way, but she stopped him with a hot lick that he hadn't expected, sending a shiver up his spine, which became a shudder. Warm, satiny palms now grasped his base. One hand was in her hair. *Oh, Jesus.* A tentative tongue grazed engorged, searing skin, which caused him to pull in air through his clenched teeth and made his stomach contract. The moment she sheathed him, he gripped the back of the sofa with both hands, dropped his head forward, and planted his feet, determined not to flip out and start pumping.

But it had been so long; it had been so long. Oh, God, yes, it had been so long. Skin against skin, the feel of wetness, not Latex, her tongue finding every sensitive ridge, every place that drove him crazy . . .

oh, girl, he couldn't help it. He had to move the way she moved, had to follow the heat of her mouth, the pulse of her hands, the swirl of her tongue, the pull and the release, which were creating colors behind his tightly shut lids.

Every exhale was a groan, each inhale a gasp. Fire breathing, quick pants, opened mouth. If she didn't back off, he wouldn't be responsible.

He was trying to tell her that, but the sentence got cut off each time, and he sounded like a broken record. "Baby . . . baby . . ."

The rest of what he needed to tell her was stuck inside his chest, blotted out by the pressure. If she didn't stop, he was gonna come. Sweat was rolling down his back. She'd found that spot just under the ridge of his head, and that made logic impossible. Chivalry was near dead. His plea was getting tighter, deeper, as he felt her gain momentum. "Baby . . ."

She glanced up, holding him in a firm grip. He turned his head and took a deep breath through his nose. She let him go with one hand. He winced. The moment he heard paper rustling, tears wet his lashes. All he could do was nod. But the feel of her hands sheathing him literally brought him to his knees. He opened her right where he dropped, pulling her hips forward, too close to the edge to even fool with the thong, which he yanked to the side before sinking deep inside her with a groan, anchoring his arms around her waist.

On the first insane thrust, she lifted to meet him, seeming just as crazed, her mouth devouring his, her arms around his neck, her legs locked behind his thighs. He couldn't help what happened next. He found himself leaning back, pulling her against him, pulling her over the edge of the sofa, lifting her, slamming his pelvis against hers, kissing her, tearing his mouth away, gulping air, head dropped back, her tightness soul shattering, her wails breath stopping. Oh, God, it was so good. He would immortalize this woman in oil, in charcoal, in whatever medium he was blessed to master.

"Ja-son, oh, Ja-son!"

With each thrust, her voice broke up his name, every exhale causing it to rise higher, from deep alto to soprano pitch. Sounded like it was leaving the bayou, running north, finding the Mason-Dixon, trying to escape. Oh yeah, he had the entire project in his mind, etched into his soul. *This* was the rhythm and blues foundation. The backbone, the spine. *Don't stop!*

Muddy waters, down home, bump and grind, backwoods, sweat pouring in the dead of winter, hollerin' fo' Jesus to jus' come get him. Thick girl, juicy thighs made for homemade loving, her mouth pure sugarcane delirium . . . breasts sweet summer melons, voice sweet, sweet tea. Aw Lawd, yeah, he had to move her to the floor for leverage. Needed to be down on the rug to git all the way down home, where she needed, something to aid his grip on her hickory-smoked, satin rump, her hair thick and natural all over the place. Perfume and woman were in his nose. Warm brown suga made him wanna smack his momma. Lace and silk skimmed his skin. A voice of his dreams reduced him to tears.

Deborah's hands swept up his back, over his ass, her legs a vice around his waist, her body begging him to pour himself into her. If she just said when, she could have it all: he'd work from sun up till he couldn't see. This was what he'd been missing . . . hearth and home.

"C'mon, pretty Deborah. Tell me when you wanna go."

An arch and a cutting gasp were her answer, which emptied his scrotum. A blinding convulsion ripped through him as she spasmed beneath him. It hit him in waves, making his voice an elongated wail with hers before he dropped, winded, eyes squeezed shut, sweat just running.

"Oh, God," she whispered, trembling and holding him tight.

He nodded, gasping for air, still shuddering, with his eyes closed. "God as my witness, I have to paint you like this."

She sat on the living-room sofa, freshly showered and naked beneath her comforter and bathed in late afternoon sun. He sat on the floor, between her legs, naked, freshly showered, a blanket wrapped around him. His eyes were closed and he was leaning back against her softness. A jar of Dixie Peach was on the coffee table, and she held a thick bush comb like it was a weapon. He could feel her warm breath against his scalp as she leaned in to make a part in his freshly shampooed hair.

"I could just go to the braiding salon," he murmured, sated and drowsy. "Was planning to do that, and to get a shape-up, too, but got waylaid." He smiled as she popped him lightly on the head.

"So fresh," she said, chuckling. "The one thing the women in my family know how to do, brother, is braid some hair."

"Iverson's?" he said, dissolving under her scalp massage.

"Zigzags, straight tracks. Whatchu want, baby?" She kissed his forehead, and he felt her heavy breasts against his neck. "I can even do a military cut, courtesy of my, uh, dad."

"He was in the military, too?" Jason said, his words drifting due to the peacefulness of being pampered.

"My dad, yeah," she said, carefully making a part.

"No, your husband, your ex," he said, smiling as her

fingers stopped applying grease to his scalp for a moment.

"Yeah," she said quietly.

"I told you I'm listening to what you say. It was the 'uh' before 'Dad.' It's cool, Deb." He stroked her calf and then sighed. "Dang, this reminds me of being a little kid in my grandma's house."

She nuzzled him. "Getting your scalp greased and Vaseline rubbed on your face and knees."

"Uh-huh," he said, laughing and snuggling closer to her. "Sunday morning, you can't be ashy for church."

"And they made you stay in church *all day*, too!"

"But they fed you," he said, kissing her leg.

"Hold still, boy," she said, laughing and popping him again with the comb.

"We gotta go get some grub," he said, biting her leg and making her squeal.

"I can't be seen out. I'm supposed to be sick."

"Whole Foods on Lancaster Avenue, right over the city limits, not the one downtown."

"Then stop messin' with me so I can do your hair, man."

He peered down at the tent his body was making with the blanket. "Then you're gonna have to work fast, girl," he said, flashing a wide grin. "Sitting between your legs and knowing you don't have on any panties is messing with me, okay?"

Chapter 9

A sense of satisfied completion spread out from her heart, like the golden rays of a setting sun, and warmed her insides as she rode beside Jason, listening to jazz. He made her feel beautiful, even in sweatpants, and held her hand between gear shifts, lacing his fingers with hers or touching her thigh, his body somehow always in contact with hers. She released a sigh and snuggled against his leather seat. He didn't even look at her like she was silly, but just leaned over and kissed her at the red light, knowing.

She wasn't sure what she expected when they got to the market, but she certainly wasn't prepared for him to slip his hand into hers. But he did it like it was the most natural thing in the world, never missing a beat as they found a cart and entered the store.

He looked around and smiled. "Okay, first order of business. Conventional means nonorganic, and you have to look at the tags to be sure you're not picking up something you don't want."

She glanced around at the beautiful produce and bright array of colors. Then she looked at the prices. "Whoa. These are definitely not conventional."

"I know," he said, touching her face. "I got it. It costs

a lot more to grow food without it being pumped up on super hormones, like veggies on steroids, and to bring it to market without pesticides." He shrugged, pushing the cart forward. "But in the long run, if you aren't eating meat, and if you factor in the cost of being on insulin, taking high blood pressure meds, and doing chemotherapy for cancer, hey, how much do you save?"

"Dang, I never even thought of it like that. You sure you're an artist and not a business tycoon or a doctor?" She smiled and began looking at the fresh kale.

"I'm an artist, trust me. I have so much crap to pull together, it doesn't make sense. House bills always lagging because I go into the painting cave and forget. The money's there. I just pile up the mail at the door till I can focus on it, and then I rack up late fees, shut-off notices . . . man. You don't know." He tossed some grapes into their cart. "These clean your blood, like garlic and onions."

"You need a personal assistant." She shook her head. "For a man who makes good money, it doesn't make sense to ruin your credit, but I also understand that to shift your focus away from your work is nearly impossible."

"Hired," he said, bagging some spinach and tossing it over the side of the cart.

"Whoa, whoa, whoa," she said, laughing. "Uh-uh."

He stopped walking. "Why not?"

"First of all, I'm not a business whiz. Second of all, I don't need to be up in your personal business like that . . . given how, uh, close we are right now, and thirdly—"

"I know, I know," he said, with a sheepish smile, beginning to walk again. "I don't have medical and dental."

She stopped walking and placed her hands on her hips. "What?"

He shrugged. "I take good care of—"

"Hold it," she said, putting her hand up. "Just wait. Don't you know you can write that expense off entirely if you're a small business?"

He just stared at her.

"You didn't know that?"

He was slack-jawed. "No."

"Jason," she said quietly. "You need to incorporate as a limited liability corporation, because if something wild goes down, you don't wanna be in the position of having someone sue you for your grandmomma's house. You need to cover yourself and keep track of all your receipts so that the tax man doesn't eat you up, baby. Normally . . . well, not this year, because it isn't a normal year, but I always get my application in to the IRS so I can do some work for them during tax season to help make ends meet, or I go work as a temp for one of the firms, just to make a little change. But I learned some stuff, and a man in your position needs to be insulated against risk."

He touched her face. "I think I'm in love."

She teasingly slapped his hand away, laughing. "Stop playin', man. I'm serious."

He was, too, but she had caught him off guard, and he was glad she'd taken it as a joke for right now. "You were gonna be a business major, right?" He meandered along, moving out of the way, watching her select fruits and vegetables just like his nana had showed him years ago.

"Yeah, I don't want to be an accountant, though. Too boring. I like marketing, and trust me when I tell you, I've sold everything from Avon to Mary Kay. That happens when you've moved around a lot. Takes a while to find a job, you know, but a sister would always get her hustle on."

He wanted to ask her if she might be able to come up with ways to market the art collective and bring in more patrons, but he thought better of it. As he watched her shop, thoughts of an all-natural juice and snack bar to go along with the art space ran through his mind. Deb had talents she didn't realize she owned, and he wanted her to spread her wings and fly in the worst way. Yet, at the same time, he would never want her to think he was using her, because he wasn't. He just wanted her to get out of the dogged, dead-end nine-to-five, but she might not understand his intent. So, he held his peace.

"C'mon. Let me show you some of the whole grains," he said, changing the subject in his mind. He moved their cart to the dried goods section. "Kamut. It's from ancient Egypt, and you soak it like beans overnight and cook it like rice, but it's chewy and nutty. You can use it for salads, like pasta salad, or serve it on the side, hot."

He watched her study the different grains the same way she'd studied the organic kale.

"Some of this I get, like I know that I can season the greens with plenty of onion and garlic, some olive oil, so there's no meat . . . maybe add cayenne pepper. And I can take herbs, hmmm . . . like basil and rosemary, fresh and finely chopped, and add them to oils to make salads pop out, but where I'm at a loss is what to do about the old-fashioned staples, like mac and cheese, and whatnot."

His heart was beating wildly as he watched her mind dissecting the old life she'd owned to adopt the new one. "If, like for a holiday," he said, becoming hopeful, "you want to make some soul food, don't think you have to give up on eating healthy, baby. All you gotta do is make sliced yams."

"With that stuff called ghee or soy butter? Then add cinnamon, nutmeg, ginger, fresh pineapple, and maple syrup, right?"

He swallowed hard and nodded. "Yeah."

She smiled and twirled around. "Hot damn, I'm on a roll." She peered at the rows of dried goods canisters. "I can do beans and rice, rice and peas. It's just how I flavor them . . . such as Scotch bonnet peppers, West Indian or West African style. No problem. Canned coconut milk, uh-huh. I can stir-fry the kale, right? Don't have to boil it. Could probably do macaroni and cheese with soy cheese, soy milk, soy butter, and whole grain pasta, right? The key is the seasoning!"

He just nodded, wondering how it was possible for a woman to give him wood in a supermarket.

"Oooh," she said, spying the refrigerated cases as they began to walk. "This Vegenaise stuff. Can I use this instead of mayo?"

"Yep."

"Then, that's what they meant about the carrot and raisin salad. Ohhh!" She rushed into the next aisle, leaving him behind, but she came back just as quickly, laughing. "I broke the code for sweet potato pie! Soy milk, yams, apple sauce, a pinch of coconut, and pineapple . . . hmmm . . . I'ma have to fool with the mix, but I bet I can get the filling to work out. Then I can use spelt four, versus bleached . . . gotta go find something to replace the shortening, though." Then she spun on him and snapped her fingers, laughing. "But I got mac and cheese: soy cheese, wheat bread crumbs, soy milk, soy butter, spices, turmeric, natural wheat-free pasta, and I'll break the code on the eggs. I need something to make it congeal. Egg replacer. But I'm gonna figure it out. You watch!"

That's just what he did; he watched his pretty Deborah race around the market like a kid in a candy store. He was spellbound as he saw her absorb all that was there, constructing and deconstructing recipes from what had to be DNA-encrypted knowledge handed down by generations of Southern women until they ventured north. She was so happy, her face was glowing. She spoke out loud to the shelves, rationalizing her choices aloud, saying, "No, if I pick this, then it's gonna need that, which is bad for you." He didn't have to say a word; whatever reading had been recommended for the class, she'd obviously done.

As he followed behind her, he loved how she took charge in the space; oddly, he loved feeling like a husband and definitely couldn't deny that he enjoyed feeling needed. Each time she turned to him, beaming, asking what he liked, his stomach did flip-flops of anticipation. He was supposed to be cooking for her, but he was more than sure that she'd mastered the art. She'd latched on to the basics of holistic food preparation and balance, using a color chart in her head, which simply awed him. He was just there to provide coaching, a little validation, and gentle steering by suggestion.

"Mostly dark greens," she said, ticking items off on her fingers as she stared down into their cart. "A bit of orange for beta carotene; some reds for antioxidants; plenty of fruit; the white veggies, like garlic and onions, as antiseptics; juices; water, lots of that; soy ice cream for the cravings; nuts for protein; soy meat substitute; Braggs Liquid Aminos I already have at home, for seasoning; vegetable boullion; soy milk; soy cheese; ghee; Ezekiel bread . . ." She looked up at him. "I know I have a lot more stuff in here than all that, but did I miss anything?"

"No, pretty Deborah," he murmured, wanting to kiss her right there in the market. He didn't care if they were blocking the aisle, and he finally gave in to the temptation.

She looked flustered and rosy when he pulled away from her and broke the kiss.

"Anything else you want in here, baby, you let me know," he said.

"Some storage containers," she said, with a smile.

He laughed. *Only a woman.* That wasn't what he meant. "I can do that."

"Well, to get all this stuff in your kitchen," she said, "you need something to put it in."

"No, baby . . . This is for you."

Her eyes opened wide, and she looked both ways, as though being chased by the cops. "Jason," she whispered. "There must be two hundred dollars worth of groceries in here. You have to put this in your house. I mean, I'll come cook and whatever, but—"

"I'm buying this for *you*." He was resolute.

"But . . . uh-uh. Too expensive."

Stunned, he just stood there for a moment. He'd never heard a woman say something like that to him in his life. Somehow it made him pin her between the cart and a shelf, and caused him to lean in and kiss her quick and hard. "This stuff is going to your house. We'll cook, and eat, and then walk down the street to class. That's the end of it."

She gulped when he turned away and fanned her face. A lady passing by with a baby in her cart gave her a discreet thumbs-up. Whew! Okay. She hurried behind Jason, who now seemed intent on getting out of the store. How did going to the supermarket together turn into an erotic expedition? she wanted to know. If this man could wet her drawers in the pasta aisle, dang! What would a romantic getaway with him be like? she wondered.

She was supposed to be washing vegetables, separating them, and filling bags so he could take half, because her fridge was only so big. She was supposed to be stir-frying kale with daikon radish and onions and garlic and Braggs in olive oil. She had carrots shredded and raisins on the counter, ready for carrot salad. She had elbow pasta bubbling in a double boiler for what was gonna be mac and cheese. She was trying to make Quorn chickenless chicken cutlets, breaded with her special blend of rosemary and basil bread crumbs, to be baked in the oven. She really was trying. She was even gonna make him cashew nut nog for dessert, break out her juicer for the man, put good dishes on the table. She woulda opened the bottle of merlot . . .

But the bags had hit the floor, and he'd found that spot just behind her ear, and his hands had found her breasts, and his breath had found her weakness, murmuring how much he appreciated every single God-given thing about her. He'd wrapped her up in strong arms, told her how her hands had felt in his hair when she was cornrowing it and pulling everything up and out of his soul through his scalp. The man was rapping hard about the future, telling her she was a work of art, his canvas, and begging her to let him work.

What could she do as he painted himself across her; stroked her to tears; and made her run like watercolors, cry out in deep, soulful blues, and shriek with white-knuckled ecstasy? Old school, raised by a Southern grandma but packaged in a new age phenomena of a body, he begged her to sauté and simmer him, braise him, and flip him till he was good and done.

They held each other, breathing hard, clothes half on, half off, sweat making fabrics cling to them. Weary, he looked up in the direction of the kitchen.

"I gotta go turn off the pasta. It's mush now," she whispered.

He chuckled deep within his chest. "Yeah . . . and I guess we oughta get another shower and put this food away before your class."

It was the longest hour and a half of his life. But he was patient. She was learning, and he loved to

watch her learn. In truth, she belonged back in
school, enjoying the freedom of opening her mind to
whatever it wanted to absorb, not at some dead-end
job. However, he respected her need to make that
transition on her own. And even though she could
have probably taught the class from the standpoint of
recipe development, he knew she needed to hear the
science behind the combinations.

Later, he'd fill in the blanks about why certain
spices and combinations were good for the body, but
for now, it was all he could do to stay awake. In the last
twenty-four hours, they'd made love so much and had
eaten and slept so little that he was ready to just fall
into a coma. A sandwich bag full of raw sunflower
seeds, and nuts, and raisins, and two apples were the
only thing keeping his blood sugar steady. Deborah
was definitely gonna have to bring some grub to his
house so they could eat while he started to get her
down on canvas.

It was the longest hour and a half of her life. She
was learning, the info was interesting, but she'd
become addicted to Jason's touch. She caught a
glimpse of him sitting in the back of the class as a visiting instructor, eyes half closed, leaning his chair
back against the wall, slowly munching on an apple,
his full mouth sucking the juicy fruit, white teeth
sending the sound down her spine, his jaw moving
lazily, like a cow chewing cud. . . .

"Huh?"

The woman teaching the class looked at her, with a
bright smile, and Deborah felt her face flush. She
gazed at the earth-mother chick, who wore no
makeup, had on a natty brown sweater over a tied-
dyed shirt, and had short dirty blond hair, and willed
her to repeat the question.

"That's okay," the instructor said brightly. "It's hard to conceive of different ways to cook what we're used to eating."

If they had paid her money, she still wouldn't have known what the conversation was about. The one thing the break in lovemaking had done, though, was give her just enough distance to finally put the food away, throw away the pasta, and fill a bag and set it in Jason's car. It was cold enough outside for his car to be like an extension of her fridge. But right now, all she wanted to do was get over to his house. She'd even been bold enough to pack an overnight bag, toothbrush and all, at his insistence. And as exhausted as she was, she couldn't wait to fire up his galley kitchen and put the scent of home back into his space.

Deborah practically jumped out of her skin when people started getting up to leave. She stood on shaky legs. She would have to remember to ask Jason what the teacher had said, because she dang sure didn't know.

Jason sat in the kitchen, one bare foot on a chair, the other on the floor as he rocked his chair back against the wall, sketch pad in his lap, pencil working furiously. Deborah, who was cooking, had indulged him. She was wearing that favorite, paint-splattered, burnt orange shirt she'd worn the first day of art class. Greens sizzled in a huge wok. The aroma of corn bread wafted from his oven. It made his stomach gurgle with need. Something saturated with basil and thyme and sage and rosemary spread muted tones of subtle memory throughout his once barren house. If he wasn't mistaken, he also smelled something sweet, like yams and cinnamon, but he wasn't sure.

The taste of merlot splashed his palate. A sigh of pure contentment escaped him as he watched her buzz around barefoot, with a glass of wine in one hand, just grooving to the mellow music of Marvin Gaye, piped through the living room and filtering into the kitchen. Then he heard her voice . . . Good God, the woman could sing?

He stopped drawing as she kept a tune, oblivious to him, her body naked and moving in a sultry sway beneath burnt orange heavy cotton. Paralyzed by the sight of her behind caressing the fabric as she belted out lyrics, he held his pencil still.

Thick, long, sensual thighs glistening with the lotion she'd applied caught the overhead lights, flashing walnut bronze, copper red, deep sienna, shadowed beauty into tight calves and delicate ankles, her voice hitting and holding high notes and able to go to a low, husky alto. A fleshy belly hidden in the shadows of the shirt, which just barely came together, a deep cleavage keeping the buttons from touching the holes, held notes long and steady. Then she bent and checked the oven, and he watched the shirt skim the very edge of the place that had given him hours of pleasure for almost two days.

He took a quick sip of merlot and began drawing, with his eyes closed.

She turned and slowly placed the pans she'd removed from the oven on the stove. The expression on Jason's face threatened to make her drop the walnut, peach, raisin apple pie she'd worked so hard on. For a moment, all she could do was watch him as she took a very slow and steady sip of her merlot and turned off all the burners.

His chin was tipped toward the ceiling, his hand was moving across the page in a passionate, intense scribble, ecstasy spreading across his face, and his lips were barely parted.

"Why did you stop singing?" he murmured and then looked at her as though coming out of a trance.

"I can't sing. I just hum around the kitchen." She sipped her wine more deeply and turned away to stir her pots.

"Gospel. Church. That's where, right?"

"I sang in a choir when I was little, but after Nana passed . . . I'm not trained."

"Don't need to be, Deb. Not sounding like that."

She smiled at him over her shoulder. "Let me fix your plate, man. Stop playing."

He slowly put down his sketch pad and stood up to go get the plates down for her, then gave a little nod toward his distended sweatpants. "Does it look like I am playing?"

She turned away and stirred her pots harder, but didn't answer. "You want greens and everything, right?"

He just chuckled, pleased that more color had risen to her cheeks. "And everything . . . yeah."

"We're gonna eat after I cooked all this stuff."

"No argument here," he said, bringing two plates to her. "But you can't blame me for having my mind blown away."

She dipped a fork in the greens pot, blew on it, cupped her hand beneath it, and offered him a taste.

He closed his eyes as he pulled the tender kale between his lips and chewed. Feeding him out of the pot was the most loving gesture she could have made as she stood in the sacred space of Nana's kitchen. Damn. The flavors spread over his tongue and warmed him from the inside out. "Wow . . . ," he murmured.

"I did okay?"

"Oh . . . girl . . . Just slap me."

She laughed. "For real?"

"Put half the pot on my plate."

He watched her smile with pride and look away.

"I hope everything else came out all right."

She began adding to his plate, loading him down

with her black woman's version of love, and he gladly accepted it, all the way down to the corn bread.

He wolfed down the grub like there might not be a tomorrow, intermittently picking up his pencil to be sure he didn't miss a nuance or a sassy twist of her mouth, the laughter spilling through him in rainbow hues. He just let her talk, floating in the zone, on her stream of consciousness, just throwing out a question here and there so she could let herself go, allow her dreams to unfold.

She was ravishing with her shirt open, her hands folded beneath her chin as if in a prayer, eyes closed, telling him her dreams, how she wanted to go back to school in the spring.

"Go, baby," he murmured. "Do that for you. Fill out the paperwork. Do whatever it takes to get the loans."

He stopped just short of promising to pay them off. He would. Shit. She only had a year and a half to go. Three little semesters. But he kept drawing, shoveling the incredible confection she'd labored on into his mouth . . . apples, raisins, walnuts, peaches. This woman served up love with soy ice dreams. She needed to go to his brother's house for Sunday dinner; the family needed to meet her. Deborah should be running the collective, if that was what she wanted; she should be his business manager, if she could stand to be bothered. She should move in, if she felt so inclined; she should be the mother of his children. Tonight he was losing his mind.

"I need to get you upstairs," he said out of the blue.

He watched her draw a shaky breath.

"I have to put the food away first," she said quietly.

"I'll help, 'cause I gotta get you up there like now. I got the dishes. You cooked."

Her smile was gentle and fading as seriousness

overtook her expression. "I've never felt this wanted in my life, and I can't begin to tell you what it's doing to me," she said in a barely audible murmur.

He stood and began picking up plates, unable to wait much longer. "Promise me you'll sing when we get up there."

She scrambled to her feet and began to nervously store the food in containers. "I . . . I can't. I don't sing, I hum. I—"

"I'll put on whatever inspires you while I work. I'll bring the wine. You can even close your eyes . . . Just walk and sing for me so I can work."

"Huh?" She stopped putting away the food for a moment. "I thought when you said you wanted to go upstairs now . . ."

He stopped scraping dishes. "Oh yeah, I do, baby. No, no, don't get me wrong." He went to her when her expression became crestfallen. "Like you can't imagine, but it's like this crazy combination process of being inspired, turned on, lit up, just nuts, but in the zone. It's a thing that I can't explain . . . can keep me on a ladder all night or up on scaffolding, and then, when it's over, it's like the best sex. Okay, stop looking at me like you're about to run screaming into the night."

She swallowed a smile and began putting the food away again. "Oh, I just didn't understand the process . . . but I'm game."

He released a rush of breath. "Cool."

She stood in his studio, looking at him work, listening to Phyllis Hyman, singing with the late, great diva, sipping wine, naked beneath her shirt, sometimes closing her eyes, because the visual was so intense. Her man was in nothing but sweatpants, his gleaming brown shoulders and back and arms working, making a sheen of sweat, which caressed him the way she wanted to. Paint was everywhere. He'd brought a small love seat in there for her, and when she tired, she sprawled on it, legs draped over it, head near the floor, shirt askew, wine on the floor, a glass in a relaxed, dangling hand, her voice caressing the strands of an old love ballad and making him work harder, until something crazy happened.

Jason just stopped painting, dropped his brushes, and abruptly got down off the ladder, several hours after he'd begun. She was almost asleep, and the next thing she knew, he crossed the room, weaving between the hung canvases, and pulled her down to him on the drop cloths.

His hard body broke her fall. His eyes bored into hers as gray dawn filtered into the studio. Wine and inspiration made his breath faint and fragrant. A half a bottle of merlot and feeling loved made her will nonexistent. His body was burning up as he parted her shirt. His groan was so agonized that she hugged him to let him know it would be all right.

Burning hands trembled over her backside, and a man falling in love arched under her weight, with a piercing gasp. A mouth filled with adoration consumed hers, whispering her name in sudden, painful bursts as she slid his sweatpants over his hips, hands shaking with need.

Paint-smudged fingers gripped her thighs, then grabbed the back of her shirt, and a paint-splattered chest strained against hers, lifting them, his body seeking a lodge within hers in frenzied thrusts. The sound he released from deep within when he found her haven and sank against her stole her reason, just like his tumble of words behind it completely destroyed her.

"Deborah, I need you, baby. Been needing you for

so long but couldn't find you. I can't go back to before now."

His voice broke as he pulled her against him hard enough to almost crack a rib. In this sacred place, his head tipped back, shoulders off the floor, arms around her like he was holding on against a personal storm, she thought she heard him repeatedly pant, "Deborah, I love you. Falling. Fell. Oh shit, don't know when, but it did happen.."

Her body convulsed with his admission, dredging his until he wailed. A united sob left them at the same time as they shuddered, and he rocked her against him as she petted his shoulders and rocked him. She wasn't sure what had just happened, but as she lifted her head from his shoulder, new tears streamed down her face. It was so beautiful that she almost couldn't look at what he'd created.

He'd immortalized her in oil. Half naked, in a burnt orange shirt, her eyes closed, a platter playing on a old-fashioned record player, her head thrown back, singing, wineglass dangling in her hand, her body lush, her hair disheveled and beautiful all over her head. Then an outline, the beginning of a new painting, on another canvas showed her standing by a window in her black lace, in hues of blue. He'd tacked up sketches of her, with her hands folded in prayer over a plate, dreams of college in the background, and signs of segregation looming over black and white water fountains to mark the era. It was a beautiful woman in the drawings, thick and sassy, eyes smoky and sexy. She couldn't believe it and just gave in to a good cry.

"Hidden dreams, lost opportunity found, forbidden fruit, the morning after, passion," he murmured against her neck, running his hands up and down her back.

"This is how you really see me?" Her voice was a

shocked whisper filled with reverence and awe as she sniffed hard.

"Oh, Deborah . . . pretty, pretty Deborah . . . I have it all with you, the whole thing. I haven't even begun to start working." He was still lodged deep within her, and his breath came as rasps against her tender skin. "I've never created in here like this," he whispered. "*Never* in my life. I've always chased people from here . . . You're the only one I've really allowed to cross the threshold." He buried his face in her hair. "Baby, I need you. Have needed you for so long."

Her fingers traced the side of his face as she looked at what he'd created, and she drew a shaky breath as she stared up at herself for the first time, feeling as though she was really beautiful. "Oh, God, Jason," she whispered through a thick, tear-filled swallow. "I've needed you all my life, too."

Chapter 10

She didn't care that it seemed to be going too fast, like a freight train running off the tracks, or that she might crash and burn. She didn't care that this was the second day that she had called out from the job on a bogus excuse. She was free and felt beautiful, and a man that she loved was up on a ladder, knocking himself out while she sang her lungs out. His home was a sanctuary, like a church, healing her, renewing her, closing up soul wounds, erasing scars in oil and on canvas.

Oh, hell yeah, she'd go downstairs and bring him up food, feed him on the ladder while he kept going . . . didn't mind a bit, if he just kept looking at her like he did. Didn't mind straightening up, cleaning out the fridge, throwing in a load of laundry so the man had a towel and they had clean sheets. Didn't care that the first floor was in semifinished mode, because inspiration had caught fire in his studio.

Every place she could swab, straighten, and make habitable, she did. Floating on air, she straightened CDs, photos, books; dusted; and pruned his plants. All he required was for her to appear with food, water, and a kiss every now and again, her voice filtering through the house. She folded his clothes, got his closet in order, and kissed him till he stopped working.

"You have to teach aikido tonight," she said, reminding him as he stared at her like she'd spoken in a foreign language.

"Oh, shit! Not now . . . I'm, I'm—"

"I know," she said, blowing him a kiss. "But you promised Wil."

His shoulders dropped. "Do you know what it's like to stop when you're on fire like this, Deb?"

"No," she said in a husky voice, "but if you hadn't stopped to teach the art class, we might not have met again. So . . . you should go. I'm one of your students, you know."

He gave her a begrudging smile, then jumped down and brushed her mouth with a quick kiss. "That's the only thing dragging me off this ladder tonight—you."

She watched him fight to keep his gaze moving from one student to the next in the class. She fought to keep her breathing steady as he sat on the mat, cross-legged, dropping gems of knowledge for his small class of wide-eyed pupils.

"Aikido," he said in a calm, controlled tone. "It comes from a Japanese trinity of words: *ai*, or harmony; *ki*, spirit or energy; *do*, system or way. Put together, it means, simply, the way of the spirit of harmony."

Deborah fought not to wave her hand like she was in church. Destiny. She knew it! Her spirit was looking for protection, self-defense, but a pacifist by nature, she really had wanted harmony . . . and Lord have mercy, Jason Hastings made her harmonize with every part of his body.

"Practitioners seek to achieve self-defense without injury to the attacker," Jason continued, almost seeming to forget his point as his eyes searched her face and then left it. "Motions are circular, not linear. . . ."

She nodded, remembering the last few days in his arms, and he shifted his gaze to the first row of students.

"In this way, your fluid movements harmonize with an attacker and turn linear aggression into circular motion via wrist locks and arm pins, and your unbalancing throws neutralize the opponent. Tonight, as we all are subject to gravity, we will learn *ukemi* . . . the art of falling."

They fell through his front door in the dark, kissing urgently, falling deeper into a well of emotion they hadn't dreamed of, falling against walls and furniture and the steps, stumbling across thresholds, falling against recessed doors and dressers, falling on a freshly made futon.

He might have achieved fourth dan in aikido, but he'd never fallen this hard, this fast, or this completely, from so far. One week, less than that, and it was all over. He was incapacitated, neutralized, his world no longer linear, his dreams splashed with the color of her skin, waking to find her still there, in his arms.

"Just one more day, one more night," he said between kisses, finding her navel. "Tomorrow is Friday . . . I don't have to teach, and you don't have class."

"I can't bring myself to go to work," she said, arching. "This is insane."

"Then lose your mind with me," he whispered, planting kisses on her inner thighs. "Stay the weekend. Let me paint you till I drop. Sunday, meet my people. Then I'll take you home and will keep my hands off you so you can go to work Monday."

Her voice bounced off the ceiling, like a slow drop of translucent color, and splashed against the floor, falling, falling, in a spiraling rainbow of stuttered whispers as his circling tongue made it impossible for her to think in linear terms.

This was big. *Major.* Meeting Jason's family, one week in. Her phone was loaded with messages from LaVern, her girl Cheryl, and her cousin, Lynn. But there hadn't been time to do more than call back and leave quickie voice mails that she hadn't been abducted and would surface soon with the scoop.

How could she call from a man's house and scream to her girlfriends that she'd been walled up in an artist's studio, making crazy love till her face was flushed, had fallen in love, and now was experiencing the ultimate *ukemi* of life! The art of falling to the max.

She ripped through her closet, panicking now, wondering how his brother, Jared, his oldest sister, Jacqueline, and his next oldest sister, Jenna, would receive her. Jared was a conservative. She put her hand on a very understated charcoal gray suit and then shoved it back in the closet. It looked like she was going on a job interview. The nurse, Jacqueline, was head of a freakin' department, okay, bold, career minded . . . Deborah closed her eyes. The other sister was Madison Avenue, New York, and she didn't have anything designer that looked elegant enough to wear at a family dinner. It was all club gear.

"Knock, knock," Jason said, peeking in the bedroom. He smiled as she turned around in a lacy white bra and panty set. "I was going to see how you were coming along, but, I must admit, now I'm not tryin' to rush you."

Panic made her palms moist. "I don't have anything to wear."

"Aw, girl . . . be serious. Your closet is loaded. I've got like five outfits that I save for gallery openings and one or two suits I wear to weddings and funerals."

She took note of his pulled-together style and closed her eyes. A charcoal mock turtleneck with a hair-width strand of midnight and burgundy running through it, courtesy of Geoffrey Bean; dark charcoal slacks; fly-ass slip-ons; butter leather belt; good tank watch; freshly done cornrows, courtesy of her loving touch; aftershave on a smooth jaw, which under any other circumstances would have made her want to jump his bones, but not this afternoon. She shoulda known the man would clean up so well that she'd feel like Cinderella sans a fairy godmother.

"I don't wanna go too conservative or too hoochie or too . . . too—"

"You go as you, all right?" he said, walking over to her and pulling her against him.

"I want them to like me."

"I only care that I like you," he murmured, gently taking her mouth.

"I don't ever want to embarrass you in front of people," she said in a small voice.

"Hey, hey, whoa." He lifted her chin with one finger and stared into her eyes until tears welled. "Don't *ever* go there. If somebody can't see what I see, then screw 'em. No . . . better said, *fuck them*. Hear? Family included." He hugged her and then broke the embrace. "The only thing that wigs my sister out, truly, is being late. Must be that paramilitary thing, her being a nurse and having to be on time everywhere. Y'all share that, so you should be fine."

With that, he left her standing in the middle of her bedroom floor, in her underwear . . . falling even harder for him than she had already.

She'd found a chocolate wool crepe dress with a keyhole neckline and long sleeves. She had set the simple design off with large amber and silver earrings and a chunky, natural amber bracelet that had cost her a mint, then had found a soft leather brown Coach purse and a pair of eel-skin chocolate stilettos.

Over her arm was a short, one-button, velvet car coat in chocolate, with a large, ornate crystal clasp. In her right hand, she clutched a pair of chocolate-hued leather gloves. She watched Jason's eyes intently as she stepped out of the bedroom, and the way he unfolded from the sofa and smiled slow and deep made her finally release her breath.

"Wow . . . ," he breathed out.

"Is this okay?"

"*Man* . . ."

She smiled and finally felt a rush of anticipation as he circled her, breathed in her scent as he helped her on with her coat, touched her hair without mussing it, and then backed away, as though not wanting to damage her in the least.

Now it was his turn to be nervous. His family put the *D* in dysfunctional. Once a month, on a Sunday, they all got together, in keeping with their parents' and grandparents' wishes. But that was it.

Deborah looked like a million bucks, which would get his brother started. Jared had been drinking like a fish since his senior year in high school, to hear his sister Jenna tell it, and was a competitive wreck. If something made one of the Hastings siblings happy, then Jared always had something smart to say about it.

Jason tried to remain cool as he drove. He had to chill and roll with the punches. This dinner was important, since Deborah would be there with him. He'd told his sister Jackie he'd be bringing company, but he hadn't had a chance to really tell her to be sure their brother eased up on the liquor. If Jared said some bull to Deborah or stated his old signifying shit,

tonight it would be on. For some reason, it mattered
what she thought of him and his family, for better or
for worse. He wanted them to be on their best behav-
ior, and as he made the drive up to Chestnut Hill, to
his brother's huge home, suddenly he worried that
Deborah might wonder why his environs were rela-
tively pitiful in comparison.

He tried to shake it off as he navigated the Lincoln
Drive, thinking of his sisters' well-appointed homes in
West Mount Airy. That settled it; he had to get his
house finished. This didn't make sense. Deborah deserved better than a futon on the floor and having to
eat in the kitchen because the dining room wasn't finished. He wondered if any of his brother's wild-ass
kids would be home, or if his brother's brood of five
hellions would be with their three mothers. Then he
wondered if his niece Kiera and nephew Kevin,
Jackie's two, would take off their iPod headphones at
the table long enough to even speak to Deborah.
Thank God Jenna was coming in from New York this
month and that they had to do Jackie's house next
month.

If Nana was living, the condition of the family
would have given her a stroke.

Jason pulled into the driveway and surveyed the
cars. His brother's Escalade was in the driveway—for
show. The man had a three-car garage. *Okay. It begins
now,* he said to himself as he walked slowly around his
ride to open the door for Deborah. His sister Jackie's
silver Beamer was there, and so was Jenna's silver Jag.
Cool.

Deborah looked up at Jason's eyes, seeing something she hadn't seen before—worry. Something was
wrong. He'd been quiet the whole drive, as though
consumed by his own inner thoughts, and she'd let

him be, understanding that feeling well, but also worrying about whether or not his turmoil had anything to do with second thoughts about her.

She looked around as discreetly as possible, quietly awed. These people obviously came from a place she could barely fathom. This was a side of town that had always been a mystery to her, and it was so far from her and her nana's reality that she had never really ever tried to wrap her brain around it. But now it looked like she might have to. Maybe Jason had sensed that as he was driving up, the reality slowly dawning within him and making him uncomfortable enough to want to turn around . . . Perhaps he just had not known how.

Her heart suddenly heavy, she yielded to his lead as they walked up the wide stone path, which had been sprinkled with salt. She was glad that he held her firmly to keep her from sliding in her heels on the slick surface. But as she stood before the massive door, she felt so very, very insignificant. The thundering doorbell just echoed the message through her soul that she didn't belong. But to his credit, Jason slid his hand in hers, threading his fingers between hers, and that slowed her heartbeat to near normal.

"Hey, bro!" a gregarious version of Jason said, flinging open the door with one meaty hand while balancing a drink in the other.

Deborah pasted on her best church smile for the shorter, thicker version of Jason, who had a horseshoe of baldness on the top of his gleaming head.

"This is Deborah Lee Jackson," Jason said, ushering her forward, "and this is my brother, Jared Hastings."

"Humph, humph, humph, pleased to meet you," Jared said, with a too-wide grin. "You're doing all right, I can see, baby bro."

"Hi. I'm Jason's sister Jenna," a gorgeous woman said, moving through the house to the foyer, in an obvious attempt to save her younger brother. "Let me take your coat. Jackie is in the kitchen."

"Thanks so much," Deborah said in her best diction. "It's such a pleasure to meet you both."

Although Jared gave her a leer before walking away to refill his drink, Jenna's smile seemed genuine, but she was so well coiffed that Deborah wished she'd gone to the hairdresser. Every strand of this woman's hair was expertly cut into a hot, sassy, short, free style, and her lithe figure looked stunning in her black mohair sweater, black wool pants, and obviously expensive shoes. Jason's sister was rocking so much ice that Deborah almost squinted, and all she could think was, *If this is a casual, at-home affair, then dayum.*

Moving like a robot, nerves so tight she felt dizzy, Deborah waited for Jason to help her off with her coat. She wasn't sure what their protocol was here, but she'd always been taught that offering to help was the polite thing to do.

"May I give you ladies a hand? Is there anything I can do to help?" Deborah smiled brightly and tried to keep her voice upbeat.

"Oh, no, honey," Jenna said, her voice easy and melodic. "Don't be silly. The caterer has everything under control."

Deborah sealed her lips and nodded. *Of course.*

"Why don't you have a seat in the living room," Jason said, seeming like he wanted to jump out of his skin. "I'll go find my sister Jackie. Let me introduce you to my niece and nephew. Want some wine?"

"No, I'm all right," Deborah said quietly, letting Jason usher her by her elbow to a room that looked like it was torn from the Victorian pages of *House Beautiful* magazine.

Two very bored-looking teenagers lounged on the expensive furniture and glanced away from the television only long enough to hail their uncle.

"Hey, Uncle J," a handsome youth said. He was dressed in full rapper gear from head to toe—sideways Phat Farm hat, leather bomber, baggy jeans, and Air Force 1 sneakers. He didn't get up but continued lounging and flipping channels with the remote.

However, his sister bounced from the chair and ran up to Jason to hug him. "Favorite uncle!" she cried.

Jason hugged her and laughed and then swung her around, making her way too short skirt flare out. "No. My pockets are empty. Go away," Jason told her.

"She's practicing to be a gold diggah, Unc," her brother said.

"Gets it from her mom, my dear sister," Jared hollered from the dining-room bar.

"Lemme introduce you to my friend Deborah," Jason said, shaking his head and trying not to laugh. "Kiera, Kevin, this is Ms. Deborah Lee Jackson."

Deborah smiled but inwardly cringed when Jason said her full name, which, in her mind, had begun to sound like a country-and-western singer's handle in front of his well-to-do people.

Kevin just gave her a tired wave. Kiera smiled and at least spoke up and said hi. But Deborah noticed something smoldering in Jason's eyes, and it took her by surprise.

"I'ma say it again, man," Jason said, looking at his nephew, who was half prone on the couch. "I just brought a lady in the room and introduced her . . . if you aren't on your feet in five seconds—"

"He'll kick your trifling ass, Kev. You know favorite uncle don't play that raggedy shit, puhlese!" Kiera said, folding her arms and pecking her neck.

"Shut up, Kiera!" Kevin said, but he got up.

Kiera smiled, triumphant. "He'll kick your punk ass, too, like he did last summer, when you thought you could tell Mom what to do in her own house—"

"Hey, hey, hey," Jason said, running his palms down

his face. "The language, KiKi. C'mon, now. And the past is the past." He extended his hand to exchange a fist pound with Kevin, who begrudgingly returned the pound. "Just want you to respect my lady. I'll do the same when you bring one home. Cool?"

Kevin nodded. "Nice to meet you, Miss Deborah. My uncle's aw'ight. But this family is wack."

Jason sighed and turned to Deborah. "There you have it."

"Hi, guys," Deborah said, with a smile, wanting to hug Jason, suddenly realizing where his case of nerves had been coming from. His introduction anxiety had very little to do with her.

As crazy as it had been, the wild exchange with the teenagers had actually relaxed her a bit. That is, until a thick, short, and very determined woman barreled out of the kitchen, wearing a DKNY winter white sweater and pants ensemble, fussing about always having to address vegetarian needs at family dinners and about the added chaos of specialty menu items.

"I'm Jacqueline," Jason's older sister said, thrusting out her hand. "We'll have a chance to talk at dinner, but for now, I'm about to get on the phone and have a hissy fit with this same damned caterer, who *knows* not to put any smoked turkey in the side vegetables. We order from them all the time—have a standing order once a month—so I don't want to hear it." She kissed Jason. "Hi, baby brother. This tofu mess is just getting on my last nerve. Is this an artistic phase or permanent?"

Jason smiled and leaned down and kissed her. "You've asked me that at every dinner for the last decade. I think it's a permanent condition, and I love you, too. Meet Deborah."

"Nice to meet you, Deborah. Jacqueline," Jason's sister said, as she waved her hand at him. He blew

Jackie a kiss as she retreated to the kitchen, cordless phone in her grip.

"Drink?" Jared hollered from the next room.

"We're good, thanks," Jason hollered back. He turned to Deborah and ushered her to an overstuffed settee. "I won't abandon you to the natives, I promise," he murmured near her ear, "but I need to go calm Jackie down so we can eat and roll. You've officially met my people."

She just looked up and nodded, and then remained very, very still as his brother came over with a glass of wine she hadn't asked for.

"So, tell us how you met," Jackie said and then looked up at Jason and glanced at her sister. "What? I want to know."

"Jacqueline, please. Can you let them put food on their plates first?" Jenna said, with a sigh, as she passed the string beans garnished with almonds. "She's always this way, isn't she, Jason? It's not you, Deborah."

"Like what? He's never brought anyone *home* officially, so I want to know," Jackie fussed, offering Deborah the vegetable lasagna. "This is vegan and has soy cheese, or whatever."

"We met at the herb store," Deborah said, with a quiet smile. "Then again in art class."

"You're back in graduate school for your doctorate?" Jackie squealed, shifting her attention from Deborah to Jason. "Finally! When? Tell all."

"Figures they met in a health-food joint," Jared muttered under his breath, piling roast beef and red potatoes on his plate and drowning them with gravy.

"No. I'm not back in school," Jason said carefully, measuring his words as he held the dish of vegetable lasagna for Deborah.

"But she said you two also met in class." Jackie

blinked and frowned as she placed the smoked salmon platter down in the center of the table.

"And the herb store," Jared said, with a smirk.

"At the University Arts Center," Deborah said as calmly as possible, watching Jason's siblings verbally corner him.

"Oh," Jackie said, her chin lifting. "I thought it was a real class."

"Pass the chicken, Mom," Kevin said, boredom resonant in his voice.

Jackie sent the baked chicken in her son's direction and the broiled salmon toward her daughter, but somehow Deborah doubted that Jason's older sister was finished grilling them.

"So," Jackie said, with a diplomat's smile. "What do you do?"

"Jackie . . . ," Jason countered, giving his sister a withering glare. "Let's have a nice dinner for once, without the bourgeois drama. All right? Why don't you update us on how you're doing or talk about current events? Whatever. Just don't start."

"Okay, here we go," Jared said, shaking his head and reaching for a roll. "Next, it'll be conspiracy theories, the litany on the diseased American food supply, and a discussion of every ism under the sun. Which one will we be accused of falling victim to tonight, Jas?"

"Uncle J's right, though," Kevin piped up. "This system is complete bull, and it's all a conspiracy."

"Oh, heaven help me," Jackie said. "And I see that your uncle doesn't mind the fact that he got his education in this warped system and doesn't mind participating in the commerce within it, young man. So, eat your chicken, and worry about your SAT scores. You see the influence you have, Jason. This antiestablishment thing isn't healthy, even if we might not like who is currently in office. People marched so we could live like this."

"I ain't leaving the good old US of A until I see folks lined up at the waterfront in Camden, getting in tires, and trying to row to a foreign country. That's some artistic rhetoric, and only the upper classes produce real artists, so give the impoverished indignity a rest, baby bro." Jared finished his drink and left the table to refill it, coming back by a winding path.

"I'm out," Kevin announced, standing, with his plate in hand. "I'm eating in the rec room downstairs."

"I feel you," Jason said, releasing a deep sigh.

"Mom, can I watch TV, too?" Kiera whined.

Jackie waved her hands. "See? You can't do anything with them. Fine. Go."

The kids fled the table.

"I personally don't think that people marched in the sixties so folks could move out to the suburbs and devolve in terms of social consciousness," Jason said, picking at his vegetables and ignoring his severely inebriated older brother. "But you didn't hear that from me."

"Don't take her there, Jason," Jenna groaned, sipping her iced tea. "Oh, Lord."

"What school did you go to?" Jackie asked, looking at Deborah pointedly. "I bet when you got your degree, you weren't thinking, Oh, my, let me pay off my student loans with social consciousness. How do you deal with him? You look so normal, and my brother is, oh, exasperating."

"I haven't finished my degree yet, and I'm thinking about going back for my bachelor's at either Temple or Drexel," Deborah said quietly. "Right now I'm at the water department. I know that the people who marched during the civil rights movement are doing cartwheels in their graves at what is happening these days worldwide." She looked down at her plate when Jackie opened her mouth and closed it.

"See," Jenna said, trying to recover gracefully.

"There are many perspectives out there, Jackie, and we have to have *open minds,*" she added, with emphasis.

"Baby bro sure can pick 'em," Jared murmured under his breath and took another swig of Scotch to wash down a mouthful of masticated meat. "Built like a brick house, though."

"Come again?" Jason said, directing his attention toward Jared.

Jared just shook his head and held up a hand.

"So, you have a great project you're working on, right?" Jenna interjected, her voice strident and her smile strained. "Tell us about how that's coming."

Jason flung his napkin down on the table. Deborah put her fork down very carefully beside her plate.

"It's all right," Deborah said in a near whisper.

"No, it's not all right for anyone to put my guest through a bunch of bull at this table!" Jason said, glaring at his older brother and eldest sister. "We're out." He stood and helped Deborah up from her chair.

"Oh, for crying out loud," Jared yelled. "Sit your narrow ass down and eat dinner. Just like Mom. Running and getting caught up—"

"Jared!" Jackie said, standing so quickly that her chair almost toppled. "That's enough. You're drunk. Just stop before this goes too far. Jason, he's sorry."

"Notice she didn't say she was sorry," Jared said and chuckled. "Whoa, Jacqueline. You're a piece of work, too, hon. Probably why both of us are permanently divorced."

"There was no call for that," Jason said between his teeth in his sister's defense. "Especially with her children in the house. C'mon, Deb. Let me take you home."

"Back to the neighborhood and back to the ghetto this time? Jason, you are going from bad to worse. Stake a claim. Fuck the sixties," Jared said to Jason's back, slurring as he stood. "I work for the mayor, not hand to mouth as some flaky artist, and last I checked, I'm in my own damned house, unless one of my ex-wives got their hooks on this one without me knowing . . . I digress."

Jared laughed and rubbed the bald spot on his head as Jason hugged his sisters, Jackie and Jenna, good-bye. Deborah tensely hugged the distraught but elegantly dressed women, who had grim expressions.

"I'm home, just like our father was, and I'm telling the truth!" Jared contended loudly. "The man worked like a dog and didn't deserve civil rights encroachment on his wife, okay."

"Take him away from the table," Jenna said, pointing, with her eyes closed.

Jason had rounded the table and was on Jared in two strides. "What are you talking about? You got something foul to say about Mom now? You are pathetic and need to sober up. You need to get some help with—"

"I don't need to do shit but stay black and die," Jared said, weaving. "Your beatnik ass needs to wake up. The only reason you got the South Street property is because *your* daddy left it to you, and Mom's mother knew our father was done till the end of time and wasn't gonna leave you jack shit. That's why you got Baring Street, Nana's house, to make sure you didn't starve. So, don't get pious and lecture me about living in the community because I had options and you didn't." Jared wiped his meaty hands on his cardigan. "There. It's finally been said, so we can all sleep at night and stop tiptoeing around the facts. He's grown. Oughta know. Was long overdue."

"What is this *my* father, *your* father shit, Jared? What happened to *our* father!" Jason yelled. He had grabbed his older brother by the arm, and Jared just peered up at him through bloodshot eyes, with a foolish grin.

"Boy's slow on the uptake, Jackie. You're the medical

professional, so you fill him in on the DNA results."
Jared yanked his arm back, trying to get out of Jason's
grip, but he couldn't. "One affair put Pop in his grave.
I'll always know that's what finally made his heart give
out. But as a proud man in his day, with all he'd built in
this town, the *last* thing he was gonna do was out his wife.
You went to Nana's to get the reminder out of his face.
Guilt probably killed your mother. That's how folks
solved things back in the day—quietly. So, when you
start that bullshit about the good old past and honorable
Negroes, you put that in your reefer Top Paper, Mr.
Artist who doesn't work for the system, and smoke it."

Jason's hand fell away from Jared as Jacqueline covered her mouth, horrified. Jenna wiped at tears, pat-
ting carefully to keep her makeup intact.

"J, you weren't supposed to find out like this. Come
back with me to my condo in Center City, and let's
talk," Jenna said, with a shaking voice, as Jason just
headed toward the door.

Momentarily stunned silent and paralyzed where
she stood, Deborah looked at the sisters and shook her
head. Then her gaze fell on Jason's older brother,
Jared. "He didn't deserve that. You said all that just because you don't approve of me," she said, lifting her
chin. "Jealousy is a nasty, *ugly* thing. I'll pray for you."

Deborah spun on her heels and went to Jason, who
was by the door, numbly taking their coats out of the
closet. He handed Deborah hers and just flipped his
over his shoulder, not even bothering to put it on, as
Deborah braced herself for the unforgiving cold.

Chapter 11

He didn't say a word. His wounds were so deep that she dared not touch him in a show of support—not even his arm—and she waited until he pulled up to her curb to speak.

"Jason," she said quietly. "I'm there for you. No matter what. I'm so sorry, baby."

She reached out to touch the side of his face, where his jaw was pulsing, and in response, he opened the car door and bolted. She didn't wait for him to round the vehicle, but rather opened the door herself and stepped out on the curb.

"I can't do this right now, Deborah," he said, pacing on the sidewalk, with his hands in front of his chest. "I've got a lot on my mind, and I have to go figure some things out right now."

Cold air cut her lungs, stopped her breath. "We're breaking up?"

"I need some space. I know it's messed up, but you heard what happened back there." He looked away from her. "I don't even know who my own fucking father is."

She watched him walk away from her, round his Karmann Ghia, and slam the car door. Icy tears filled her eyes, and the blur of his car pulled away, burning rubber.

His cell phone was blowing up on his hip, but he couldn't see through the tears, didn't want to see. Just wanted to drive, loop the parkway, take his mind and body away from where he was right now.

It all made sense, all the nights his grandmother had tucked him in bed, her warm hugs rocking him, telling him that no matter what anyone ever said about him, he was loved. Thick, gospel Sunday morning love in the form of grandmom's hands, which had always absently caressed a bored little boy's face, put crayons and pencils in his fists. She'd tell him to draw her a picture during extra long services and sneak him gum and mints, even though eating in church was forbidden. She'd let this child have a room all to himself, where he could draw on the walls as long as he did his chores, forever saying, "Dream, child, and become. . . ."

Explaining why his father always seemed angry . . . because he worked so hard. Explaining to an adolescent why his father didn't understand art, seemed to hate it, and actually seemed to take it as a personal affront. Explaining to a young man roaming the globe, searching for something that he could overstand, not understand, that no, the system, as it were, wasn't fair, and the old folks agreed with him. But this same wise sensei had promised him that his mother had loved his every breath, even if she couldn't raise him, until her heart just gave out from compounded grief. Then she'd explained about Jesus and forgiveness until tears ran like a river down her dignified, wrinkled face.

"You knew, Nana!" Jason shouted, pulling up to Jenna's building. "Why didn't you tell me? I deserved to know!" He clutched the steering wheel and rested his forehead against it. Bitter tears streamed down his face as he closed his eyes and took in deep, shuddering breaths. "I miss you so much, Nana. Why didn't you just tell me?"

Jenna sat at her kitchen table in her immaculate condo, eyes red, twisting a tissue and intermittently sipping her tea, with shaking hands. "He was an artist, and he lived in the house on South Street," she said quietly. "Dad had been caught for the millionth time, and Mom, God bless her, fell in love with the gentle soul who had a studio . . . was active in the Civil Rights movement, and she became pregnant with you."

Jason couldn't even lift the mug to his lips; the trauma of what his sister was saying was so profound. "What was his name?"

"I don't know . . . The whole thing was *so* taboo," Jenna practically whispered into her mug. "Mom just made us swear that we would all always get together for family dinners once a month as brothers and sisters, no matter what. That's the only reason we do, I guess."

"Well, it was a bad idea," Jason murmured, his voice a million miles away as his gaze went toward the Center City skyline. "Then again, maybe she knew that would be the only way I'd finally find out. The ancestors are deep."

Jenna nodded. "It wasn't a fling, Jason." Jenna stared at her brother and waited until his gaze met hers. "One time I heard Mom crying and telling Nana that she loved him, but that she couldn't leave Dad and hurt all of us other children, that she couldn't head to Canada to be with him in Toronto. He was so decent that he wanted to be sure you would be okay. He left all he had, his house on South Street, to Grandma. He put it in her name outright to let her know he wanted his son and her daughter to have somewhere to go in case my father continued to dog our mother and she got put out. I can help you check the property records. His name would be on the deed before the property was put in Nana's name."

"Thanks," Jason said, with a swallow. "I wouldn't even have known where to begin. All this time I thought it was from Nana's people and that that was why Jared was so pissed off about the way the property got split up during the funerals. Now I really get it. Slow on the uptake. I really was Mom's oops baby." He looked away as everything in the room blurred.

"You're *not* slow on the uptake. This *was* a conspiracy, Jason, to keep you in the dark and to keep skeletons in the family closet."

Jenna broke down and lowered her head to the table and sobbed as Jason's hands covered hers. "Don't you understand that's what's wrong with Jared? He was the eldest and had to know that his father treated our mother so poorly that she went somewhere else for comfort. All his life he has lived in the shadow of the all-powerful Jared Hastings, Sr. Dad took Jared out on the town with him, and he saw what was going on! He knew the other side of it. Plus, Jared's faith in women was completely torn to shreds because his mother had done the unthinkable, in his mind. He's been drowning that pain in Scotch ever since. Then here you come, Mom's favorite, Nana's baby, the one to protect from the world. Jackie felt robbed when she lost her grandmom to you, and then Mom died. Our sister has been going through life like she's been cheated. God knows, after what she saw Dad do, she doesn't trust men. Me . . . I did what you did. I ran."

Jason looked up at the ceiling, blinking back tears, and gave up. Speaking was impossible as his sister stood and came to him and bent down, hugging him.

"You're my baby brother with a heart of gold, and

Jared is sick. Jackie is neurotic. You should have never been told like that, and not in front of your new girl-friend. It was so ugly. Deborah was right. I'm so ashamed of what this family has become because of this secret."

Jason petted his sister's back and pulled her into his lap, rocking her, swallowing hard. "I've . . . I've got a whole piece of me missing, Jenna. Family roots out in the world." He clung to her. "How do I sign my work now?" He buried his face in her hair, so choked up that he was going blind from tears, as she completely dissolved in his arms at his question. "Do I put Hast-ings on there, or what? I don't even know his name."

She'd set the alarm and gone to bed numb, a prayer in her heart, and she'd curled up into a little ball. In the morning, when the alarm blared, she knew that she would simply touch the top snooze button and stare at the gray dawn filtering in through the window. Color had escaped her life, fled it. For one whirlwind, glorious week, she'd seen magenta and jewel green, yellow and aqua.

People were still blowing up her phone with stupid messages about *their* agendas, never realizing or seem-ing to care that her life might be falling apart. They'd been that way all through her divorce, still leaning on her for this or that, giving temporary ear time to things that had wrung out her soul, and then launch-ing into their litany—as though she had the emo-tional stamina to address any of it. The one thing she knew for sure was she wasn't answering her father's terse messages inquiring into her whereabouts. She didn't need to be judged right now, just held.

Jason had been wounded so deeply, her man might never care to come back, and she didn't know how to help him, if she could, or if it was even her place.

Deborah snuggled down deeper under the covers, wishing that she didn't have to let her feet touch the floor again. Then she immediately cancelled that wish, thinking of people who were paralyzed or permanently bedridden.

No. She'd survive; she'd get up in the morning and go back to the grind, just like she would keep going to class, would fulfill her self-improvement mission, and would stay on course to getting back into school. One of her fellow students from art class had mentioned a lead. The fiasco at Jason's brother's home had also taught her that money doesn't equal class, just as her nana had always said. She'd learned that she had more class, more compassion, and simply more couth than people who could run paper rings around her with their money and degrees. She'd had a week to dream. *Bless Jason for that.* He'd also shown her that she had a voice, something important to say, and that she was sexy and valuable, all the things she hadn't believed before.

Deborah let out a shuddering sigh and fought back the tears, remembering something else her grandmother firmly believed: For everything there was a reason and a season. Some people came into your life for a reason; some for just a season; others for a lifetime. Huge tears rolled down her cheeks. At least this man had appeared in her life, even if the reason was to show her that she needed to strengthen her sense of self-worth. At least they'd had a brief season, a glorious post–New Year's week. He hadn't walked away because he was a jerk. The way this had gone down had everything to do with what was going on with him, not with some deficiency within her. But she so wished that she could wrap her arms around him and help him through this hard time. However, he'd made it clear that it wasn't her reason or her season.

What color was heartbreak? she wondered. It was painful shades of gray.

Jason was wrung out by the time he put his key in the door at three AM, and he stopped short, remembering that he'd definitely cut off all the lights when he'd left to go pick up Deborah. Glancing up to the third-floor apartment, he let out his breath hard. Wil was home. *Damn. Not now.* That was the last person he felt like dealing with.

Annoyed at the encroachment, Jason slammed the door behind him and paced through the house, smelling food cooking.

"You need to leave a brother a message if you're gonna raid my refrigerator," Jason said, flinging his coat on a kitchen chair.

"Well, hello to you, too, dude," Wil said, with a wide grin, as he looked at the microwave. "I thought I might have missed out on catering leftovers from your monthly family dinners. And you actually cleaned this joint while I was gone, man? Looks fantastic, even if you did take a sledgehammer to the dining-room wall. If I didn't know better, I'd swear—"

"I'm not in the mood, all right. Drop it." Jason walked away and bounded upstairs, needing space.

Wil was right on his heels. "Hey, man, I'm sorry. You don't look right and definitely don't sound right. What gives?"

"I found out my life is fucked up, man," Jason said, rummaging in his drawers to find an old T-shirt and pants that he could paint in. "Like I needed confirmation. I held down your class. I'm out."

Wil leaned against the wall. "Something way profound happened. Talk to me."

Jason shrugged, yanking off his sweater and pulling on the ragged T-shirt. "What's to tell? My big brother drops a bomb on me, says that my old man ain't my father. Some other dude, who none of us know, is. So, I guess I'll just be signing my oils from now on as J." He flung his sweater across the room, kicked off his shoes so that they slammed against the wall, stripped off his pants, and put on his jeans, breathing hard. "Like I care! Whatever. The asshole didn't have to do that shit in front of Deborah, though."

Jason zipped up his jeans and went into the studio, brushing past Wil.

"Don't touch your work while you're like this, man," Wil said quietly, leaning against the wall. "Don't bring that kinda energy into your sanctuary." He glanced around and shook his head. "No, man. Step out into the hall. I'm seeing masterpiece-level work unfold. You'll ruin it."

"Who cares, man! It's just a gig, just a stupid commission to keep the lights on!"

"Step out of the studio until you pull your head together!" Wil shouted. "You might be able to take me in martial arts, but I promise you we'll fight all over this house if you try to blot that beautiful woman out. Is that Deborah? Huh! Answer me!"

Jason looked away and hurled a brush at a window. "Yeah."

"She didn't have shit to do with your foul-ass brother."

Jason closed his eyes but didn't answer.

"I'll help you renovate the house, I will knock out every wall, down to the support beams, if you need to work this out, but don't screw with your gift, dude. It's not done, and you know it. It's against the code . . . unless it allows you to create something good from it, that is."

"How was London? You're back early," Jason said offhandedly, looking out the window.

"Shitty. Why else would I be home early and needing my old job back?"

Jason ran his hands down his face and walked out the door, slapping the light switch on the wall. "Sorry to hear it, man. For real."

"I'm going downstairs to finish heating up food," Wil announced. "I'm putting a pot of hot water on. Jasmine, green? Name your poison."

"Green."

"Good. Now we're getting somewhere." Wil raked his locks. "The food isn't from a caterer, is it?"

"No," Jason said, giving Wil his back to consider. "Deborah made it."

"And I suppose you have no doctor's note, Ms. Jackson?" Deborah's boss said, folding her arms over her ample bosom.

Tired of cowering, Deborah lifted her chin and bent the truth. "No. I didn't feel well enough to even go."

"Hmmm . . . that's a problem, because—"

"Why?" Deborah said, without blinking. "Policy clearly states that I need a note *after* three days, Ms. Brown, the operative word being *after.*" She stood and looked hard at her beefy supervisor. "Let's not play games. I've had a decent record, I haven't even taken all of the vacation time that is due to me, and I never took a sick day. I'm here on time daily, and I stay late most days. If this is going on my record, then call in the union rep now, and we can pull these damned books apart for everybody and see if there have been any inconsistencies across the board."

Her supervisor was on her feet, pointing a fat finger, her beady little eyes glaring behind thick, black-rimmed glasses, and her greasy hair moving with her head like it was a helmet. "Listen here, Deborah

Jackson. You won't get anywhere in this department with an attitude like that."

"Good," Deborah said between her teeth.

"What did you say?" Her supervisor glared at her. "You are so close to being insubordinate, it isn't funny!"

Deborah thrust her shoulders back and stood up straight so that she was a full five feet eight inches tall. "I said good. It's good that this won't become a safe hiding place for me, because I'm going back to school to finish my degree. You're right. I'm not going anywhere here at all." She shook her head. "I'm no threat. Trust me."

Her supervisor opened and closed her mouth, flustered.

"Are you done? I have work to catch up on from being out *sick.*"

All eyes were on Deborah as she flounced out of her supervisor's office. LaVern was coiled and lying in wait, ready to launch a viper attack and to get the scoop.

"So did you get in trouble, lady?" LaVern hissed through her teeth as Deborah slid into her chair.

"No," Deborah said flatly. "Good morning, LaVern. How was your weekend?" she added, sarcasm dripping.

Somewhat taken aback, LaVern hesitated. "You feeling okay? No need to be salty with me just because you got in trouble with Miss Thang."

"No, I'm not feeling okay, LaVern. I had the flu," Deborah said, not bothering to glance at her coworker as she spoke.

"That's not what Doris Reiger said. She said she took Friday off and was in the supermarket out where her sister lives, on account of the bar mitzvah they were throwing that weekend for her nephew, and she said she saw you all hugged up in Whole Foods, with some hunk."

Deborah stopped typing and turned to stare at LaVern head-on. "Did the heifer get pictures?"

LaVern nearly spit out her coffee. "Girl, you're too much. I told her it couldn't have been you, because you were all gaga over some raggedy-ass, broke artist."

Pure fury imploded inside Deborah's chest. She leaned in to LaVern. "Then I hope you run and tell Ms. Brown that it wasn't me Doris saw, because if I find out you did, we can step outside, old school. Try me. I'm a sister under a lot of stress."

Deborah stared out of the bus window, in a daze. What was wrong with her? She'd told off her supervisor and threatened a coworker, both very foolish things to do for a woman who wanted to stay gainfully employed and didn't want a prison record. But with God as her witness, she would have kicked LaVern's narrow tail today and gone to jail. The word *no* had a ring to it, and standing up for oneself felt good.

She chuckled sadly to herself, thinking of her little cousins and her girlfriend's children when they had turned two years old. Little kids, once they learned the power of the word *no,* would say it to everything just to have it ring in their little ears. Do you want a piece of candy? No. How about a cookie? No. So you want a kiss? No. Do you want a present? No! That was just how she felt today. Deborah, do you want a man? No. Do you want to be gainfully employed? No. She stood and held on to a pole, and a guy almost knocked her down as he passed by. Normally, she would have just let it go, but today was not the day.

"Yo! The pharase is *excuse me.*" She looked the teenager up and down.

"My bad, Ma. Damn, you ain't gotta get all bent."

Deborah told herself to get off the bus before she said another word and got her behind beat down or shot. But it felt good to at least be acknowledged as a human being and not a doormat. "That's right," she muttered to herself. "No."

When the telephone rang, she had to fight to get the paint-splattered shirt over her ruined tank top and make a dash for it. The arms of the shirt were inside out. She'd learned in class one not to wear anything that she minded getting soiled. Without looking at the number that flashed in the display, she answered, breathless—hoping. A male voice made her grip tighten, until she realized who it was.

"Hi, Dad," she said, flopping down on the edge of the bed, thoroughly disappointed. She closed her eyes and waited for the reprimand.

"I tried to call several times before I left a message, but you didn't pick up."

"Then how would I know you called until you did?" she said, in no mood for his pious lecture.

"Don't you think that it's time for you to be getting yourself together and not running the streets, after a divorce?"

"Happy New Year to you, too," she snapped in a brittle, uncharacteristic tone. "Will that be all, sir? I have a class tonight and need to be on my way."

Silence crackled on the line for a moment.

"I'm your father, and you need to monitor your tone of voice."

"Roger that, sir," she said, slicing him with the military lingo she'd picked up from him as a child.

"I'm glad to hear you're back in school," he said. "Is that why you weren't available?"

"I am back in school, sir, and the rest of my whereabouts are on a need-to-know basis. Last I checked, I was grown. What is your need to know, sir?"

"Because I'm your father and—"

"Save it!" she shrieked, completely losing it as tears

filled her eyes and her voice cracked. "Just stop it, Dad! You don't care about me, and you know it. You have blamed me for her dying since the day I was born—but I'm over it and you. I don't care if you hate me! I don't care if I'm a big, fat disappointment in your life! I don't care. You want a relationship? Then stop grilling me like I'm in the army. You want a loving, kind, caring daughter? Then recognize that I was *always* that for you. But I want a father who is there for me in return."

She'd meant to be strong, meant to hold back the emotion and give him the same cold shoulder he'd given her. But instead, she was sobbing like a little girl and rocking, her words coming out in hysterical jags. "I love you sooo much, and you never even came to see if I was all right when my husband left me! Where's the cavalry, Mr. Decorated War Hero?"

Blood had drained from her knuckles. She was on her feet, leaning over, screaming in the phone, hiccup–crying into dead silence, but she couldn't stop herself. It all had to come out tonight.

"What about those dads who clean shotguns for their girls, huh?" Mucous was making her slur her words like she was drunk, and she wiped her nose with the back of her hand, shouting at the tops of her lungs. "What, because I'm an Amazon, you think he didn't work over my heart, take my dignity, or rob me blind of what little I had financially speaking? Oh, that only happens to small, petite, pretty girls, right? You're the only one who loved someone and had them leave you, like Mom did by dying, right? Well, I lost a mom *and* a dad, and I only had Nana, and then she died, and I was left with nobody! That's how my ex got to me, made me follow him all around the country like a lost puppy dog, a stupid lost puppy! I was one!"

Breathing hard, she dropped to the floor, sobbing her eyes out against the comforter. Then the strangest sound she'd ever heard came through the phone.

She'd expected a dial tone, but it was an older man quietly crying.

"Oh, baby, no, no, no," a broken male voice said. "Please, baby, don't cry. Daddy didn't know all that was going on . . . I swear. I'm coming up there. You hear me, pretty Deborah?"

The dam inside her broke, the verbal connection had been made, years of heartbreak cascaded over the edges of her sanity, and she wailed like someone was murdering her.

Chapter 12

Her nose looking like Rudolph the red-nosed reindeer's, her eyes a bit puffy—cold compresses and Visine notwithstanding—Deborah braved the sleet and freezing rain and walked a block to class. It wasn't about Jason. This was about not allowing herself to be chased away from something she wanted, refusing to be derailed. There was a nice woman named Susan in the art class, and last week Deborah hadn't gotten her card. God willing, tonight she would, and she'd begin looking into a new job and going back to school in earnest.

Deborah hunched her shoulders inside her bomber jacket against the cold and tugged her hat down so far, she looked like she was about to rob somebody.

As insane as the session on the phone with her father had been, and although it had emotionally wrung her out like a rag, it had lifted a lot of weight from her spirit. Darryl Lee Jackson had listened and even apologized and had promised to visit her. Firsts across the board. He'd said he loved her, and that meant the world. Even if he never came to visit, all the hurt that had been stacked up within her for years had got cried out on the phone with someone who, for the first time, seemed to realize just how much he had contributed to that.

Yet, it wasn't about remaining a victim. That was the old Deborah. The new Deborah was empowered, could say what she meant and mean what she said—tactfully at times, blunt at others—but she didn't have to fear her own voice. *She mattered,* and she knew that now. *Her* vision of *herself* also mattered. She didn't need another set of approving eyes to validate her, no matter how handsome they might be.

Why hadn't she understood that before, she wondered, when it was such a simplistic concept?

Deborah sniffed hard, swung open the heavy, leaded-and-beveled-glass and oak door to the arts center, and went inside, a new woman.

"You're honestly not going?" Wil asked, his tone gentle but incredulous.

"No," Jason said quietly, staring down at the platform he was varnishing. "I just did one class . . . It's better this way. My head isn't there."

"They'll be real disappointed, man," Wil said and then slipped out the bedroom door.

Jason continued to slowly add strokes of glossy sealer to the blond wood, his newly straightened-up bedroom a reminder of Deborah. He stopped and rolled his shoulders, answering Wil, who was long gone. "Too late to worry about causing disappointment, man. Already did that."

"Oh, you poor thing," declared Martha, one of the older ladies in the class. "You should be home, in bed, with some hot tea."

Deborah just nodded and gave her classmate a weak smile, not wanting to admit to a near stranger that she'd had a complete meltdown before coming to class. "Thanks, but it's just a cold." *Yeah, hot tea in bed. That would be nice, but not in the way Martha probably meant it, and it definitely isn't gonna happen with Jason.*

As she spied Susan entering the class, however, it was all Deborah could do to maintain her cool and not mug the woman. Remembering her manners, and allowing Susan to get settled, Deborah finally approached her and smiled.

"Hi, Susan. I was hoping you'd be back this week," Deborah said, leaning against the long table so as not to tower over the short blonde.

"Deborah! Last week was a hoot. I wouldn't miss this class for the world. How are you? Catching a cold?"

"Yeah. What can you do?" Deborah said, with a shrug. "But I wanted to see if we could still exchange numbers . . . I meant what I said last week. I hate my job and would love the opportunity to go back to school. But without a good job, I can't afford it."

Beaming, Susan began excitedly rummaging in her purse for a business card. "Actually, I have an agenda. You seem to be so good with people—diverse people— and you just put everyone at ease and you came in so professionally pulled together that first class. So, I was wondering if you'd be interested in interviewing for something that is sort of like a marketing position at Drexel?"

"Are you serious?" Deborah said, digging in her purse for paper and a pen to scribble her contact information down for Susan.

"How does minority recruiting sound?"

Deborah threw her head back and laughed. "That's awesome!"

Susan thrust out her hand. "You get me your resume right away, lady. All right? The position is entry level and doesn't pay that much, but as an employee, as long as you keep above a C average, you go to school for free. You meet prospective students . . . The director is the one who travels. Sorry about that part. But as college fairs happen and what have you, you basically are a host who rolls out the red carpet of hospitality and invites people to galas and makes them feel that coming to Drexel U would be a good choice." She folded her arms over her chest, with a huge grin. "Finding people with good energy and enthusiasm is really hard. Resumes smezumes. I have a feeling that you're the kind of person who, once committed, goes above and beyond, just because it's the right thing to do."

Without thinking, Deborah gave the woman a big hug and then danced around like a little kid. "Thanks so, so, so, so much for the tip. Oh, you have no idea! This is right up my alley. I know Philly. I can tell young people all about the city but also make their parents feel at ease. Oh, girl, you don't have to worry. I'll get my resume done right up at Kinko's this week, and I'll have it in your hand before next class." Deborah hugged herself. "Susan, I can't tell you why, but trust me when I say, I needed this tonight."

"Good. Then we have a deal. You get me your resume ASAP."

"Done." Deborah sighed and began to move back to her desk. "Oh, should I address the cover letter to you or the director, the boss?" She waited, holding the pen above Susan's card.

Susan just shrugged and gave Deborah a quick wink. "Either-or. Since I'm one and the same."

Deborah covered her mouth and Susan gave a belly laugh, but there wasn't time to say more, as a cute, quirky-looking guy who was all arms and legs and dreadlocks bounced into their class. All the women gave each other curious looks.

"Hi, my name is Wil. Just in from London, loves, and I'm Jason's roommate." He leaned back on the desk and shook his head, with a big, chipped-tooth smile. "From the expressions on all your faces, he's already ruined the lot of you. I don't feel the love, ladies." He sniffed his underarms theatrically. "All right, I could use freshening, but remember this: He's just the good-looking one. I'm the one with talent."

Everyone laughed hard and warmly began to welcome and accept their replacement. Finally, as Wil went around the room, redoing introductions, Martha sighed. "Tell me, Wil, that we won't have to do still life," she said.

Wil pressed his hand to his chest as though aghast. "That cad. Tried to weasel out of the foundation basics, did he? I'm shocked beyond measure. Unheard of in an entry-level class." He pulled his T-shirt hem down beneath his bulky sweater and brushed off his chest as if it were suit jacket lapels. "First, he hijacks the minds of me class, turns them against me, spoils them rotten, and now no still life?"

More hearty laughter echoed throughout the room, and the women exchanged winks, signifying that Wil had endeared himself with humor.

"But he was going to read our paintings," Liz said, her voice baleful. "I wanted to know what my swirls meant."

"And my competition brought psychic readings of canvases and other cheap parlor tricks to my institution of higher learning?" Wil said in a loud, fake Elizabethan accent. "Oh, the slings and arrows of outrageous misfortune, milady, but I would say your swirls are born of deep passions."

"Oh . . . brother," Deborah said under her breath, laughing as Liz giggled and blushed.

"A nonbeliever in my midst," Wil said, his expression filled with mischief, which widened Deborah's eyes. He covered his eyes with one palm. "I have seen your image before . . . I am getting a name . . . a letter. No, don't tell me."

Mortified, Deborah froze and then slowly began to shake her head no.

"Fair maiden, that name is pretty Deborah!"

Deborah closed her eyes.

Susan nudged her. "Damn, he good."

Deborah packed up her supplies after class like her apartment was on fire, and maybe it was. Her mind sure was. She was trying to get out of there before Wil cornered her, yet she couldn't mess up her new networking opportunity with Susan. Both women agreed to meet one night later in the week when it wasn't sleeting. As Deborah headed to the door, Wil blocked her from leaving, drawing stares.

"Deb, just one word, maybe two, please," Wil said, pressing his hands together like he was praying.

"I really have to—"

"Did you make the pie?"

For a second, she just looked at him and then laughed. "Yeah, I did."

"Aha! I knew it. It was my Cinderella test. The glass slipper fits you . . . but our prince is well broken, milady."

She wanted to tell him to stop with the bad Shakespeare routine, but how did one chastise a truly good soul, which Wil seemed to be? It had to be a nervous habit, like taking on a persona to play a role in front of all those eyes. But the thing he'd said about Jason being broken needed clarity and seriousness.

"How is he?" she finally asked.

Wil's smile faded. "You were there at ground zero when it 'appened. Terrible."

"I don't know how to reach him," she admitted, beginning to pick at the nap of her gloves.

"That makes two of us . . . I was hoping you had

some special something I don't own." Wil sighed. "Do you love 'im?"

"What?"

"It's a yes-or-no question, very simplistic, really." He asked again, this time using phony sign language. "Do you love him?"

"I . . . I . . ."

"Stuttering in sign language is hard for me to mime. Let me see. I . . . I. . . ." Wil said, his tone growing peevish.

"Yes!" she said, closing her eyes. "Ohmigod, Wil. I don't know you and it happened so fast and I don't know what to do. I wanna kick his brother's ass, but not as much as I want to just hug Jason, but he won't let me. He's like this wounded bear. Yeah, I love him."

Wil let out a hard breath, and his shoulders dropped two inches. "Gawd. That makes two of us. He's me brother. Me only family worth a damn. I can't rationalize this for him or cheer him up with bad jokes and beer. So, I figured I'd go to the only woman I've ever seen him remodel a house for . . . *Nana's house* . . . and the only one that he's ever painted like you." Wil stared at her deeply and for a long time. "The man loves you, Deborah. That's all I can say. Ride this storm out with him, if you can. It's not fair of me to ask, but like I said, he's me brother."

She'd heard Wil and had left several unanswered messages for Jason. She'd left them open, not pressing, just saying that it was her and she'd be there for him if he needed to talk. Then she left him alone, not wanting to add additional stress to his life by freaking out or sounding desperate. As long as Wil was there and coming to class, she knew Jason was physically all right at the very least.

Crazy as it was, she had even started a letter and

then had realized, this was lunacy. If a person was in that much pain, they had to emerge from their own cave. She'd pray for him and hope for the best; that was all she could do right now. In the meanwhile, she would remain focused. Susan had asked for a resume. As soon as she'd arrived at work, she'd made a call on the sly to Drexel University to find out what she needed to do to matriculate, and she had even called her old alma mater to find out how, if she got in to Drexel, she could transfer her credits there.

Settling down at her desk early, she became the list master this new, sleeting day. But that was part of the plan. She'd read somewhere that the only way to eat an elephant was one bite at a time. So she made a list.

Therefore, every day she would follow her six-week class schedule, learn new things, but also tick off at least one "to do" on her achievement list. This way, she wasn't stagnating, wasn't waiting, and wasn't losing her mind. This thing with Jason in deep cave mode could go either way. People deeply hurt sometimes lashed out and became toxic, and she was trying to be healthy. Sometimes they went backward, to old lovers, crazy as it sounded, back in time, to where they perceived it was safe. Or sometimes they developed a layer of protective Sheetrock around their hearts that was so thick that it was damned near impossible to penetrate. She'd lived that all her life with her father and knew she couldn't go there, banging her head and heart up against a stone wall.

The only problem was that every class Wil would be bringing her frantic updates. Although Jason's friend had the best of intentions, she was going to have to draw the line with that, too.

Deborah kept typing, her mind a million miles away. She looked up at her supervisor, who'd come to her desk, with arms folded, drawing stares from coworkers. All eyes seemed to say, "Ooohhhh, you in trouble"!

"Some man is here to see you, Ms. Jackson, and this is highly irregular."

Jenna sat at Jason's kitchen table, glancing around. "I haven't been here in so long . . . It's so different, Jas. Wow."

"I'm working on it little by little," he said, taking the kettle off the stove.

"Have you called her?"

He didn't respond.

"You should," his sister pressed. "I don't care what Jackie said . . . She seemed nice. She was a hundred percent in your corner. Made us, rightfully, all feel like dirt. She didn't curse, didn't stutter. She just said you deserved better and that she would pray for us."

He didn't say a word; he just poured the hot water over Jenna's tea ball.

"Can I see your studio?"

Jason looked up for the first time. "Why?"

"Don't shut me out, Jas." Jenna began to wring her hands. "I don't care what the rest of the family does or thinks, but me and you were always tight." Tears rose to her eyes. "I didn't do this. I didn't hurt you."

"You didn't tell me, either," he said calmly, sliding a jar of honey toward her.

Jenna lifted her chin, and the tears were gone; so was the warble in her voice. "I want you to stop and think for a moment, Jason." Her tone had gone from apologetic to big sister. "I was thirteen years old, thirteen, when I learned. That's how much older than you I am. Right?"

He looked away as he leaned against the sink.

"What kind of a burden do you think that was on a kid, huh?" Jenna folded her arms over her chest. "Yes, you were a baby, but I was a young, adolescent girl who adored her father and thought her mother walked on water, had to be a saint, because she was Mom." Jenna pushed away from the table and stood, chuckling sadly as she began to pace and rake her short, stylish hair. "Wounded? Puhlease, Jas. I went buck wild and did half the school, I was so angry. The only reason I'm halfway okay at this juncture is that I got therapy."

Now she had his full attention.

"You went to a shrink about this?"

Jenna smiled. "Yes. After I kept pushing people away, running all over the globe, and messing up my life, yeah."

For a long while, they said nothing. Jenna walked over to the table and retrieved a small envelope from her bag.

"I went to the land and title office at city hall this morning. His name is Christopher Nesbitt. He's from Barbados, and he came to Philly by way of D.C. There were previous addresses listed, and Nana said he was in Toronto." Jenna's voice became gentle as her eyes searched his. "We are still brother and sister, Jason. Blood doesn't make kin. Love does. Anyway, you know that from Wil. He's more brother to you without any biological connection than, sadly, Jared will ever be. So, even if I just became your half sister, does it matter as long as we still love each other?"

Jason went to her and pulled her into a hug. "No . . . it doesn't matter. Thank you, sis."

Jenna kissed his cheek. "Show me your studio?" She looked up at him. "I envy you. So do the rest of us. Haven't you figured that out by now?"

Jason's embrace slackened. "Why? You guys have it all going on. I'm just living—"

"You, dear brother, are living your grand passion," she said, touching the side of his face. "Don't you get it? I went into advertising because that was the only way I could think of to tap into my creativity. Jackie and Jared never even let theirs bloom. That's partly why they're so frustrated." She pulled away from him and placed the envelope on the table. "Sure, for some people, those professions are their art . . . but you weren't around when we were little. Mom was an artist, a fine one at that."

"Mom? Our mother, who worked in—"

"Look at this kitchen, Jason. Our mother could do ceramics, oil. She was gifted. But in that day, how did an African American female artist express her talent? Think about it. Her work was called crafts, and only degreed men of means made what was called art. You know that field has as many isms as the next, and art is so freakin' elitist."

"That's what I've been trying to tell Jackie and Jared!" Jason raked his hair, feeling the tight cornrows Deborah had placed there. His hand slid away as new awareness filled him. "That's why Nana encouraged me, too. . . ."

"Yes, honey," Jenna said, getting choked up. "That old girl walked in the marches with Martin, did her day's work and went to church, tithed for the cause, gave money to the NAACP, and hoped with all her might that she'd live to see a generation experience a dream deferred. I know. I never argued with them, because their sickness was so deep, and I didn't want it to bubble up and hurt you at a dinner table." Jenna looked away. "I'm sorry I wasn't braver."

Jason shook his head. "No, Jenna. You are brave. I'm proud of my big sister. Thank you."

"I'm proud of my baby brother. You've honored all your parents . . . Mom, Dad, Christopher Nesbitt, and Nana."

Jason swallowed hard. "That means a lot coming from you. It means a lot that you're telling me that here in Nana's kitchen."

"Your father was an artist, J." Jenna patted the envelope. "I would place money that's how they met, him and Mom. His occupation is in the paperwork."

"Oh, wow . . ." Jason began pacing.

"You've never gone treasure hunting up in the attic here in grandma's house, have you?"

He stopped pacing and stared at his sister for a moment. "No. Too painful. I just closed the space off and figured I'd get to it one year."

"Everything artistic thing Mom ever made, painted, or created, she sent to Nana's, before Dad could trash it. To him, art was synonymous with Christopher Nesbitt and had to go."

"Including me," Jason said quietly. Now his lengthy name made sense, too: Jason Christopher Nesbitt Hastings. He was the only one of his mother's children with such a long handle, the only child told through subtle implication not to ever speak his middle names around his so-called father. The tapestry of his life came together so clearly now. "Like I'm sure Jared has said, this gives a whole new meaning to being the oops baby of the family."

His sister's eyes glittered with compassion, and she let out a weary sigh, but she didn't answer the charge that they both knew was true. "You get your creative gift from both sides. You have to use the talent God gave you through the people who made you. Don't listen to crazy people. Our brother and sister are crazy. Consider the source, Jas. They have a lot of issues that stem from this whole family debacle. Listen to your heart. Listen to Wil. Let the anger go, and paint, man!"

She strode up to him and hugged him. "I'll come help you fix up this house so you can create. I'll take a couple of weeks off. I can manage contractors in here, with Wil helping, if you need this to be completed . . . You need completion, closure. You understand? As long as your environment is all crazy and chaotic, your energy will be that, too."

He closed his eyes and nodded. "Oh, God, Deborah said that to me . . . said I needed to get my taxes done, get an accountant, set up as an LLC."

Jenna shook her head and laughed. "Damn, Jas, you'd better marry that one."

He opened his eyes and stared at his sister hard.

She opened her mouth and then covered it with her hand. "Oh . . . my . . . God . She's the one, isn't she?"

He looked away. "I . . . I . . . like, I'm not sure. It happened so fast. I don't know. Like, Jen, it's too hectic right now, too crazy. Feel me?"

"Advice from one previously crazy person to one on the border of insanity. Don't run."

Their gazes locked.

"I mean it, Jason. Don't run."

"I just need a little time to think. A week is too short."

Jenna relaxed. "Okay, I'll buy that. A week is too short. Let it germinate, but not without care, watering, and feeding."

Jason relaxed. "Okay, I can do that." He let his breath out hard. "Wanna see what I'm working on in the studio?"

Sunshine spread across Jenna's face. "Yes."

Deborah almost fell on the floor when she came around the corner section of gray cubicle barriers. Her father was standing there in full uniform, shoes shined like glass, and enough braid and metals on his chest to open a parade for the president. *Major Jackson has come to town.*

His chin was high, his eyes forward, shoulders back, and his hat was under his arm, and at his age, he was still as tall and handsome as ever. Instant tears filled her eyes.

"You came," she whispered, overcome by emotion.

"You said the cavalry didn't come. I took exception.

We have always been here," her father said, speaking in the plural as though he had the entire U.S. armed forces at his beck and call for her. "You just never said how badly you needed us." He opened his arms. Deborah barreled into them. "You think I wouldn't come directly when my baby girl was crying her eyes out? What kind of father would that make me?"

She hugged him hard, wetting his uniform, so glad that he didn't seem to care.

"Can an old man buy you breakfast?"

"They won't let me off till . . . two hours from now."

He shrugged. "How bad do you need this job, Deborah? Really?"

She looked at him, astounded. "Really badly, like paycheck to paycheck. Reality check, Daddy. I'm serious."

"Roger that," he said, with a sigh. "Then, how about a family emergency? Even in the military, they grant those for administrative personnel in noncombat roles and during peacetime." He glanced around sheepishly. "Last I checked, the water department wasn't in an armed conflict."

"You haven't been in the trenches here or in the ladies' room," she said, with a wide grin. "Lemme go tell them I'm leaving and get my coat and purse."

She bounced with each step. Her daddy had come to see about her!

Jenna stood in the center of his studio, with her hand pressed to her heart, staring up. Then, all of a sudden, tears began to stream down her face, and she walked out and stood in the hall, overwhelmed.

"Jesus . . . oh, Jesus, I never knew," Jenna said, shaking her head.

Bewildered, Jason remained very still by the door. "Sis, what's wrong?"

She waved him away. "It's been years since I've seen

your work, *years,* Jason. The development is insane,
brilliant. Why are you just banging around in Philly, in
exhibits, and doing small commissions?" She whipped
out her BlackBerry. "I'm your big sister, and I know all
the right people in New York. You need an agent."

She took her dad home with her and showed him
her small place. She was so pleased when he smiled
and said she kept a nice home. They walked at his brisk
pace to Abbraccio's, a small restaurant at Forty-seventh
and Warrington Avenue. The large windows and comfortable atmosphere of the restaurant was perfect for
the easy communication that had befallen them. All
she wanted to do was let him know she was getting herself together, but she fell into the old trap, rattling off
accomplishments and seeking his approval, hoping to
keep him smiling and with her just a while longer.

"And I'm taking self-defense and art," she said, with
a big smile. "Even healthy cooking. And, oh, this lady
I met in class is a director of minority recruitment and
said she'd accept my resume. So I have to get right on
that. I'm going back to school, Dad. You'll see."

He smiled sadly as he stirred his coffee and gazed at
her. "Deborah, you look so much like her . . . I'm sorry,
baby. You don't have to impress me. I did that to you.
Don't get me wrong. I'm proud, baby. Real proud that
you're doing things. But you're fine just as you are. You
do those things if you want to, but not because you
think I'll inspect your life. Not anymore. We clear?"

"I don't know what you mean." Deborah's hands
became tight around her mug of tea, and nervous-
ness invaded her stomach. "Plus, I don't look anything like Mom. I take after your side."

He shook his head. "I loved that woman so much,
sweetheart, that looking at you was like looking at her
ghost. There's pictures of her that your grandma kept

for me . . . when I couldn't manage it all. From when she was a little girl, from when she was a teenager, then at your age now. It's the eyes. Her mouth. Same voice. All you got from me was height and color, but the rest is her. I could never look in your eyes without asking why the love of my life had to die on a delivery table. And it wasn't right, wasn't fair to you."

She didn't know what to do with her father's deep confession in the near-empty restaurant. He'd said he couldn't manage, which was the same as couldn't deal. She'd never known Darryl Lee Jackson to be unable to deal with anything in his natural-born life. Rather than speak, she took a shaky sip of tea. Her world and every paradigm in it were shifting, and even if what had been there before wasn't healthy, it was known. This new territory frightened her.

"When you have a little one," her father said slowly, talking into his coffee cup, his gaze averted, "they look up at you with these eyes of expectation, eyes of hope, eyes of complete trust, and, baby doll, I was so close to the edge of despair that I couldn't look into your eyes and not see your mother's. I don't expect you to understand me, but I couldn't handle that. I'd let her down . . . had let her die. I didn't get her the right doctors, I guess. It wasn't that I didn't love you . . . been thinking through it all since I talked to you last night and all the way up here on the train. Wasn't sure what I was gonna say, though."

He drew in a shuddering breath, took a slurp of coffee, and then swallowed it, with a wince, like he'd tasted hard liquor. "My mother held the pieces together, Deb. Your other grandma was dead." Two big tears shimmered in his eyes. "Wasn't till you let loose on me like you did that I came to know how much I'd hurt you, suga. Was never my intention. I was running from my own hurt. And that's gospel. Mom told me that years ago, but I couldn't hear it, rest her soul in peace."

Deborah reached across the table and clasped his hands. "Daddy, I love you. I don't know what it was like for you. She must have been something so special. You had a right to your pain."

To Deborah's horror, she watched the two shimmering tears in her father's eyes fall. The sight of her normally stoic father crumbling due to the subject matter made it difficult for her to breathe.

"She was that," he said plainly, not even bothering to wipe his face. "But I've been foolish. Wasted time looking back, and her parting gift to me—which was you—I cast aside."

"No," Deborah said, squeezing his large, rough-hewn hands. "You listen to me, Daddy. You were there plenty of times. I was being overly dramatic." Panic made her breaths shallow. She wanted him whole, not hurt.

"You sound just like her," he said, with a sad chuckle. "'You listen here, Darryl Lee Johnson.' Then she'd deliver the law. That was your mother. That's you. No, pretty Deborah, my only baby girl, it wasn't all right what I did . . . but you have your momma's and grandmomma's heart, a heart of forgiveness, a gentleness that surpasses all understanding." He wiped at more tears and took another deep slurp of his coffee. "I came up here to check on you, and here you go forgiving me. How's that for a twist?"

She smiled through tear-blurred eyes. "I'd say that's what family's for."

He nodded. "I have some things down South that belonged to your mother and me, and to your grandma . . . things that I wouldn't give you while you were married to that ass."

They both looked at each other and smirked.

"I'm glad you didn't," she said quietly, squeezing his hands and smiling. "But I don't need anything. I'm—"

"You're going back to school, right?" he said, cutting her off.

"Yeah, Dad, so I can't—"

"Then you need to be able to go on your own steam." He stared at her. "I've got pictures and silver and china and furniture for you when you're ready, Deborah. But I'm not talking about those sentimental things . . . You take your time going through your mother's wedding trunk and your grandmother's items."

"I thought her sisters . . . I thought you—"

"Got rid of everything?" He shook his head and sighed. "Have my child, my girl child, out in the world, all alone, with nothing left for her?" He stared at her, his eyes brimming with new tears. "I must have come off as one mean-spirited bastard."

She closed her eyes and shook her head, tears falling and her throat so tight, she couldn't speak.

Warm, rough hands covered hers. "I didn't want some guy around who didn't have enough respect to meet me eye to eye and ask for my girl right, a guy who up and ran her to Elkton, Maryland, to marry her on the fly just because her grandma had just passed and he thought she was coming into money. I didn't want him to take what was yours."

Her father squeezed her hands until she opened her eyes, and he leaned forward to wipe her face with his fingers. "'Cause, see, I couldn't come between man and wife. No father can. But if he took my child's one hundred and fifty thousand dollars from the sale of her grandma's house and her mother's insurance policy, then went after the china and silver, I'd have to shoot that rat bastard and go to jail."

He smiled when Deborah went slack-jawed and didn't blink. "I didn't want that on your conscience, baby girl." Her father patted her cheek. "I just needed to know that hostile forces had cleared the area and were really gone before I could call in the true cavalry. A Dreyfus Fund."

Chapter 13

Jason stood in the attic, listening to the echo of silence. The stillness was like stepping through to another dimension, where the dust-covered sheets were like altar cloths.

Half afraid of what he'd find, he took his time reveling in the quiet of the house. Wil was gone; Jenna had left and would no doubt begin banging and hammering away with contractors very soon. He knew that much about his play brother and half sister. They were relentless.

But so were his fears and his nagging doubts. Who had his mother been? Who had his father been? What had they dreamed, what had they given up, and what had they risked? How did they endure it? That was what he needed to find out, needed to ask someone.

His grandmother, a proverbial pack rat, seemed to have folded and shoved many lifetimes into one small, dormant space. Like a high priestess of ancient tombs, his nana had preserved treasures in sarcophagi of plastic, double wrapped with tape, revered in sheets, packed in old newspapers. A museum of history lay before him, a wasteland of hopes salvaged by a diligent archeologist of dreams. Nana's hands had kissed wishes good-bye and entombed them, to be rediscovered and unearthed a generation later.

He knelt before his mother's trunk as though opening a shrine. Plumes of dust and the faint hint of feminine scent lingered. He traced an ancient photo with his fingers with the care of an archeologist removing a delicate fossil fragment from the earth. "Mom . . . ," he said aloud. She was beautiful, like all queens of her era. He could see his brother and sisters and even himself in her face, her expressions replaying through genetic sampling and rebirth. His niece Kiera also had her mouth.

But this tomb had been rightfully raided by his sisters. His mother's dresses and jewelry had been removed and now resided in major metropolitan museums—the suburban homes of his siblings. No, that was not what Jenna had sent him on a quest to find. The link to his art, the Holy Grail of who he was, had to be in this sacred space, according to the treasure map left by his sister.

Jason stood and closed the trunk with care and began opening boxes one by one. Five-by-seven and eight-by-ten oil paintings revealed themselves in hidden recesses. A box of what appeared to be balls of newspaper held ceramic work, and another held stunning glass fragment mosaics.

"Oh my God . . . ," he whispered as he went to a heavy board and moved it, only to find a nude of his mother, her back turned, eyes closed, lush tropical plants all around her, and her face tilted toward the sun. "It's not just hers. It's his." Jason stooped quickly and peeled back the brown butcher paper and reverently touched the signature, CN. "Barbados," he murmured, reading the word beneath the signature.

Overwhelmed, Jason went back to the trunk, this time his eye keener, his hands slower. He began removing items until he got to a small cigar box at the bottom. Without opening it, he knew. *Letters.*

The sunlight was waning by the time he finished reading the last one, as each letter had required him to sit back and reflect. *Tragic* was the only word that came to mind. A mother's love, a grandmother's conflicted involvement, a lover's pleas . . . then silence. No more art. No more romance. Thirty years of silent agony, and the spirits yearned to speak.

He stood and gently tucked away the treasures, vowing to give Jenna a private attic tour when they both could cope. But something had awakened in him. It was the missing panel. Adrenaline rushed through him as he hurried down the steps, switched off the light, and locked the door at the bottom of the narrow stairs.

His panels had visual representations of music for every emotion . . . but he'd left out grieving. He'd forgotten the good, old-fashioned, cathartic funeral, where prostrate mourners had to be hauled away by ushers, where gospel choirs rocked the house of worship to a sudden frenzy, Pastor raising the Word over his head, pointing and shouting and whooping so the people could get it all out. He'd forgotten nurses in white uniforms, with fans and tissues, somebody trying to go home to Jesus with Grandma. *Just climb right in the casket with her. Lawd, take them, too!* Beads of sweat rolling down fat necks and damp collars. Tissues blotting oversized cleavages. The amen corner, with hands raised and eyes closed. Ecstasy Mahalia Jackson style. The center aisle a place to file down to pay last respects or get the Holy Ghost, whichever came first.

Fried chicken being fixed down in the common rooms by grandmommas still living. Everybody sobbing as they smell collards and mac and cheese, knowing their family rock would go next. A prayer in every heart. *No, Jesus, don't let 'em take my grandma . . . not our family historian, not our family healer, not our family matriarch, the baker of loaves that could feed the masses. Pass over our nana. Let the plague find some other tent.* Not a dry eye in the house as tambourines slapped big booties and meaty palms and the pianist loosens his tie. Because home-going was a serious musical affair in his community. Praise dancing, praise the Lord, praise in half note, staggered claps, double rock choir sways.

He was sobbing and working. He didn't care, because all he needed now was some gospel—just some church. He kept composing in his head as he rushed to his clock radio and flipped stations until he found what he needed in his grandmom's house.

She hugged her father at the Thirtieth Street Station and laid her head on his shoulder, loving how some things about him hadn't changed. Old Spice aftershave filled her nostrils, and he was still that tall, solid oak tree trunk.

"You act like I'm going overseas," he said, smiling, petting her hair. "This old man is on desk duty."

"I just . . ." Her voice trailed off.

"I know, baby," he said, his voice becoming strained. "You come see your old man real soon, when you can. Just a request, not a command . . . I'm trying to get better and mend my ways."

"You be safe," she said, allowing him to finally pull away as they called his train. "I'm coming down there real soon. I promise."

She watched him smile, nod, and turn in a way that tugged at her heart. She didn't move but remained rooted where she stood on the marble floor. There was no one in the train station but the two of them. So much time had gone by without them understanding each other or knowing each other. She wondered about his friends, his favorite dishes, what might make him laugh . . . What was his life like down in Virginia?

If he'd allow her, she'd share her life with her father, because he probably wondered those things about her, too. If Jason was still in her life, she might have liked to introduce him to her dad . . . but that was impossible now. How could she go to Jason with this amazing discovery when he'd just lost his father and his entire identity along with it? A shiver ran through her, and it made her want to turn and finally leave the station, but she couldn't.

Long after she watched the escalator carry her father away, she remained, watching where he'd been, hoping that he'd be around for a long, long time.

It wasn't until she was at her kitchen table, resurrecting her past life on paper, that she realized how much experience she actually had, how many good courses she'd taken, and how many good references she really did have. Dang! She'd always been the hustler and the financially responsible one! What had her ex been talking about? And she'd listened to the fool? Who was crazier, him or her? she wondered.

Between deep concentration and intermittent disbelief, she also realized how it was time to shed the old people, places, and things that were toxic in her life. Just like the diet change, she needed to go on a friendship diet. Drama free.

She knew that as she listened to a voice mail from crazy-ass LaVern, asking who her new man was, speaking about her father. She knew it was time to wean old relationships when Cheryl called up, angry that Deborah hadn't called her back and let her borrow her purse so she could style out to the clubs with it. And it was definitely time to put distance in her relationship with her drama queen cousin who needed a babysitter so she could roll up on her baby's daddy with her girls. Naw.

Deborah kept her focus on the papers strewn on the table. Kinko's was open all night. She'd have that resume together and a decent cover letter, too. Then she'd have all her information in files and ready to go for when her application to school arrived. What her father had done still hadn't really sunk in. Yet, if she could put it away and work her way through the last semesters, she'd have a good job, plus her education and a little something for a rainy day.

She looked at the telephone and willed herself not to go to it. Jason had his own problems, wasn't interested in hers, didn't want to share his with her, and had made it perfectly clear where he was at. Her gaze sought the window. But wasn't part of a life partnership, a friendship, about going through thick and thin with someone? That was the thing, she mused. Only Nana could have answered that question.

"Man, don't you think you need to slow down?" Wil said, his voice filled with concern. "Like . . . you're delirious. All night you were blasting gospel. Now you've got a duffle bag packed to jump on a flight to Toronto." He opened his arms. "Like, when are you coming back?"

Jason shrugged. "I don't know, man. Just don't let Jenna in here with a wrecking ball. I want to do the renovations in here myself. I figured that much out last night. I've got to work some things out in my head, and I'll sleep on the plane."

He wasn't sure what he expected, wasn't sure what he was looking for, but it certainly wasn't to have Deborah haunt his every thought and dream while he was in the airport, on the plane, and now in a cab, whirring down the pristine Canadian streets to a destination unknown. But how could he offer Deborah a permanent place in his life when he didn't know who he was? He needed answers before he went any further. Shame, hurt, humiliation, shock, anger . . . He'd experienced the color spectrum of emotions, and he didn't need to put her through that while he got his head together. She deserved better than that.

The same resonant questions haunted him, though: Who was his mother, really? Was he just the result of a fling? Did the man actually love her? Who was his father, really, and by extension, who was he? How could he ever envision going forward with his own family one day, having his children ask about his parentage, if he couldn't draw a complete picture and had only a white, blank canvas as an answer? Nesbitt had to know. His father owed him that; the rest didn't matter.

Oddly, he wanted to thread his fingers through Deborah's as a sense of déjà vu claimed him. He needed her reassuring warmth beside him to stave off shivers of uncertainty. He wanted her to see this city, which seemed as though it had been built inside an endless, living green park and along waterways. He wanted her to witness the delicate balance—the dichotomy between all the glass and chrome skyscrapers and the old stone and brick, whose historical dignity had been preserved.

There were so many museums and galleries, and he wanted to show her how this ethnically diverse paradise thrived, with art and music and academia as its pulse. He also wanted to weep into pretty Deborah's hair and tell her all that he'd discovered . . . and to ask her what his life would have been like if his mother had brought him here with her and Christopher Nesbitt.

A profound soul ache threaded through him as he

realized too late how he needed Deborah's gentle kiss, as well as her urgent one, to quiet his disquieting thoughts. But in his state of self-consumption, he hadn't bothered to call her.

The decision to just pick up and go had been erratic. Initially, he'd called it spontaneous. The address on the letters was ancient. If his father still lived there, he probably had a whole new life, one unmarred by an illegitimate son.

When the taxi stopped, Jason hesitated, not sure if he should climb out or pay the fare. He looked up at the walk-up apartments, which were in a vibrant West Indian neighborhood, amid small cafes and vendors, and then took a deep breath and paid the cabbie.

On the curb, Jason studied the return address on the yellowed letter, forever branding the distinctive penmanship into his memory, and then allowed his gaze to match the address to the apartment numbers. Dredging his soul for courage, he flung his backpack over his shoulder and jammed the letter down deep in his army fatigue jacket pocket. Taking the brownstone steps two at a time, he steeled his nerves and rang the bell.

No answer. He leaned on the bell, a sense of quiet desperation sweeping through him. He'd come all this way. Maybe the man was dead. Maybe he'd moved. Maybe his wife and a whole new family would answer the door. Maybe he should turn away. Maybe a very unflattering representation of what he'd imagined his father to be would open the door. Jason turned to bolt down the steps. An old woman, with her hair tied up in a scarf, yanked the front door open.

Jason stopped mid-descent and stared at her dark brown face, which was creased with lines, and the way she clutched her housecoat, shutting it against the blast of cold air.

"Eh?" she said quickly and then discharged a volley of French.

"Christopher Nesbitt," Jason replied, trying to resurrect his foreign language skills as the shock eased.

"Oh, le professor! Qui, qui, he is avec l'Universite de Toronto. Rue St. George."

"Merci," Jason said, his eyes filled with unspoken appreciation.

"You are one of his etudiants from les Etats-Unis?" she asked, attempting to speak to him in English. "I will have the apartments ready soon, but Monsieur Nesbitt did not say—"

"No, no," Jason replied, finding it hard to even speak "I'll find him at the university. Don't hurry yourself at all. Merci, merci." He jogged down the steps and began running, frantically looking for a cab.

If he had known the streets, he would have run all the way to St. George Street on foot. His father was alive, was a professor at the university, and he hadn't blown the man's cover. The place where he had just been was clearly some sort of studio or retreat where visiting art students resided. The taxi couldn't get him to the university fast enough, but as he looked at the endless rows of hundred-year-old, Ivy League–type buildings, he wondered if he'd ever find Christopher Nesbitt within that labyrinth during his lifetime.

Hopping out of the vehicle, Jason stood on the wide stone pavement. Then he meandered along the immaculate, cobblestone walkways of the campus. Finding a posted campus map under glass, he figured out where he had to go—100 St. George, the art department.

Memorizing the directions, he ran. Just flat out ran, as though someone or something was chasing him. Anticipation and cold air clipped his breath. Vine-covered buildings and new chrome construction were becoming a blur. He rushed through the doors of a massive brick structure that had steepled peaks, like those on a London cathedral, and hunted down the administrative offices. Surely, a secretary, an administrator, someone would know Christopher Nesbitt's schedule.

A startled older woman, with auburn hair and half-glasses, looked up. Jason didn't even wait for her to ask him who he was.

"Uh, there's a professor here by the name of Christopher Nesbitt, and—"

"I'm sorry, monsieur, but the semester has started, and his classes are all full," she said, seeming annoyed by Jason's intrusion.

"I just need to talk to him for a minute. Can—"

"All his would-be students attempt that, but you will have to make an appointment. Le professor is extremely busy." She folded her arms over her chest, resolute.

Jason's shoulders slumped. "All right. When can I—"

"Next Tuesday, at—"

"Lady, I flew all the way here from the United States and—"

"Oh. American. This explains it," she said, with disgust. "Well, before you made your flight, did you think to have the courtesy to e-mail l'professor, or call this office for an appointment, or to even see if he was available?"

Jason closed his eyes and ran his palms down his face.

"It's all right, Marie," an amused, deep male voice said.

Jason opened his eyes and found himself staring in a mirror that distorted time. Thick, unruly white hair stood where his wild Afro normally would have been. Eyes that slowly registered shock, eclipsing all amusement, matched his own. Caramel skin weathered with age stretched over a bone structure that could have been his, the hue several shades lighter but from the same palette.

"Professor, I am so sorry," Marie fussed, standing. "I tried to tell this student that there was a list, protocol. But he is American and barged in here, demanding—"

"It's all right," the professor said. "He's my son."

Deborah walked out of her cubicle, with her head held high and just an old coffee mug, her coat, and her purse. Ms. Brown clutched a resignation letter in angry, trembling hands, along with Deborah's request to serve out her two week's notice using every vacation day and personal day she was owed by the department. She walked past coworkers without even turning, her head held high, her shoulders back, the Jackson military dignity in each step. She was a free woman.

The sense of complete freedom that washed over her put pep in her step as she made it to the street. The urge to phone Jason caused her fingers to tingle. This was such an incredible change, so empowering that her lungs felt like they were bursting. But she'd vowed to give the man his space. She refused to even ask his housemate, Wil, anything. No. She was on a mission, a life-changing tear. Drexel University was her next stop. She already had on interview gear— her best charcoal wool pants suit—had her resume in a neat portfolio, and could also pick up her application while there. Why wait for the mail?

Now that she was free of her old job, free of fear, free of toxicity. There was nothing she couldn't do!

Catching the subway-surface trolley from downtown, she got off at the Thirty-third Street exit and braced for the cold sunshine that awaited her above ground. A shiver of anticipation ran through her as she walked briskly toward the administrative buildings on Drexel's campus. She was almost running and had to slow down so she didn't get all sweaty. She wanted to be perfect. Even if Susan couldn't see her today, she would glimpse a confident, pulled-together woman who was right for the job.

But when she approached the outer office and spied Susan's grim expression just beyond the secretary's shoulder, anticipation turned to tension. Something was wrong.

Susan stood, walked around her desk, opened her office door a little wider, and came out to the front desk, rather than inviting Deborah to come in.

"I just came to drop this off, like you'd asked," Deborah said, hesitating and then digging in her portfolio.

"Oh, Deborah," Susan said, with a sigh, briefly closing her eyes. "University politics and budgets . . . There's been a hiring freeze. As soon as it lifts, you're here, lady. I just can't move right now. Can't hire a soul."

It took a moment for the information to sink in and for Deborah's vocal cords to follow the command from her brain to speak. "I totally understand," she said as calmly as possible. "In the meanwhile, I'm going to be sending in my application for school."

"Good," Susan said in a rush, her shoulders slumping in relief. She hugged Deborah hard. "I'm so glad you didn't do anything crazy and spontaneous." She released Deborah, with a smile. "Thank you for understanding. We should do lunch one day really soon."

Deborah pasted on her best professional smile, hugged Susan quickly, and stammered an excuse about why today was not possible for that to happen. She willed her footsteps to remain slow and steady as she left Susan's office, panic sweat making her blouse stick to her. The moment she got outside the building, she started running. She had to find a newsstand, get a paper with want ads, go find a cybercafe to post her resume. Calling her dad to get him to rush a funds transfer was out. He'd just pledged his faith in her to be responsible; now she'd gone and done something ridiculous and unplanned like this.

She wanted to call Jason and tell him about the bizarre turn of events, tell him how she'd put the cart before the horse and how it had run her behind over. Then she realized, maybe she'd done that with him, too. He was definitely the cart before the horse. Deborah just shook her head.

"Well, at least you've got an updated resume," she muttered to herself, with a sigh, and then dug in her purse for a mass-transit token.

His father drank espresso, while he allowed his tea to cool, untouched, mesmerized by the long and colorful story Christopher Nesbitt was telling him, with tears in his eyes.

"Don't hate your other father," Nesbitt said philosophically. "He was a victim of the era. Thought he could do certain things as a man, and there'd be no real repercussions. His affair terminated in an abortion, but not before the woman made herself known and shattered your mother's world . . . which is the only reason she allowed herself to come to me, despite the fact that I'd admired her for years. Had loved her at a respectful distance." He sipped his espresso and looked out at the icy street beyond the frosted window. "In a way, it was the best and the worst of times. Your mother wasn't a word that I detest being used against any woman."

"But having an illegitimate kid must have been—"

"Do *not*," his father said quietly and firmly, setting down his cup, "*ever*, ever use that term when speaking of yourself or another human being."

The two stared at each other.

"Jason," his father said, without an apology in his

tone. "You're not *illegitimate*. That's a carryover from the old British caste system. What makes a human being legitimate? Your mother chose to keep you, which, in my mind, is a legitimate decision. You were born, you were made, and you are a human of value and worth. That alone legitimizes you in the eyes of the Creator." He shook his head. "No, no. And what your mother and I shared was completely legitimate—love."

"I don't want to sign Hastings on my work anymore," Jason said quietly, wishing he'd known this great man all of his life.

"Don't do that, son," Nesbitt said. "It would break your mother's heart and would dishonor her memory, as well as all she sacrificed to keep all her children together."

"I don't understand." Jason folded his arms.

"Then overstand, mon." Nesbitt smiled. "Gotcha. You didn't think an old beatnik philosopher could go there, did you? Hmmm . . . son, I've lived all over the world, have heard all the rhetoric and discussion and passion and zeal, and I agree with as much of it as I disagree with. But the question is not about right and wrong, but truth. What is your truth?"

Eager to please this new mentor for some unknown reason, Jason leaned forward and encircled his tea with both palms. "Like, I'm not really a Hastings. I'm a Nesbitt, right?"

Christopher Nesbitt put a finger to his thick lips as he sat back in his chair. "Yes and no. Follow me. . . ." He leaned forward, his intense gaze boring into Jason as he drew on the table with his fingers. "Your mother named you Jason, in keeping with the way all her children's names begin with J."

"Okay, that I can live with," Jason said, carefully sipping his tea.

"Then she gave you my full name and Hastings, the surname she'd elected to keep, the name people would see, to preserve her dignity, your dignity, your stepfather's dignity, and that of your brother and sisters'. On the outside, you are Jason Hastings. What you are on the inside, by both blood and name, is Christopher Nesbitt. I can live with that, and so could she. It was her truth. It gave her peace. And she had built Hastings's name in the community long before all of this business occurred. If it hadn't been for her, he wouldn't have had a good reputation, a solid practice, or community goodwill. This I know to be fact."

His father sat back and folded his arms. "If you change your name to anything, add Warren, your mother's maiden name, to the list. Your Nana Warren kept my sanity, sent me pictures, and accepted my calls and letters . . . sent me the funeral program." His voice became thick with emotion, and he stopped to take a sip of his espresso to steady himself. "Lotta years, son, lotta memories. I know Nana Warren and your mother sent you back to me."

"I don't wanna lose touch with you, man," Jason said, his voice reduced to a murmur by emotion. He wanted to ask if he had other brothers and sisters but thought better of it.

"No need to, son," Nesbitt said, forcing his tone to become upbeat. "Come up here. The galleries are fantastic. I travel . . . You've got an exhibit. I'll come visit you in Philly. I have students at the apartments all the time, if you need working space. I want to learn you, catch up. Fill in the blanks and white spaces. You've got family in the Caribbean, over in Montreal. You've got . . ." Christopher Nesbitt's voice trailed off as new tears shimmered in his eyes and his voice betrayed him. "You've got her stamped all over you, and I can't even begin to tell you how much I loved that woman. Come by the house, and I'll show you."

* * *

Numb, she found herself standing in Thirtieth Street Station, with an Amtrak ticket in her hand and a very small overnight bag. She wasn't going to ask for help but wanted to see what had been locked away in storage for years. For some reason, she needed to just walk through the past so that she could face the future. She was unemployed and had nowhere to go during the day, so visiting her father just seemed to make sense.

They pulled up to an old Victorian home, and his heart raced as he wondered what untold stories had happened here. *Why would a lone bachelor up in years stay there?* he thought, that is, until Christopher Nesbitt turned the key and pushed open the leaded- and beveled-glass door.

Art from all over the world besieged Jason's senses. Velvet settees and Queen Anne chairs had to make room for Ashanti stools and Ghanaian thrones. The walls were stark white, and exquisite pieces were front lit by canister lights and recessed lights. Exposed beams gave the cathedral ceilings additional height. Each room looked like it was designed more for gatherings and discussions than for personal, intimate living.

Nesbitt dropped his keys in a flat, round African woven basket on a Chippendale desk in the grand foyer and bade Jason to walk through.

"I just entertain here . . . teach . . . have people in from overseas to attend artist conclaves and discussions. Musicians, painters, writers, sculptors," said Nesbitt. "I don't discriminate, as long as they're cool people and are true to their craft."

He walked Jason through the massive dining room and into the kitchen, and hung their coats on huge antique brass hooks by the backstairs.

Nesbitt went on. "It's just me. Never settled down after your mom. The world became my family. I married my craft. Each piece of art became one of my kids. Just a bedroom, bathroom, and studio space are upstairs, and the third floor is a series of guest rooms for when people travel here from overseas. You're welcome to stay as long as you like." He looked at Jason, with expectant longing. "The guest rooms . . . my room . . . and the basement office all have work from her. The basement studio is for visiting artists and is bare."

"I'd like to see her," Jason said quietly. "I'll stay the night, and maybe real soon, you'll come to Philly so I can show you what I found in Nana's attic."

The two shared a knowing smile as Nesbitt nodded. "I'd like that, Jason. Thank you."

"I didn't expect to find you home during the day," Deborah said and laughed. "I was gonna leave a note on your door and then hang out until later. I thought I'd have to track you down at the Pentagon, if that is possible."

"Come in here, you crazy girl. What are you doing on my steps?"

Her father laughed and hugged her, but she noted that his complexion was off and he seemed a little gray in pallor. His voice was rough, and he had stubble on his chin, like he hadn't shaved yet. She followed him through the town house and into the kitchen, taking off her coat and studying every detail of his form in his gray sweatpants, shirt, and black slippers. Her father in slippers at four in the afternoon? Uh-uh.

"Daddy, you feeling all right?" she asked as he put water in the tea kettle.

"Put your coat in the closet, and have a bite to eat." He'd spoken to her with his back turned.

Deborah didn't move as she studied the bottles of medicine on the counter. "Why don't you let me make you something and you sit down?" she said in a tense, quiet voice.

"I just need some tea to settle my stomach. Not really hungry. But I can take you to dinner, or I can order you something in."

She went to him and made him turn around and then touched his face. "You're sick, aren't you?"

He pasted on a too-exuberant smile. "Now, baby, don't you go worrying about hypothetical scenarios. Just a little stomach problem. They've got me taking stuff that makes me nauseous."

She hugged him, not believing a word. "You had chemo today, didn't you?"

He laid his cheek against the crown of her head. "Yeah," he whispered. "But that don't mean nothing."

"Oh, Lord . . ."

"Now see," he said, holding her tighter. "That's why I didn't want to say anything to you."

"You need somebody down here to take care of you, Daddy." She looked up at him. "I'll come. I'll—"

"No. You don't reorder your life like that, sweetheart. Ms. Catherine does a fine job on Tuesdays and Thursdays, when I have to go. So far, the old man is holding his own." He lifted his chin with pride. "Prostate, stomach, liver . . . My past has caught up with me, but it ain't over till it's over." He touched her cheek, wiping away the tears. "I'm glad you came, glad you know, but I don't want you feeling sorry for me or reordering your life. Got your name on everything, in case. But until then, you keep all your plans. You promise me that?"

"I—"

"No, Deborah," he said firmly, kissing her forehead and then holding her away from him by her upper arms. "You meet you a nice fella. You fall in love. You get married. You have yourself a good career. Have babies. Don't you come down here and wait for your old man to kick the bucket. I'm not going down without a fight . . . They said maybe two years, and I'ma prove 'em wrong and double that. Watch me."

The urge to wail was so great that she had to make fists with her hands by her sides. But the need to comfort her father in the only way his personal dignity would allow won out. She nodded, tears glittering.

"All right, then, Mr. Darryl Lee Jackson," she said, with a shaky voice that soon became firm. "You're gonna let me go through these cabinets like Grant went through Richmond. You're going to tolerate my presence as I go shop for healthy foods that will nourish your cells and give them oxygen. You are going to allow me to prepare you a week's worth of highly flavorful, nourishing food . . . and then you're not going to be stubborn and refuse to eat it. You are going to introduce me to one Ms. Catherine so I can show her what I've learned and she can follow recipes that will double those years the doctor projected. That's an order, sir."

A slow smile tugged at her father's mouth. Warm arms encircled her. A kiss crushed her hair. "Order accepted with full appreciation, ma'am," he whispered against the crown of her head. "If you stay until I can hold food down tomorrow, I'll also take you to the storage bin so you can see everything. Thank you, God, for giving me a baby girl like you."

Chapter 14

Three days in Toronto had changed his life, had altered his perspective forever. He could see more than a career trajectory. He could see a life tapestry, a model for living, and could, for the first time in his life, envision travel and teaching as something tangible, something real, and not as a trap. A philosophical old artist had demonstrated how a certain amount of conformity was in keeping with the Eastern disciplines he'd learned, yet within the so-called confines of that conformity was a certain enviable freedom. It was the ultimate in *ukemi* . . . falling, flowing with the circular energy of the universe. To be a rolling stone was one thing; to use all that you'd gathered in your travels to put down a stone foundation was something else.

World politics, world religions, technique, and artistic messages had kept them up until the wee hours of the night—bonding. Sharing. Revealing. Communing. He'd learned from *his father*. The magnitude of the miracle was so great that it required testimony.

There was only one person he wanted to share this with. Pretty Deborah.

* * *

"No, man," Wil said, his voice sad. "She didn't come to the center this week, after art class. I guess once she found out I'd be teaching, she just left."

Jason pushed off the kitchen counter, worry making him pace. "I called her at her job, and they said she didn't work there anymore. She's not answering her cell, not answering at the apartment. I'm not trying to panic, man, but if she left her job . . . you know?"

"Deborah *quit* her job?" Wil's expression was a combination of disbelief and fear.

"That week we hung out, she gave me every way to contact her. It was like we were one, you know?" Jason said, not caring if he sounded freaked out. He was.

"She'll turn up, man," Wil said. "Look, maybe she went somewhere to lick her wounds, too. Until she surfaces, let's keep moving forward. We get this joint in shape. We get the collective in shape. We get the artists in the collective to put real sweat equity into the house on South Street so it can come alive to the vision."

Jason nodded, but his thoughts were still searching the streets of Philly for her.

"You weren't supposed to get snowed in down here with your old man," Deborah's father said, warming his hands over a bowl of her homemade vegetable soup. "Been over a week, almost ten days, chile."

"I'm not leaving until Ms. Catherine can make it back and forth reliably, so you're stuck with me."

He gave her a peevish grin. "I guess I'm blessed to have a live-in drill sergeant who won't cook meat and only does organic. Carrot juice and herbal tea. My coffee gone. I'm already in the hospital. *Man!*"

"Don't act like you don't like my cooking," she said, laughing. "That's your third bowl of soup."

"Okay, okay, I like what you fix, but I just wish you

wouldn't ruin it by explaining what it was. Just let me be ignorant, and I'll be fine."

"Oh, this from a man who ate military grub for years, those dehydrated, fake food packs, or whatever they call 'em." She folded her arms, with a wide smile.

"Those meals were state of the art," he fussed, dipping a section of Ezekiel bread in her thick soup.

"Uh-huh. But aren't you glad I made you let me go to the market before we headed out to the storage unit?"

She walked into the living room, where he sat in a recliner, watching CNN and eating her soup, and hugged him from behind, angling her body around the huge leather chair so he could peck her cheek. She sat on the wide arm and laid her head against his, just letting her warmth and life force flow from her arms into his, quietly praying for God to spare her daddy.

With Wil as the primary crew, the paint job had been completed in a day, and the floors had been restored to a high gloss three days after that. The most striking attic pieces had been unveiled and hung with reverence throughout the living room, dining room, foyer, and the new basement space.

Exposed basement brick and beams and ancient furniture, which had been sent out to be reupholstered, created extra flow space below the living room. He and Wil had had too many beers one night and had opened a hole in the floor. A spiral staircase to the basement from the living room as a secondary way down had just felt right, so they had gone with it. A blond modular desk, files, and a new computer had been put in the basement space. It was time to have a real office and to handle his business. Phone lines, computer lines, another stereo, and a flat-screen TV had gone down there, too, along with a bar and Persian rugs.

The dining room was a celebration of his mother's legitimate choice to create him. He had created a space for her; she was no longer hidden in the dark, under dank sheets. His father would be proud to see Janet Warren's nude oil capturing everyone's eye from every point in the room. A spotlight of recessed lighting was on her, and the masterpiece had been positioned so that she coyly peered around glass blocks, the same way she peered around tropical ferns in her lover's painting.

His grandmother's cherry-mahogany dining-room table had become the centerpiece of the room. Like an altar, it was littered with stacks of candles captured in wrought iron. High, formal dining-room chairs redone in burnt orange, with gold swaths of African fabric as tiebacks, all contrasting and coordinating with the hibiscus in his mother's hair, flanked the glistening table.

Floating shelves in the living room held objets d'art, just as the china cabinet was now a striking foyer piece filled with ceramics and glass designs. Stained glass glistened in moonstruck windows. Copper pots danced with ancient cast iron on overhead hooks in the kitchen. Every now and again, Jason would stop to run his hand over the surface of the refrigerator as though it was his touchstone. He missed Deborah so much, it hurt.

But forging ahead and not allowing despair, Wil lost his mind and pulled up in a truck filled with plants, claiming one of the collective members had told him that life energy was required everywhere. Brothers who knew their craft were tightening up the bathroom, but it had taken a crystalologist to come in and adorn the walls with a positive energy mosaic and medicine wheel.

Benches hit the porch, along with crystal wind chimes and wrought-iron torches. Four determined artists lifted a bed platform and moved it according to the whims of a true feng shui healer from the dojo until there was complete harmony with the chi of the universe. Wil's third-floor apartment space got a dramatic makeover just by being cleaned down to the baseboards. That seemed to be all the energy shift required to chase away the mice.

Crews of artists worked like chain gangs, inspired by the vision of having dignitaries flow from the Rhythm and Blues Fest grand-opening gala, to be held on the Avenue of the Arts during Black History Month, to their space for the after party. Jason would bring a piece of Toronto to Philly, and a mirror and glass sign read TORONTO ON SOUTH. Neon white lights backlit the French windows, showing off Toronto's sexy stained-, leaded-, and beveled-glass panes.

The house on South Street, which had just been a quasi-hangout before, would now have a brand-new, gleaming juice bar of amber wood; a gourmet menu of holistic foods; hand-painted stools; a Bose sound system; café tables; and a cyber space of networked laptops perched on high, circular tables and connected to a dedicated server so that ideas could be pitched on the fly. It would be there for writers who stopped in to create over a latte once the party was over.

Art would grace the walls, appropriately tagged. Bookshelves would compliment the upstairs reading/ conversation space. The second floor would have sofas, walls strewn with art, sculptures, and an open mic for the jazz band and poets. The third floor would be more conversational gallery space.

He'd come back on fire, inspiration driving him as much as his worry for Deborah. With each day that passed, he became more focused, more obsessed with every detail. He prayed that she was all right, prayed that she would surface before long, before February, when Christopher Nesbitt came to town. His home, their space, had to be right for that moment. People would go to the grand opening, then to Toronto on South, so that his colleagues could also have a chance to do some high-level networking and could showcase their talent. Then the inner circle would go to his home, as would his father. She was his right arm, a part of his rib. The entire exhibit was a tribute to her and to generations of women like her, who had been the backbone of male inspiration.

"Deborah, where are you?" he whispered in the darkened kitchen and then closed his phone.

He hadn't been able to work in the studio during all the renovations and hadn't told Jenna he couldn't find Deborah. He'd deflected his sister's inquiries by divulging what he'd learned about his real father, and then he'd let her overwhelm him with her platinum Rolodex, her connections that, she'd insisted, had to come to the gala and back to his gallery for the private party, where the champagne and wine would flow. He'd left the catering to her.

Tension knotted his spine as he climbed the stairs. This Sunday was his turn at a family dinner, and while he usually just took everyone out to eat, Jenna insisted that peace and healing in private were needed before his event. Not even the kids were invited. His well-intentioned sister hadn't seen the new space yet and had made her decision based on the progress of the gallery, but the concept put him in a cold sweat. All he'd need was to break Jared's neck while supposedly breaking bread.

However, all of that was moot. The project was far from finished, and February was only weeks away. If he didn't get it together, there wouldn't be a party, period. Launch his career into the stratosphere? Yeah, right. He had to finish what he'd started and deliver.

Like his grandmother probably would have said, he'd put the cart before the horse. Right now he had professionals working on his taxes and his business structure. He had fixed up his house for a huge party and had invested a mint in restoring everything at the gallery. But he would probably be sued for noncompletion of a major contract if he missed the event deadline. As it was, he was dodging probing calls from his big client at the Rhythm and Blues Fest. Jason ran his palms down his face. He was screwed.

He looked in the room that he hadn't entered in more than ten days. Deborah was everywhere. She was the sensual promise of falling in love and of lovemaking in a panel of deep sienna hues, which was next to its balanced mate in cool blues—*The Morning After.* He remembered the black lace and silk and how the sunlight had kissed her skin. Then he saw her dancing in nightclub blues, singing her heart out, and then draped over a settee, exhausted, wineglass dangling, her burnt orange shirt open and exposing her voluptuous breasts.

Deborah in oil stood at his table, with dreams deferred in blues, her hands folded beneath her chin . . . but she needed a mated panel of vibrant hope. He just didn't know what that would be. There was blank canvas there, but the funeral in deep blues needed a fiery opposite. The collection lacked balance. The yin and yang were off. It needed to end in the number nine, too, the number of completion, as Joyce from the collective had told him, and she was always adamant about such things. What would be the centerpiece then?

His deadline was in a little over three weeks, and he'd hit a wall. He couldn't even begin to sketch, he was so burnt out. Tomorrow was Sunday, and he also had to pull his head together for the dreaded dinner and order in from a restaurant in Chinatown that had vegan options and also delivered. There was just too much going on. He was bone weary.

"Nana, what would you do?" he whispered, looking

at the funeral mural. The answer stared right back at him. *Go to church.*

"I'm fine, Daddy," Deborah said from a credit card pay phone in the train station. She fingered the gold cross that had been her mothers as she spoke to her father. "Yes, I promise to charge my cell phone as soon as I get home. You call me after your next session, all right? Call if you need anything, okay? I love you."

She closed her eyes as he told her how much he loved her and said good-bye. She didn't care what happened. She was going to church today—in what she'd worn to work the day she quit. She was getting off that train in Philly and heading to the eleven o'clock service. Today she was gonna give it over to the Lord, was gonna holla and put it on the altar. The minister had better preach till the ushers had to lift her up and carry her out. She had gotten too close to her daddy and too many years had passed to lose him now.

Deborah swallowed hard and gripped her ticket as her train was called. So much understanding had passed in the quiet hours between her and her father . . . as they sat in the kitchen, or when she rested on the sofa while he reclined in the La-Z-Boy. They'd watched television together in silence, argued over sports teams, and told stories with just smooth jazz on in the background. They'd broken bread in the kitchen while she cooked and he watched and commented, poking fun and teasing her to keep from misting over, as she reminded him of his long-gone wife just by the way she commanded the space.

Time had become truncated and had disappeared. Old hurts had got purged, and hearts had filled with deep appreciation. Broken fences had been mended.

The angels had danced and played with the lights
during the ice storm.

She'd learned so much about a woman she'd been
inside for nine months but had never been allowed to
know until now. He'd shared her mother's letters to
him while he was away at war. He'd given her jewelry,
keepsakes that had been locked away inside his heart
and hidden in dust-covered boxes. The yellowed,
sepia-hued pictures in dusty albums had brought her
to sobs that he couldn't comfort; the cleansing flood
had to come out when she saw that she wasn't fat as a
child. The weight gain was recent, but in the last ten
days she'd lost almost fifteen pounds and had toned,
not even sure how. Shopping bags and luggage in tow,
she boarded a train to Philadelphia, looking like a
bag lady, holding photo albums, her greatest treasure.

But just remembering how her father's voice had
become tender when he spoke of his wife put tears in
Deborah's eyes as she stared out at the gray, icy land-
scape. The unfeeling man she'd thought he was, was
a hopeless romantic like her, just hidden behind
layers of protection. She just hoped that this morning
the good Lord would give him some additional protection, if she prayed hard enough.

Jason vaguely remembered a church Deborah had
mentioned over on Forty-sixth . . . on Hazel Avenue,
Cedar . . . He couldn't remember but would find it. He
certainly wasn't going to drive all the way up to where
his siblings went, halfway across the city, where things
were high brow and staid. His grandmother's store-
front refuge in old Mantua was gone and now boarded
up. An Asian convenience store was next to it.

No. This morning he needed to hear gospel music,
needed to hear the Word, needed to feel like there
was hope, and had to say, "Thank you, Jesus." He'd

been blessed beyond measure. His life had been rede-
fined, and a missing piece had been unexpectedly
given to him, like pearls cast before swine, but he
wouldn't fly in the face of grace. Today he would be on
his knees, would go to the rail if they called him, and
would lay it all down. And he would also ask that God
keep His eye out for a sweet, beautiful, kind woman
named Deborah Lee Jackson . . . put her under an
angel's wing, make her forgive him for being a complete jackass and pushing her away.

Oh yeah, he was going to church—Windsor knot in
his silk tie, charcoal VIP meeting suit, and good shoes.
This was serious.

She sat right up front. She had gotten there early,
her shopping bags and overnight bag with her, but
she didn't care. Wasn't missing a thing. When the
choir started up, the minister saw her face and
nodded. She could tell from his concerned gaze that
he clearly knew there needed to be some words
spoken beyond the usual.

The minister peered at her bags. He probably
thought she was homeless by the bundles of posses-
sions by her feet and the frantic expression that she
knew had to be on her face. It coulda had something
to do with the way her hands were shaking as she
clasped a tissue and then shredded it. She'd been on
her knees since she'd got there, jumping up only to
sway with the choir and belt out every spiritual and
hymn.

Then the man got to preaching. Deborah wrapped
her arms around herself and began rocking slightly
and nodding.

"I was gonna start off by talking about the company
we keep, and how that can take us down a slippery
slope that's off the path. But then I saw a young sister

in here who inspired me to go on and talk about something different. Is that all right, church?" Her minister leaned forward and opened his arms, his robe billowing out.

"Go 'head, Rev. Take your time!" a woman shouted from the back.

Deacons nodded their sleepy, calm nod, murmuring, "Thas all right. That's all right, Rev."

"'Cause I'ma tell you, folks, we's living in some hard times. Amen?"

Amens filtered throughout the sanctuary to spur him on, beginning a dialogue that would ultimately hit an emotional crescendo. People waited as the minister chuckled and took several deep breaths, shaking his head. "Had to make sure it was all right," he said.

"Yes . . . flock," he said, his voice dropping to a patient baritone as he spoke into the microphone. "Home ain't what it used to be. Some of us ain't got no home!" he shouted, suddenly exploding and beginning to walk as he whipped the congregation up. "Storms of change, floodwaters of tragedy, tides of destruction done took mothers and fathers and daughters and sons and babies and grandmothers away from here before their time!"

The minister swept a billowing arm across the pulpit, with flourish, as people shouted, and then he jumped up and down to make his point. "They gone! Wiped out. Everybody you might have loved or cared about. What you knew as a child might no longer exist! Some children never even got to know home. If you had a home as a child, in these times, you were blessed. Thank you, Jesus! Your house might have fallen down, got repossessed, got boarded up, or been washed away in a storm! Momma might be on drugs; daddy might be a molester. Faces are missing at the dinner table! You done buried so many family members, you can't go to another funeral. I know! The family rock is gone. Nana done went on to glory with Momma, and you left here to deal in this wicked world as a motherless child!" He shook his head and flung open his Bible. "Children, we gonna go home to Jesus today, because in my Father's House, there are many mansions! We gonna talk about it." He pointed to the lectern. "Ain't that what it says?"

Sobs began to wrack Deborah's body as she waved her tissue in agreement.

"Doors may have closed in this world, but you got a home!" the minister yelled. "There's a home that neva goes nowhere. There's a Father that don't never leave you! Won't leave you, can't leave you, because he promised He wouldn't do that to you! He pays his child support, gave His Son. That's how much He loves you! Church, you know what I'm talking about. He's the rock, was grandma's rock. That's how come she could be yours!"

Deborah was on her feet, swaying as the organ worked with the minister's voice. Her hand was in the air. Distraught parishioners who had lost husbands, sons, mothers, and children shouted for the minister to tell it. Nurses were marching up and down the aisle like pastoral soldiers and prayer warriors. A light buzzing had begun in Deborah's ears. She couldn't open her eyes. Her daddy was gonna die. He had the dreaded sickness, cancer. But she was blessed; they were blessed. They'd had time to rediscover each other and share how much they loved each other. "Thank ya, thank you, Jesus!"

"So you'd better get right with those people who ain't gone yet," the reverend called out, pounding the pulpit. "Ya best git right with your real Father, too," he exclaimed, now pointing up. "Ya better bury the hatchet, let bygones be bygones, and be glad ya'll still here to argue," he added, with a loud snap in the microphone. "Because, just like that, a car accident in the middle of the night, a phone call from an emergency room, a stray bullet or heart attack could make time evaporate. Then y'all gonna be in here with me, trying to climb in the casket, when you had time to get it all straight before it was too late."

He mopped his brow as the fervor of the congregation reached new heights. "It works like that with God, too. God is fair. He's patient. He'll wait. 'Cause He knows you gotta come pass His way in the end. So, when you get there, I hope you know Him, just like you best try to untangle some of these family dramas. You best open your heart and get humble. Best say, 'Thank you for waking me up in the morning, for that job I'm complaining about, for the breath I breathe, for my tribulations that teach me, for the people who do love me but who I haven't made time for!' You better look inside your heart today and ask how many blessings you have walked past, like it was your birthright, not realizing that it was *the grace* that gave it to you! It was a gift! Because your Father loves you for no other reason than the fact that you're His.

"I came here today," the minister screamed, jumping up and down, "to tell you about *my Father!* Have mercy! You got a problem? Give it to Him! You lost your home? Give it to Him! Somebody you love is sick? The doctor gave you bad news? If they got an addiction . . . if they're running on you, taking you through changes, or if they might be missing in action, might be lost to the streets, then tell your Father! He wants to have a conversation with you about what's going on in your life! Wants to sit down in your living room, at your kitchen table, in your dining room, in your bedroom and say, 'It's gonna be all right.' He can make it all right! Can't he do that? Who knows what I'm talking about in here this morning? Can I get a witness!"

Her voice had somehow fled her body in sobbing chants. "Yes, Jesus!" The minister didn't lie. Somebody was sick with cancer. Somebody needed help beyond the doctor's skills. She had gotten right with her daddy before it was too late. Yes, somebody was missing: a man who'd stolen her heart. Somebody she loved had fallen out with his family and had lost his mind. A man with talent had run away, not knowing who'd made him. "Help him, Father God!" she cried.

Yes, Jesus, she was blessed beyond her wildest dreams. "Thank you, Jesus!" she yelled. The Father had provided for her when she had not expected it, in a way she couldn't have fathomed. In the midnight hour, Father God had made a way out of no way. She didn't have to go back to a job she hated. God was sending her back to school, no matter what! Both her earth father and heavenly Father were there now. "Thank you, thank you, *thank you!*" she cried.

She'd called Jesus to the table to eat dinner with both of the men in her life, to enter her kitchen and drop healing in her pots. She had prayed for Him to join them in every heartfelt conversation; had asked the Lord God to anoint a studio, a town house in Virginia, and to walk into a recreation center; had invited Him to be on the telephone. He'd been there when she had buried the hatchet with her father and had resurrected the best memories of her mother and grandmother. She'd prayed over medicines on the counter and prayed up her father's townhouse. She knew that whatever God's will was, her daddy would be with her momma again in heaven, so you couldn't begrudge the man's peace after years of heartbreak. She had asked God for Jason's peace, too. . . .

Deborah's arms were in the air. Someone was lifting her up as she tried to climb up to the sky, shouting "Jesus!" and screaming that she wanted to go home.

Music was in her marrow, and tambourines jerked her spine. She was moving, guided by angels in white uniforms, who stroked her hair. Minister was calling people to the rail. The choir was rocking. Her face was hot. She was going in and out of consciousness. Someone put a cold compress on her face. She was crying and laughing and waving her arm and didn't care. So much had happened, and Father God knew it all.

Jason held her and rocked her as nurses kept bringing tissues and compresses. He couldn't stop crying as he tried to calm Deborah down in the small anteroom behind the main sanctuary. He'd seen her as he slipped in the back of the church, but she'd never seen him. She'd been riveted to the sermon, which had soon caught fire within him, too.

Her hair was all over her head, her chin was tipped up to the ceiling, her fists were clutched, and her eyes were squeezed closed. All he could do was rock her and keep pushing her hair away from her fevered face. He was so blessed, so blessed . . . He'd had a chance to get right with his biological father, his half brother and sisters. He now had a chance to get right with Deborah and get right with himself. He'd been blessed beyond measure with a gift that came from a place beyond him. God had answered his prayers, and he hadn't said thank you for any of it.

The rail called him as the minister's voice became strident; he had to get right with his first Father . . . had to forgive Hastings, too. Had to let the anger toward Jared and Jackie go. Had to turn it over, do what Nana woulda said, what he'd seen her do Sunday after Sunday without fail.

Now that he knew what that dear woman had had on her heart, how could he deny the urgent altar call? Her daughter, his mother, had died of a broken heart. Nana's grandchildren were in turmoil. She had done a day's work for folks who didn't rate her as a human being or think she had problems, much less care that she did. Nana had been half crippled by arthritis but had raised a toddler for her daughter, a love child. She had kept her daughter's lover at bay and had prevented him from destroying a family, but had respected him still without judgement and had saved his art and letters to one day give his son. The woman had been bent but not broken till the end because she had called the Father to her house on a regular basis and had gone to His house every Sunday without fail.

"Yes, Jesus." The words slipped from Jason's lips in a tense murmur. His eyes were closed, and tears were streaming down his face.

An usher slid in beside Deborah as soon as Jason stood. Torn, he didn't want to leave her after just finding her, but he had to. Two elderly nurses stroked his back, urging him forward, murmuring, "Go 'head, baby. Go to the rail," in that same timbre his nana would have used, had used, breaking him down, opening him up, wearing him out.

Jason half stumbled forward, oblivious to the applause in the aisles. Light through stained glass filled the sanctuary with prisms of color. The music made them dance behind his lids. He couldn't see anything but the rail and black-robed arms opening up to receive him. The minister had him, holding him tight as he lost it.

"That's right, son. It's all right now. Just come on home."

Chapter 15

They sat in the cold in Jason's car, which was parked in front of his house, just looking at each other for a long time.

"You first," he said in a voice so quiet she wouldn't have been sure if he'd said anything if she hadn't seen his mouth move.

"No," she murmured. "Before I get into all of what I have to say, I need to know where you are."

Jason nodded. "That's fair." He leaned his head back against the seat and briefly closed his eyes. "I'm humbled. I'm blessed. I'm emotionally wrung out. I'm in a real different place than I was, and I am very, very sorry that I took you where I did." He opened his eyes and just shook his head as he took up her hand. "Deborah . . . I went some places that may take me hours, days to explain, but if you'll hear me out, I'll leave no stone unturned."

His hand trembled as he cupped her cheek, and his eyes searched her face. "I learned a lot. I learned that I need you." He touched her hair, his gaze holding hers until she looked away. "Will you come inside and let me tell you what happened?" He held his hands up as though being frisked by the cops. "And I swear I won't touch you. I just have to explain to you why things went down like they did."

She finally nodded. "All right . . . and then . . . I have some things I need to say, too."

Deborah steeled her nerves for what she might hear from Jason as they got out of the car in the late afternoon sun. Although she'd been through an indescribable experience in church that morning, now, at two o'clock in the afternoon, she was standing on Jason's porch in the cold, and the shadows of the past were flitting through her mind, a past filled with men who walked, couldn't deal, said they'd changed their minds. She supposed that Jason would explain his turmoil, talk about his religious experience, and then, because of his newfound salvation, let her down easy. She braced her heart for the probable loss.

He opened the door and unexpectedly clasped her hand to usher her through it. She stopped and gaped, unable to synchronize what her eyes were seeing with her thoughts and fragmented heart.

"I had to go all the way back to the beginning," Jason said, pointing to a beautiful china closet tastefully filled with delicate ceramics and glass art. "My mother was an artist, a creator," he murmured, gently leading Deborah forward. "So is my father."

He took her into the living room and told her about his trip to Toronto and the apprehension that had claimed him, then turned to her and closed his eyes. "I didn't know until I got on the plane how much I wanted only you to be there with me."

Jason dropped her hand and moved to the wall of glass block that separated the living room from the dining room. "All this art on the walls is from them. It was hidden in the attic. Then I found this," he said in a quiet, pained voice. "He loved my mother."

Deborah gasped when he stepped aside so she could see the stunning nude that graced the dining room. She covered her mouth.

Jason looked at her and nodded. "I know. I had the same reaction. I found it in the attic, hidden away, like it didn't have the right to exist." He swallowed hard and held on to the back of a chair, speaking to her while looking at the painting, then slowly explained his grandmother's involvement in preserving the past for him here, how this house had been a warehouse storage unit for him, a place of discovery. "She was so wise. She knew if it was willed to me, then I'd know what I needed to know, and even if I sold it, I'd have to go through everything before I did."

He didn't look back. He just began walking toward the kitchen and then took Deborah down to show her his office and the overflow guest area, his voice low, introspective, talking to her but also, it seemed, to the unseen spirits that had molded his life.

"I stayed with my father for three days," Jason said, walking a zigzag path through the office and then going upstairs. "When I got back, I couldn't find you . . . so I threw myself into the positive, hoping."

She followed him, understanding completely. She had just experienced the miracle of rediscovery and had somehow known that she was supposed to quit her job when she did—not for another job, but to have time to spend with her father. God's hand was orchestrating things.

"I wasn't dodging your calls," she said quietly as they entered his bedroom. "I had to go see about my dad . . . He's sick, Jas, and I didn't pack my charger. I turned my cell off on the train to save the battery, in case he wasn't home once I got down to Virginia . . . and I got stranded. I never turned it back on. I never called home to check my phone messages." She hugged herself.

"Oh, baby . . ." He came to her and hugged her, rubbing her back. Now he understood better why the Spirit had taken her over in church. "I would have gone with you. I will take you down there to see him. Anything you need to do, I'll be there . . . would have been there, too. I know what a father means."

"I didn't think anyone here in Philly really cared about me or where I was," she said quietly, finally relaxing enough to hug him back and lay her head on his shoulder.

"I cared," Jason murmured. "Deborah, when I came home and couldn't find you and then found out you weren't working where you had been and hadn't come to class, I panicked. I thought maybe you had gotten laid off, had quit, or, worse, had moved, and I couldn't allow my mind to go there. The fear that you might have done that was eating me up alive, so I worked off the stress. I fixed this up for us. I fixed up the gallery for us. I wanted to show you when I found you that I'd treat you better than the others had treated you."

She looked up into his eyes. "What did you say?"

He closed his eyes and cupped her face, placing a gentle kiss on her forehead, the bridge of her nose, and finally her mouth. "Deborah, pretty Deborah, I've learned so much about wasting time, running from what's good for me. Baby, I'll treat you better than my stepfather treated my mother, better than my half brother treated his wives, better than your ex-husband treated you, and better than any other man who didn't appreciate you did. Just give me a chance to show you that I'll be there through thick and through thin. Let me meet your father the old-fashioned way before it's too late. Let me honor you the way a man is supposed to honor a woman, with my full respect. I don't care what you've heard about how men can be. I'm telling you, I'll be better than."

The kiss began slowly and then deepened. She didn't care that she'd come into his space with a wall built up around her emotions, because he'd crumbled it at her feet. But this time, the warmth that he'd ignited in her heart was radiating out, claiming the rest of her body.

"I missed you so much," he whispered hoarsely against her hair and then pulled away, as though in pain. "I know I don't have the right to put my hands on you, and you probably don't want that from me after all I've put you through, but stay with the family and eat with us this afternoon, okay?" He drew in a steadying breath and crossed the room. "I fixed up the bathroom, finished it," he said, opening the doors. "So, if you . . . Well, it will be nice in here for you if you ever use it."

He walked away quickly, causing her to follow him, with her hand over her heart. The kiss had been so sensual, it had dazed her, and his confession had been so hot, it had left her on wobbly legs. He was practically bouncing off the walls, and her mind needed time to gather all the different bits of information he'd tossed out. He would meet her father the *old-fashioned way*. What was he saying? She dared not hope. No, she had to be tripping. Then she pondered all that he'd told her, including his deeply personal account of his visit with his father and the intimate details of his mother's life. She stood in the doorway of the studio and finally found her voice.

"Jason . . . oh Lord . . . When?" She slowly walked toward the painting of the church funeral, and tears welled in her eyes. Then she turned away swiftly, covered her mouth, with a gasp, and closed her eyes, making the tears spill. "That is *exactly* what that feels like."

"I started it when I began going through the attic," he said, his voice distant as he leaned against a ladder.

"I missed Nana so much, and I knew you'd missed yours so much. I did us in church, over the one casket, hollering . . . gospel choir in the background. Our grandmothers might have been different people, but they were cut from the same cloth, so I merged them."

Deborah just shook her head and then turned back to stare up at the painting. "It's beautiful. I thought I'd die when she passed."

"Me, too." He sighed and pushed off the ladder. "I found a bunch of my mom's letters, read so much that filled in the blank spaces in my life. The whole thing was a deep experience, Deborah."

She nodded. "It was something we both had to do alone."

"Baby . . . what did you discover on your personal journey?" he asked, remaining across the room, as though intentionally leaving space between them.

"So many good things," Deborah whispered. "And they all came out in church this Sunday morning." She took her time and told him about all she'd learned about her father and their relationship. She told him about how she'd lost it on the telephone and about all that had been bottled up. She told him about the risks she'd taken with her job, about how her father had shown up there, about the disappointment of not being able to interview for the new position, and about how that had worked out, nonetheless. This time, for the first time in her life, she didn't feel like she needed to hold anything back. When she was done speaking, his eyes were glistening with unshed tears.

"That is beautiful," he whispered. "Just like you. Deborah, you may not see it, but it's your spirit that's gorgeous, too. I don't know how to describe what I'm seeing, but I can see it."

He walked toward her but then, oddly, passed by her and touched a blank canvas that hung next to the

funeral blues painting. "I saw it come out this morning," he said, touching the striking oil in hues of blue.
"This one is one extreme. The music, the emotion of
grief." He closed his eyes and pressed both palms to
the fifteen-foot blank canvas. "This morning was release, praise, fire of the spirit leaping up to reach
Heaven . . . the music, the preaching, helping the ecstasy. I saw it, and for the first time, because you were
there as part of my catalyst, I felt it."

Jason opened his eyes, leaving her stunned silent as
he walked to the next blank canvas, which was beside
the one depicting dreams deferred. "This one shows a
woman of that era denied, blues, her hands clasped
and her mind drifting to what could have been but
what obstacles wouldn't allow . . . a woman like my
grandmother, yours, our mothers. I couldn't figure out
what to put there until just now." He shook his head.
"They held out for the future. The children. Hands of
the ancient reaching down, angels . . . just like you did
in watercolor that first day in class. A baby . . . a woman
graduating, you, the next generation marrying, the
colors vibrant, life affirming. Yeah. A palette of fire
colors."

He spun as she gasped, nodding. "The centerpiece!
I saw it! All the colors brought together, a fusion, your
watercolor, Deborah, life, the layers of life, the rhythm
and blues of life, heartbreak and heart swell, confu-
sion and clarity, obstacles and victory, passion and
consequences. It's all the full palette . . . That's what
our lives are. Take out one color spectrum and it just
isn't balanced. The angels move between the layers of
the unseen, never leaving us." He turned to her.
"That's what I learned while I was gone, while you
were gone." He ran his palms down his face. "I have
to paint."

"But your family . . . ," she said, not sure what to do.
Her body wanted to press him against a ladder. Her

heart wanted to burst out sobbing and confess how much she loved him. Her mind knew she needed to ground him and handle the next pressing issue—company for dinner.

"Oh, shit, oh yeah. Uh . . . food."

"I'll cook," she offered. "When are they coming?"

"Four, and no, I didn't invite you here for that. It's not right." He dashed through the studio and hit the stairs. "I have menus somewhere in the kitchen drawers."

Deborah rushed down the hall, behind him. "Well, at least let me set the table nice for them. How many are coming?"

Jason looked up, bewildered. "Huh?"

"How many family members are coming? Tell me so I can set the table while you sketch."

"I don't know. Uh, me, you, Jenna, Jackie, and Jared, if he comes . . . Wil. I don't think the kids are coming, last Jenna said."

"Six," she said, reaching up into the cabinets to find six midnight blue plates and then gathering flatware. "Do you have place mats or napkins? How about a little gold ribbon left over from Christmas or something that I can tie these knives, forks, and spoons off with?" She waited a beat. "Scratch that. Uh—"

"Ask Wil. His lady, Evelyn, wrapped gifts for her family up there, and knowing Wil, after they broke up, he didn't throw anything out . . . unless she went in there after him. But we cleaned his apartment, which was a sty, so everything could have gone."

"Give me his number," Deborah said calmly, placing two steadying hands on Jason's shoulders. "Breathe. I'll find the menus, I'll order, I'll call Wil and run up to his apartment, and you go up to the studio and get to work. And I'll fix the table. All right?"

She could see that all nonartistic thoughts were leaving his brain. It was the most incredible thing to watch his eyes glaze over. He got a faraway look in them and just nodded, agreeing with her but clearly not having heard a word she'd said.

Almost an hour and a half had gone by while he was sketching in an ecstatic trance. Feet bare, in a comfortable pair of jeans that weren't too bad and a crewneck sweater that Deborah had found, he had passed inspection for dinner in his own home. He was in heaven. Something smelled fantastic, too. The doorbell rang. He could hear Wil's voice booming in the background of his mind. It was all good.

Deborah's voice finally brought him out of his reverie, and he stood up like a zombie, conflicted down to the last cell in his body. He didn't want to leave *the zone* but had to. He left his pad on an easel and walked away from the drawing, with a sigh, and then hurried down the steps to see that his sister Jenna had arrived first.

Jenna rushed him, with a hug. "Look at this place, Jason!" She whirled around. "Oh my God! Just look at it!" Then after fanning her face and laughing, she turned to Deborah and Wil. "I'm so sorry," she said, thrusting out her hand. "I'm Jenna. We met at my older brother Jared's house." She gave Deborah a big smile.

"And I'm chopped liver?" Wil said, with a big grin. "Jason did *not* tell me his *younger* sister was drop-dead gorgeous."

Jenna blushed and chuckled shyly. "Go on, Wil. You need to stop. We've known each other for years." She waved her hand at him. "He needs to stop. I've known him forever."

"But ain't rediscovery grand," Wil said, wiggling his eyebrows. "You look good, girl . . . I haven't seen you in ages. Come tell me what you've been up to. I just got back from London."

"Hey, hey, that's my sister," Jason said, half joking and half serious as Wil took Jenna by the elbow and walked her toward the living room.

"Last I checked, she was grown," Wil said, with a wide grin. "And how."

"Should I leave my sister in the clutches of my horny best friend?" Jason said in Deborah's ear while everyone was laughing. "Then again, she's thirteen years his senior, and he might be the one in trouble."

"Come help me in the kitchen," Deborah said, laughing. "My name is Bennet, and I'm not innit."

"Great position to take," Wil called out behind them, but everyone stopped as Jenna shrieked and ran into the dining room.

Jenna sucked in a huge gasp and spun to look at Jason. "You did this of Mom from memory? Or a picture you found? Can I have a copy of the picture, *please*?"

"I didn't do it," Jason said quietly. "My father did." He looked at Jenna. "There's so much I need to tell you guys that I found out, and I'm not sure even where to begin, but he isn't a monster. He really did love her and didn't take advantage of her."

"Wil," Deborah said, touching Jason's shoulder as he choked up. "Why don't you take Jenna on the house tour? Then we'll all meet up in the kitchen, dish up the food from the cartons, and Jason can give us a rundown about Toronto."

"Okay," Wil said, his eyes filled with both compassion and gratitude.

Jenna smiled and went to Deborah to hug her. "I like you so much, lady. I'm glad you came back and didn't give up on our crazy family." She left Deborah's side and followed Wil through the house as he pointed out her mother's art pieces like a museum curator.

Jason's arms drew Deborah close, and he nestled his cheek against her hair. "Thank you. I couldn't do it just yet . . . got filled up."

He was thankful that she just nodded, knowing, just like she had found gold ribbon to tie off the flatware against midnight blue plates, had cut funky shapes of burnt orange upholstery fabric left up in Wil's place to set the plates on, had gone and found flowers from some source unbeknownst to him, had arranged huge sunflowers and goldenrod in one of his mother's showpiece vases, had discovered hand-painted wine-glasses high up in the cabinets and had hand-washed them so that they sparkled brilliantly, and had ordered the food. And now that he was downstairs, he was sure that she'd created a pie.

This woman that held him had known how to put the finishing touches on him and his life. Deborah Lee Jackson was a ground wire, a balance beam of support. She was a quiet force that had taken him by storm, had entered his spirit, had set him back on the right path, and in this moment, standing in the dining room after what she'd just done, he knew he couldn't live without her.

"The place looks good, Jason," his sister Jacqueline said slowly as she shed her full-length mink for him to take.

"Parking's a bitch around here, though," Jared complained, stomping his feet to get the slush off his shoes in the foyer.

"It's nice to meet you again," Jackie said crisply, looking through Deborah. She noticed Wil cozying up to Jenna and scowled. "But I thought that *this Sunday,* given the nature of the things that need to be discussed, it would just be *family?*"

Jenna stood up and folded her arms. Jason drew

Deborah to his side and held up a hand, his expression serene.

"I've been to church today," Jason said, with a smile. "It's all right, Jen." He sighed. "Here's the thing . . . I owe Jared a thank-you for teaching me a lot." In a surprise move, he walked over to his brother. "If it wasn't for you, man, I might have missed out on meeting a great man who is getting up in years. Thank you. It hurt, but thanks for that gift. I forgive you for the last dinner. It's over."

Jared was speechless and held his body rigid as Jason hugged him and then let him go.

"Y'all," Jason said, waving everyone into the dining room. "I've learned that family is about a vibration of love. In that regard, Wil is a brother, too. Deborah is family to me. She's been my rock. So let's all sit down, bless the food, and break bread as one family."

Slowly, tentatively, everyone joined hands around the dining-room table, and Jason said a blessing that included thanks for everything and everyone he could imagine.

Jared raised an eyebrow and glanced at Deborah as they sat down. "Sounds like the man had a *real* religious experience," he muttered, scowling at the painting of their mother and then studying his wineglass. "Tell me that you have something stronger than vino up in here, Jas. If I have to stare at our mother naked, I'm thinking Scotch, Bourbon. I can't do fruit juice and tofu, too."

Jason shrugged. "When I got back from Toronto, getting to the state store slipped my mind." He passed seared string beans with garlic down the table, toward Jared.

Growing totally irate, Jared thrust the dish toward Jackie. "All right, then. What was on your mind when you did this . . . this . . . abomination of Mom, huh?

Why didn't you put some clothes on her or put her in a nice dress?"

Jenna, Wil, and Deborah held their breaths as Jackie lifted her chin in pious, silent agreement.

"Because I didn't have the honor of painting her," Jason replied calmly, dishing brown rice onto his plate. "From the artist's perspective, he captured her as he saw her . . . in the beauty they shared."

Jared held his glass of cranberry juice, mid-sip. "Say what?" As understanding dawned, he slowly pushed back from the table. "Noooo . . . tell me you didn't have the fucking unmitigated gall and audacity to—"

"No, don't, Jared!" Jenna screamed.

Wil was on his feet. Jason dropped his napkin, frozen by sheer disbelief.

"Oh, God, don't," Deborah whispered.

Jared had stood, pitched his arm back, and flung a delicate, irreplaceable stem glass that had been created by his mother, and that was filled with cranberry juice, toward a priceless, irreplaceable work of art. Wil made a dive across the table like he played for the NFL, got cranberry juice in his face and across his chest, and then caught the glass in an across the table slide that wiped out the rice and string beans but saved the painting.

"Are you crazy?" Wil shouted.

"That's why *he's* my brother," Jason said, standing. "Thank you, man."

Jenna gripped a fork like a shank. "I will stab your big, stupid, alcoholic ass up in here, I swear, Jared! That's my mother, too!" Jenna rushed forward, but Jackie grabbed her arm. Then Jenna slapped Jackie so hard that her older sister's head jerked back.

Wil blotted the cranberry juice on his face and set down the almost lost stemware. "You need to put that crazy bastard out, man. You don't need that type of energy up in your home after all you've been through."

"You're calling me a bastard?" Jared said, incredulous. "You've clearly got the wrong brother! C'mon, Jackie. We don't have to take this shit."

Jackie was still holding her cheek as she stood, tears glittering in her eyes as Jenna brandished flatware at her. "This is why I don't ever want to see you nig—"

"Stop!" Deborah yelled, barring the entrance to the dining room and stopping Jackie's words. "Do you hear yourselves? You're family. Please stop on the Lord's day."

"What are you, Mother Theresa?" Jared shouted, trying to get around Deborah.

"She's right," Jason said, making everyone stop moving. "I'm sorry."

"You're what?" Wil and Jenna said in unison.

"I'm sorry," Jason repeated quietly, firmly, calmly. "For you, this painting represents pain and fear . . . and knowing you were coming, I shouldn't have put it up. For me, it represents a time in our mother's life when she discovered a part of her dreams and made me." Jason let his breath out hard. "No matter what, we're still family, and we're all we've got left. Each other. There's kids, my nieces and nephews, and then their kids will come along. Do we want to pass on this legacy of not speaking to people, or do we want to heal?" He walked over to his brother. "Man, I know what happened had to be awful for you."

"You have no idea," Jared said through labored breaths, his face becoming red as his eyes filled. "After everything happened, *my* father wasn't good for anything. He was *never* the same. I couldn't do anything to please him like before. Couldn't get him to give me the time of day, no matter how many awards I brought him," his brother said, his voice breaking as Jason pulled him into a hug. "I tried, too, tried to put the family back together, and the shit wasn't possible!"

Jason hugged him harder and rocked him where

he stood. "I know, man . . . I know. He's proud of you. We all are. You set the Olympic bar in the family, set the pace for accomplishment."

Jackie covered her face and wailed into her hands, and Jenna and Deborah went to her. "Oh my God, Jas," she screamed. "I was in high school! They both died. My momma just clicked off feeling and everything was the new baby and she practically lived at Nana's house, my grandma's house. This house is where *my* grandma used to live, too. She wasn't just your nana. You got the best one. Her! Nana! It wasn't right!"

Broken moans filled the dining room as Jenna began to rock. Wil helped Deborah gather and comfort both women.

"I have letters," Jason said, breathing hard, fighting not to break down. "Mom's letters, which show how much she loved you, and I know Nana did, too, because she kept everything tight. Nana wouldn't let her just run off to Toronto. Mom couldn't do it. Nesbitt told me, and he respected her decision." He held his older brother tighter as Jared's sobs became bleating. "They all got hurt up. Does it matter who started it? Who was right or wrong? We were all kids! None of us had a choice about anything. We just picked up and played the hand we were dealt. But we have a choice now. I choose to love you. C'mon, y'all . . . Don't leave. I want you in my life."

Faces got washed; the rice and string bean dishes got tossed. A floor got mopped. Homemade pie got cut and served in the kitchen, with herbal tea and coffee. Hearts mended as eyes saw pictures and read letters, and more sobs cleansed hearts. Art got told as a story and a journey throughout a home that held so many memories that it was bursting at the seams.

"I'm glad you caught that glass," Jared said, wiping

his face and hugging Wil near the door. "I don't know what I would have done the next day, once it sunk in, if I'd destroyed the painting."

"It's all good, man," Wil said, giving him an embrace. "It's cool."

Jason nodded and hugged his siblings. Jackie clutched letters and held a piece of ceramic art for her curio shelves like it was a prized museum relic. Jenna held a self-portrait of their mother. Her tears were flowing, and she was so overwhelmed that she couldn't say good-bye.

"This is for you, man," Jason said, handing Jared a cigar box from the attic.

"What's this?" Jared said, his voice gravelly.

"Open it. This was part of Nana's stash."

Everyone gathered around Jared as he gingerly opened the lid. In an elderly woman's scrawl, there was a note that read: *My first grandson's achievements. I am so proud, Thank you, Jesus. Let that boy reach the stars!* Beneath the weathered notepaper lay a lock of baby hair, a tooth, a silver spoon, and a xeroxed copy of seemingly every school award Jared had ever received.

"She was so proud of you, man," Jason said as his brother peered up at him with bloodshot eyes. "Anything up there that you all want, you're welcomed to it. I've been blessed."

"Thank you," his brother whispered and then put his fist to his mouth for a moment. "Three wives, five children, and I didn't have a soul to see about me . . . care about me, you know? Only thing I had was the firm."

Jackie and Jenna went to him and held him.

"That's not true, big brother," Jackie whispered. "We love you and are gonna get you some help."

"Every step of the way, we'll be there with you," Jenna promised and kissed his cheek, wiping away tears.

"I've got your back," Jason murmured. "You call me day or night, hear?"

Jared nodded. "I'm a pretty good attorney . . . and I've got your back, too. All right? You're my brother. Gonna make sure you get insured and protected right so no one can come in and take from your priceless collection. Those agents and art dealers are barracudas. You need somebody to go over your contracts to be sure they're not robbing you. Call me. Free. Family rate." He turned to Deborah. "I was *not* talking about you or signifying. I'm so ashamed of how I've acted in front of you, but I'm so glad he's got you."

Deborah went to Jared and hugged him and just allowed silence to speak for a moment before she pulled away. Jackie swept her up next, and it was all Deborah could do to fight the brimming tears.

"I'm so sorry. You're the best thing that has ever happened to us," Jackie said. "I didn't mean to treat you like I did when we met. I'm glad you're part of this family, just like Jason's dear friend Wil."

"It's all right. It all came out the way it was supposed to," Deborah said. "Thank you for letting me be a part of you all."

Jason and Wil shook hands and yanked each other into a brotherly, one-armed embrace.

"I've got an old jazz collection up there, a lot of seventy-eight platters . . . Thelonious Monk, man. They're yours," Jason said.

Wil stared at him. "No way. Those are—"

"Yours," Jason repeated, ignoring Wil's wide-eyed surprise. "Why would I hoard them? Jazz is all you, man. Nana loved you, too."

Wil let go of him, raked his dreadlocks, swallowed hard, and headed for the door. "I'ma say good night, folks. I . . . I just, you know. I love you, man. Thanks."

Wil slipped out the door, and one by one, the Hastings siblings followed him. Jason stood on the porch, his stomach to Deborah's back as his arms encircled her.

"This was the best family dinner we've ever had in the thirty years I've been alive," he murmured into her hair. "It wouldn't have been possible without you."

"You all did the hard work. I just chaperoned."

He fell quiet and hugged her tighter against the cold. "Don't go home tonight."

"Okay," she whispered and closed her eyes.

Chapter 16

He'd turned her nude body into raw canvas beneath the brush flickers of his tongue, his soul-dissolving kisses adding splashes of color-stained tears to the midnight blue sheets, her cries fire-orange sunbursts. Patient hands molded her hips, her thighs, her breasts, spreading warmth through her as though she were pliant clay . . . Moistened at the wheel, her mind spun as she followed his lead, literally caving in on herself under his touch.

Building her pleasure from the mattress up, he lifted her hips, steady hands caressing the lobes of her backside, turning her into a natural bridge, her arms splayed at her side, her fire breaths now a chant as her thighs trembled and she clenched her stomach muscles. She thrashed from side to side, his tongue painting, painting her insane, painting her iridescent gasps, opening her deepest magenta-hued flower, making it spill passion, varnish his sheets, and lacquer his tongue.

Weak from his kisses, her voice had become glass art, shattering, splintering, and then gathered together by a deep moan, cemented by his baritone whispers between her legs. She wanted him inside her so much that tears shellacked her face. Needing to feel his hair, she'd ruined his cornrows, her fingers making the parts fuzzy.

Pleasure glazed, pleasure dazed, fired white hot, she opened for him, her expression agonized as she reached for his shoulders, rushing him, pulling him up her body, etching him with her nails, her inner thighs a pulse against his hips, telling him that he was better than all the others, worth whatever the consequences were.

He dropped his burning face against her cheek, feeling her pour herself all over him . . . just like in the studio. He was done. There was no coming out of the creative process, not now, not when Deborah's perspiration-soaked belly slid against his. Not when her drenched hibiscus drew him in toward paradise, causing him to shudder as he entered the gateway of unending tomorrows. How could he stop when her breasts cushioned his chest, her erect peaks grazing his tortured nipples, her hands sending spasms up his spine?

Sweat ran down his face and dripped off the end of his nose and coursed down his temples. His back was wet, his shoulders slick as he moved against her so slowly that she sobbed. Every thrust felt like he was being stabbed in his chest, he wanted to release so badly. She pulled every hue he could imagine up his shaft until he swore it was staining his sweat.

"Jason, I love you," she whispered in a thick gasp, sitting up to take his mouth.

Her kiss, her words, her body tensing to reach his lips broke him, made him drop to his elbows, then just gather her in his arms, his pacing ripped to shreds.

"Oh, baby, I love you," he said into her mouth, then against her neck, his hands entangled in her mass of thick hair. "Deborah, oh, God, Deborah . . . You're better than anything or anyone I've ever known. . . ."

There were so many more things he wanted to say, but blinding color was carving his scrotum. He'd begun moving against her so hard and so fast, he'd lost his timing, pace, rhythm . . . had lost the art of falling. He was plummeting . . . couldn't move any way but linearly, unbalanced, and she seemed to know that, as her pelvis met each thrust with a grinding, circular motion that begged him to say her name. Then he splattered into pure creative essence, heaving, hollering, and holding on to her through every agonized shudder till there was nothing left.

She woke up to the smell of tea on the nightstand and a note. Deborah blinked and reached for the note, her body sore from pure overattention. She couldn't overstand, understand, couldn't do anything—could barely reach for the note and her tea.

It was simple and beautiful, and made her smile. He'd drawn a red heart and an arrow pointing up and a smiley face, and then he'd jotted a few simple words: *I'm upstairs at Wil's. Coming back soon.* She smiled and brought the cup of tea to her and sipped it, realizing that it was cold, and then wondered how long she'd been knocked out.

After taking a few unsteady sips, she headed for the bathroom. By the time she'd washed her hands, splashed water on her face, and began to swish toothpaste and mouthwash around in her mouth, she heard Jason reenter the house. She chuckled quietly to herself as he bounded up the steps like a big kid and then crossed the room. Two knocks and he was through the bathroom door, beaming.

"What did you do?" she said, eyes wide.

"Military cut. Wil put a nice fade on it and taped the

neck pretty cool, I think. Can't find a barber open on a Monday." He spun around. "So? I pass inspection?"

"Oh, baby, why would you cut your gorgeous hair?" She went to him and ran her hand over the low cut, feeling the bristles nip her palm. "I loved it."

He kissed her, with a smile. "It's not for you. It's for him."

"Who?"

"Your dad," he said, unfazed, while hunting for a towel. "He does chemo on Tuesdays and Thursdays, right? No need to freak the man out by having some knucklehead go down there to see him, wearing an Afro out to here, or Iverson's, so, hey. I know what time it is . . . He was in the military, like, what? Twenty-five, thirty years?" Jason rummaged around the bathroom. "I gotta shave, too . . . find something conserva—"

"Whoa, whoa, whoa. When are you talking about—"

"Today," he said and stopped moving around to stare at her. "We go to your spot, get your clothes, drop off all the photo albums and stuff that's in my trunk. We drive down. You stay with him through his Tuesday session. I'll get a hotel, not presuming, you know and—"

"I have to prepare him for this, and you don't have to go today, baby. I mean, I was just down there, and Ms. Cath—"

"Deborah, I *have* to go today." Jason let his breath out hard. "Because after Wednesday, when we come back up . . . or if you need to stay through the week, I have to go back to work. My shit is raggedy with the project, and I have to finish."

She folded her arms over her chest. "You don't have to do this. I know you promised but—"

"I have something very important to ask the man, aw'ight!" Jason turned around and began rummaging in the medicine cabinet, muttering.

She touched his shoulder and stilled him. "Jason,

you have to work and finish this project. You don't have to prove to me that—"

He held her face, almost squishing it. "Let me do this, baby. Please let me just . . . Lemme keep my word, all right. Then, after that, I'll get back to work, but I can't think or work or concentrate unless I follow through on what I said."

"Okay," she mumbled and then grabbed his wrists. "You're squashing my cheeks."

"Oh, my bad," he said, letting her go. He paced in the bathroom. "Have you seen my towel?"

She picked it up off the edge of the sink.

"Thanks," he said as he grabbed it and headed for the shower.

"Want me to come in there with you?" she offered, remembering the glorious days they'd spent while he was working in the studio.

"No, not this time, 'cause we've gotta get on the road."

Deborah just watched Jason from the corner of her eye as she held the MapQuest directions for him and he fidgeted with CDs as he drove. He was so frantic that he was making the hairs stand up on the back of her neck. He must have changed his clothes five times, and then he'd insisted on going to Whole Foods to bring groceries to her father's door—even though she'd assured him the man was stocked to the gills from when she'd been there. Still, Jason had said it was a matter of protocol to bring something. Yeah, they'd had the same grandmother in principle, it seemed.

But the man grilling her for hours on the road about her family, like he was prepping for the game show *Jeopardy*, was so endearing that she kept needing to touch him. Then he'd hurt her feelings, initially, by telling her to get off him, only to frantically admit that he couldn't go into her father's house with wood—

and that was what her touch produced—so she had to get off him.

Deborah folded her hands in her lap and tucked away a smile. Her dad had put up a fuss about the visit, acting like the Military Police had wrongfully arrested and detained him, but she hadn't let Jason hear that part of the conversation. He was on a mission.

Jason was so nervous that he bounced the little Karmann Ghia into her father's driveway, coming perilously close to kissing the bumper of his black Lincoln, and then he briefly shut his eyes.

"Baby, it's gonna be all right," she said, holding his arm.

Jason nodded and began to open his door and spun on her when she reached for the handle. "Are you crazy?" he said through his teeth. "Stay there till I come around. I don't want him tripping because he saw something like that!"

She held up her hands like she was being arrested. "Okay," she whispered and wanted to kiss him so badly that she had to hug herself.

Jason bolted around the car, collected Deborah, and almost slid and fell while trying to pop the trunk to get the groceries, which were probably frozen from three hours at twenty-two degrees on the highway. But she bit the insides of her cheeks and never changed her facial expression. Before they hit the steps, her father was at the door, dressed like he was going to work—in full uniform—although he was semiretired.

"Oh, Lord," Deborah breathed.

Her father looked Jason up and down. "You Jason Hastings, here to see about my baby?"

Jason lifted his chin. "Yes, sir."

Her father tilted his head, inspecting every inch of Jason down to his shoes, then grunted, with a nod, turned on his heels, and left the door open, striding into the house.

"See," Jason whispered. "That's why I cut off the 'Fro. I ain't crazy."

She couldn't argue with him. Her father had never got a chance to preview her ex, and since they were both military, they spoke the same language. Now it was her turn to be nervous.

Jason fell back and let her go up the steps first and then shut the door softly behind them, but he rushed to help Deborah off with her coat, watching her father watch him. The old man nodded, with another indecipherable grunt.

"Hang 'em up over there," her father said, without fanfare. "How was the drive down?"

"Oh, it was nice, Dad," Deborah said, going to him and hugging him. "It was sunny and—"

"Good," her father said, kissing her cheek and cutting her off. He folded his arms over his barrel chest. "Where you from?"

"Daddy!" Deborah shrieked, not expecting the uncharacteristically territorial, protective display.

"Sir," Jason said, risking stepping close enough to extend his hand. "I'm from Philly."

To her horror, she watched her father grip Jason's hand like he was attempting to crush bones before he released it.

"What part?" her father asked, gaze narrowed.

"West Mount Airy, but down in Powellton now."

"What do you do job wise?"

Deborah tried not to cringe . . . She'd told Jason to wait, arguing that she needed to broach the subject of their relationship by degrees with her father.

"I paint and—"

"Okay," her father snapped, cutting Jason off. "This here is my baby girl. Plain and simple. I don't know what she told you, or what you think, but she's got a father who ain't in the ground yet, hear? I'm excellent with munitions, and I will blow your punk ass away if you hurt her. I ain't got nothin' to lose. Know that? Embrace it as a concept, boy."

"Dad! Oh my God, what has gotten into you?" Deborah's hand flew over her mouth. He'd never acted like this before in his life. She turned to Jason, who hadn't flinched. "I'm sorry." She turned back to her father. "Daddy, please . . ."

Jason piped up. "It's cool, Deb—"

"It's cool? It's what?" Her father looked like he was about to ask Jason to step outside.

"Hold it!" she said more loudly than intended. "I don't know what's happening here. I don't know why it's happening."

"He knows," her father said, practically growling.

Jason nodded. "Yeah, I do, and I would, too."

"Somebody explain it to me, then!" Deborah looked between her father and her lover.

"You're his baby girl, and somebody already treated you wrong, and he wants to be sure that never happens again, and I can dig it," said Jason.

Deborah looked at her father, who drew her to him under one arm.

"You ain't taking my daughter through a lotta bullshit, I ain't worked so hard for some flaky artist trying to find his muse to come and try to rob my baby of whatever she got, and you ain't leaving my child out here pregnant and by herself, just because she told you I'm sick!"

She gasped and took note of her father's resolute expression, knowing that he thoroughly believed all he was saying, but Jason just nodded.

Her father nodded toward the grocery bag on the floor, by the door, with an angry jerk of his head. "She was just down here, and if you came in my damned door, dragging groceries, I know Deborah done cried all over your shoulder . . . and I don't care what the hell you talked her into doing with you to comfort her. I will put a bullet in your ass, boy, if you jack with my girl! You think I was born yesterday?" Her father let her go and squared off against Jason. "Think I ain't seen it all, from the Philippines to Kuwait! Sheeit, and ya thought you was coming down here to see some weak old man, didn't ya, huh? Fooled your ass, didn't I?" He pointed toward the kitchen. "Tell me what's on the table?"

"Oh, my God!" Deborah said, rounding her father and standing in front of Jason.

"A Glock nine-millimeter, sir," Jason said calmly.

"You've lost your mind, Daddy!" Deborah cried.

"Naw, I ain't," her father said, his Southern drawl by way of North Carolina coming out as he got whipped up. "Shoulda shot the first one and made you a widow when that fool took your little house and all my sweet baby girl's dreams. Now this one has come sniffing like a vulture, thinking her old man is dead in the ground and she's ripe for the picking. No. Not this time. I love you, darlin', and if the cancer don't kill me, standing by and watching this surely will." He directed his attention back to Jason. "Ain't what you expected, is it? So, what'd you come down here for?"

Tears stung her eyes as she went to her father and tried to calm him. "Daddy, what happened wasn't your fault, and Jason's not like that. . . ."

Her father hugged her protectively. "None of 'em seem like that, but they all dawgs."

"Sir," Jason said quietly. "I don't know how you feel, but I will, hopefully, one day if I'm blessed with a daughter. All I can say is why I came here."

Her father tensed and lifted his chin. "Yeah? Why? Other than to try to fool with her mind?"

"I came to ask you to give me your blessing to marry her."

"What!" Her father headed toward the kitchen.

Deborah's body blocked him. "What?" she asked more quietly.

"Have a prenuptial drawn up, Mr. Jackson, sir," said Jason. "Have your lawyers make sure I can't touch anything she owns before we get married, if she'll have me. If you want my taxes, my Schedule C's from my self-employment filings, I'll fax 'em to you from my accountant's office. I swear to you, sir, I'm not a struggling artist playing her or looking for a meal ticket. Deborah gave me my vision back. And I invite you to come up to my major client's black-tie event in a couple of weeks. I'll send a limo for you, sir, no less than what I'm doing for my father from the airport. I'm not trying to impress. I just want you not to have to deal with Amtrak.

"This here," Jason said, stammering, "it belonged to my mother. She never got to really wear it, but my grandmother kept it in the attic . . . and I added more stones to it, sir . . . but it's thirty years old. I'll promise you on my mother's grave, I won't hurt her, will see her back to school, whatever she wants to do."

Deborah was paralyzed where she stood. Her father turned away from the kitchen and his pursuit of a firearm to look at Jason carefully.

"You ain't on drugs, don't have no diseases, and ain't gay?" her father asked.

Jason shook his head no. "No, sir." He stood up taller.

"And, your grandma, the one you mentioned, she living or dead?"

"Passed on, sadly, sir," Jason said, thrusting his shoulders back, still holding out the ring. "Was a God-fearing woman, raised me in the church, and I rededicated yesterday. Ain't gonna lie. It had been a while, but Deborah made me go back."

Her father nodded and raked his close-cut silver gray hair. "Can't be mad at you for that . . . sounds like your grandmother was like my mother."

Jason nodded.

"Go over there and get that ring, and lemme see it," her father said, too proud to back down, but too relieved to let the opportunity pass.

Deborah stood between both men, tears streaming down her face, unable to breathe.

"You made her cry," her father fussed. "You need to give her the danged ring and hug her or something."

"Sir . . . I . . ."

"Oh, I ain't gonna shoot you. Would leave a stain in the rug."

They sat at the kitchen table, laughing, hugging so close, they were practically sitting in the same chair. She kept turning the huge, three-karat, emerald-cut diamond in the kitchen light, marveling at the way Jason had created small mosaic blocks of semi-precious stones, sapphire, ruby, topaz, citrine, in the wide platinum band. There were so many colors that she lost count as tears blurred her vision.

"When? How?" she asked, pressing her face against his shoulder while her father insisted on making the tea.

"Don't ask the man his business," her father said in a strange turn of allegiance. "Y'all always want the details, and sometimes the magic is in the details."

"Thank you, Mr. Jackson," Jason said, making her father smile.

"I want you two to go on up and drive safely," Deborah's father said when Jason came from the hotel to rejoin Deborah at the house. "Make her stop worrying. Everything is in the hands of the Lord, and I'm a tough old dog. Y'all been here since Monday. It's Wednesday . . . I've lived through another treatment.

So it's time for you two to git. Ms. Catherine will take good care of me."

Jason threaded his arm around Deborah's waist, stilling her protest, as he glanced at an older woman who had on a nurse's uniform, but who also had a deep tenderness in her eyes, suggesting that she went way beyond the call of her profession. The two men shared a look.

"Deb, I think your father is in good hands," Jason said.

Deborah stared at the caramel-hued woman with a soft voice and gentle eyes. She so resembled her mother that it was eerie. "All right," she said, conceding, and feeling both happy and sad at the same time. She walked over to Ms. Catherine and simply hugged her. "Thank you for taking such good care of my stubborn dad . . . I don't know what I'd do without you."

Ms. Catherine hugged her hard. "Oh, I make him behave," she said, with a smile. "I'll be sure he eats."

"Y'all talk about me like I'm not in the room," Deborah's father fussed.

"Maybe . . . maybe you'd come to Philadelphia for the event, too, Ms. Catherine?" Deborah asked, glancing at the older couple, then Jason. She chose her words carefully so as not to embarrass the older woman, who was clearly from a generation that kept all such liaisons very discreet. "If Jason sends a limo on Friday, you all could rest up at the Ritz-Carlton or do some sightseeing . . . then relax, and we'd send a car for you to take you to the event."

"Whatever you'd like, sir," Jason chimed in. "Whatever makes you most comfortable."

Darryl Lee Jackson drew his paramour of many years into a light embrace, causing Catherine Johnson to beam up at him, with deep appreciation. "I told you my daughter was one of a kind. Her fiancé ain't half bad, either."

* * *

Only after they'd hit I-95 North did he begin to relax. Only after they'd become ensconced in the privacy of his Karmann Ghia did it hit him: pretty Deborah was going to marry him . . . He'd asked a woman to marry him. He'd almost gotten shot by the major. Only after she'd begun squealing, expressing her feminine appreciation in high-pitched non sequiturs and repeating his name in alto, did he realize how long a drive it was from Arlington to Philly.

He tried to keep up the conversation with her, but all the blood was draining from his brain. He offered short explanations for phenomena that really had a long story behind them—like the fact that he had friends in practically every art skill area, so having her ring designed and made was something that could be done in a day or so by a very, very good friend. He tried to focus on anything other than getting at her the way he wanted to right now.

But she didn't understand that the way she stroked his leg and kissed his neck and kept turning her hand in the sunlight, saying, "Oh, Jason," was messing him up. She couldn't possibly know that the moment her dad had said yes, and she had thrown her arms around his neck, it had taken his clear focus on the gun on the kitchen table to keep from kissing her like he wanted to.

He let her rehash the entire experience, draw parallels, find metaphors, discover signs in the universe, trace evidence of the distinct hand of God in all things, point out the coincidences, and observe the lessons learned. He was beyond intelligent conversation. His contribution had been dumbed down by a mind-numbing erection. At this point, all he could say was, "Uh-huh."

* * *

"You were awfully quiet on the way home," she said, closing the door behind him as he dropped their bags.

"Uh-huh."

"Everything okay? I mean, you seem like you have a lot on your mind."

"Uh-huh . . . I do."

"What, baby? What's wrong?"

It didn't make sense to pull his woman to him that hard, or to kiss her that hard, or to drag her halfway up the steps without letting her take off her coat. Didn't make sense to be banging into doors, stumbling blind, fighting with too many winter layers, needing her skin under his palms so badly, his hands were shaking. Didn't make sense that he couldn't catch his breath and was still drowning in her kiss, just like it didn't make sense that he'd needed her like this for three days in Virginia. Didn't make sense that he hadn't used a condom with her so many times that he couldn't bring himself to do so now.

He sank deep inside her, coat still on, shoes still on, pants shoved down to his thighs, her dress hiked up, her underwear in shreds, her voice a shrill echo, making him arch. Sense? What was that? Discipline? He didn't own it. Not with her. Not in her. Not when she was squeezing his ass under his coat and she was really wet for him. He came so hard and so fast that it stole his breath before shame washed over him.

"Damn . . . I'm sorry," he said, panting into her hair. He could feel her cheek lift into a smile and just shook his head. "Baby, I'll make it up to you. Just gimme a minute."

She stroked his close-cropped hair and kissed him slowly and deeply. "I'm flattered . . . So *that's* what was wrong with you. Dang."

* * *

She sat up, squinting at the morning light. Jason was on the phone, walking in an agitated circle. Shoes, coats, clothes were all over the floor, and intermittently, he would kick a discarded item out of his way. She watched, trying to figure out what had gone wrong.

"I *don't* work like that," he said, veins visible in his neck even though his voice was overly calm. "No. Three days before the event, you can see the work. No. It's not ready. Yes. It will be ready by the deadline, and I'll let your crews know what kind of hanging anchors you'll need. I don't care if she is the executive director! I said, I don't work like that. No, you pull out the contract. I know what it says. This is weeks early, weeks! No." Jason walked back and forth like a caged tiger. "Nonnegotiable. I'm in the studio, and this conversation is throwing off my concentration. Yeah, yeah, you, too. Yeah, we'll touch base next week."

He clicked off the telephone, leaned his head back, and rubbed his neck. Before he could even get the telephone back into the saddle, it rang in his hand. He clicked it on and answered, with a snap. "Yeah?"

Then he groaned.

"How the hell do I know what hors d'oeuvres go best. Jenna, Jenna, you're going neurotic on me again. Please. I have to get in the studio. No, sis, they . . . oh, my God, Jen. Stop stressing about canapés and vegan dishes. I can't make decisions about what? No."

Deborah watched her fiancé pace and rake his fingers across his scalp.

"When did they turn the lights out on South Street?" said Jason. He began rummaging in drawers. "Oh, shit, I think I saw a bill for . . . I was busy! Yes, I have money. I just . . . Okay, okay, the lights will be back on before the event. Yes, I promise. When did the phone lines go out there?"

He stopped hollering and looked at the telephone in his hand for a second. "Jenna! Jenna!" Then, all of a sudden, he hurled the phone and began rummaging in his pants for his cell phone. It was vibrating when he found it. "Yeah, the house phone just went out. I know that will look sick if the client calls and my line is disconnected. Oh, hell no! I can't entertain any prospective clients while I'm in the last weekend, trying to finish. Jenna, Jenna, listen, don't do the guilt thing. Hey! No, if I'm not going to let the people who paid for it see it, then . . ." He closed his eyes. "Oh, my God . . . dinner? When? No! Tell 'em I have the flu!"

Deborah remained very still as she watched Jason hop around the bedroom, trying to put on a pair of boxers and search for bills that had been shoved into mystery drawers.

"Stop," she said after a moment.

"Huh?" He looked up, eyes frantic. "Go back to sleep, baby. Everything's—"

"Falling apart and you need help." She got up and began picking up clothes off the floor.

"I can—"

Deborah held up her hand, with a smile. "You're on a deadline. I've been trained by the military, my dad. Go take a shower. Put on your work clothes. I'll bring you some tea and breakfast. I'll find the bills. I will make a stack. I'm gonna go to the Dollar Store and get a notebook and some files. I'll pay the phone bill with a credit card. Gimme your wallet so we can get the phone back on before a client calls again. I'm going to start a filing system in your office down in the basement. I'll separate house bills from the Toronto on South expenses. I'll have a paper version for backup and an Excel spreadsheet on the system in your office. I'll have a system for mail sorting. Bills versus solicitations, contracts, or personal correspondence."

She didn't miss a beat as she marched into the bathroom to find a towel. "Give me the cell phone, and I'll screen while you work. Once we get the house line on, you call forward to the house line so I can answer it, and I'll give you your phone back so you can call me without leaving the zone for food, water, whatever. Got it? I'll call Jenna back, and we'll get the stuff ordered for the after party. We will also need to develop a committed work schedule for anyone working the gallery. No more fly by night. I want a real schedule, backup people on standby, and contact numbers for everybody. You trust me?"

"Yeah . . . ," he said, calming, his shoulders dropping two inches. "But I've gotta get to my accountant to fax your dad the stuff I promised, call about your prenup—"

"I can make those calls, and hold off on the prenup. My dad . . ."

"I don't want him to—"

"Breathe," she said. "I'm going to buy a calendar. I'm going to make people schedule with you around your deadlines. I'm going to make sure you have room to breathe. All right?"

"I feel like I can't breathe sometimes, Deborah."

She touched his face. "I know you do . . . because you're a product to the outside world, a commodity, a machine that cranks out this fantastic stuff." She hugged him and allowed her hands to sweep up and down his back. "They don't understand the genesis of brilliance, and they want to rub all the shine off you. But I will back 'em up like a bulldog. Diplomatically, of course. You do you. How about this? You create, and I'll delegate and manage."

"I can't do this by myself anymore," he said, hugging her hard. "It grew. It's bigger than it was before, and it has gotten out of control. Like, I can't even wrap my mind around things I should, like Toronto."

"The gallery—"

"No," he said, holding her so he could look at her. "I want to go there, show you after the gala . . . want to take you there for our honeymoon this spring. I want you to see the campus and decide if you might wanna spend a semester there. If it's too far from your dad, we can defer that, but—"

"This spring? You wanna get married this spring!"

"Well, yeah," he said and then smiled. "Breathe. How about this? You create the wedding, and I'll delegate and manage."

"This spring?" she squeaked. "Spring is six weeks away."

He pulled her to him. "I want your daddy to walk you down the aisle."

She looked up at him and then closed her eyes, knowing God had found the best man for her, the one better than them all.

Chapter 17

The man had worked like an absolute dog for three weeks solid, and she had had to practically force him to eat. Most times he'd been so paint ravaged that he'd slept in the studio, drenched in rainbow hues, funky, evil, not wanting to even make love. She'd kept the wolves away from the door, and soon a lot of very unhappy people had begun to realize that Jason Christopher Nesbitt Hastings had a formidable screen worthy of the Pentagon. *The artist was at work.*

Yet, for all his genius, she could feel Jason's hand trembling slightly as he clasped hers beneath the table in the grand ballroom of the Park Hyatt at Bellevue. His father seemed equally as nervous as he sat, looking at the stage, waiting for the panels to slide out on cue behind the music awards presenters as music legends came to the stage amid thunderous applause.

Deborah looked at the handsome duo—they were almost mirror images of each other in tuxedos—and then took note of her father's proud, unblinking gaze and the regal woman who clutched his arm—stunning in her gold gown. The Hastings sisters and Jason's brother, nieces, and nephews; Wil; and the whole family took up two VIP tables, at a thousand dollars a plate, and she wondered if she could ever pull off a wedding that would make his sisters look like they did tonight. Rapt.

She was so proud of Jason and had told him so many times, but toward the end of his commission, he had closed the studio doors, had had a panic attack, and wouldn't let her see what he'd been creating. She hadn't pushed. She had just got his father on the telephone and had slid the cordless in there so they could talk the foreign language of artists. By the time the trucks sent by the client came to pack everything in crates and to move it, she thought Jason might need a sedative. Then, for three days, he crashed and burned.

"I'm proud of you," she whispered. "It's going to go perfectly. Watch." He didn't answer, but now his leg was bouncing under the table, and it looked like his bow tie was strangling his Adam's apple, it bobbed so hard. She squeezed Jason's hand as Marvin Gaye's signature song filled the sound system and the curtains swished back to reveal the first two panels.

Deborah didn't hear what the awards presenter was saying; she was monitoring her soon-to-be husband's pulse as the audience gasped and murmured their appreciation. She looked at Jason, then at those who mattered to him, before assessing the tables of music industry greats and local dignitaries. All it took was one slow nod and a slow smile from Christopher Nesbitt for the tension to drain out of Jason's body. His siblings sat slack-jawed. Her father murmured, "Damn," his voice deep and resonant. Then she watched her father simply shake his head. Ms. Catherine had a gloved hand pressed to her heart. Nieces and nephews leaned forward, with their mouths open. Wil just closed his eyes, as though the image was too much. *Then* she looked up and froze.

The music, the lighting, the moving black-and-white sketches of her, which danced across the midnight blue drapes, beside the fifteen-foot canvases, made it look like she was walking up to a lover in a club, sliding onto a bar stool, smiling, looking over her shoulder to take a number, agreeing to a dance, and then stepping into the large oil and sliding into his arms. The way the lighting and video directors played with Jason's imagery made it come alive. The genius of it was so profound that her hands went to her mouth as she leaned forward.

Then she saw the raw, sensual half sketches of the couple rolling, falling, kissing; of a man passionately taking a woman, perfectly timed to Marvin's wail; and of a woman wrapping her arms around herself as he got his hat, slid it onto his head, and left, an image that merged with the large oil of her in lace the morning after, in blues.

The audience was on their feet. Nesbitt was hollering, "That's my boy! Yeah!" Then, as the crowd settled down, a new pair of awards presenters came out and two more panels emerged from the wings. Stevie Wonder, Earth, Wind & Fire, Teddy, and other greats kept time with dancers boogying in the clubs, sweat flying—courtesy of Jason's attention to detail—butts shaking. People were slow dragging, a couple in a corner was necking, and a woman, Deborah, was leaving alone, trying to hail a cab on a cold, wintry sidewalk. Then she watched that melt into a woman drinking wine as Phyllis Hyman's "Living All Alone" played, into Deborah reaching for the telephone, her poses suggesting various forms of despair, until she merged with herself, passed out on the settee.

People screamed, they hollered, they clapped, and they cried, forcing the awards presenters to nod and wait until the ecstasy had subsided.

Selections from the O'Jay's *Ship Ahoy* album opened the dreams-deferred piece, and as message music from the era played, raw footage of Martin Luther

King and Malcolm X speeches, newsreels of marchers being beaten and hosed, and defending themselves from the dogs set upon them were juxtaposed to sketches of Jason's grandmother taking off her apron in the kitchen he would eventually rebuild . . . of a young woman at the table, his mother, who then became Deborah, who then became his niece Kiera. Deborah squealed and began crying.

Deborah sipped air as she watched herself stand up from the table and walk forward, with books in her arm, then a cap and gown, tossing them with what seemed like hundreds of butterflies. Jason's mother, smiling, became one of the butterflies, taking off with wings, and then his grandmother flew away, nodding. He'd sketched her turning in his arms, with her stomach big. Then he turned, holding a baby, his father gripping his shoulders in support while the butterfly that was his mother landed on his father's shoulder and kissed him on the cheek. Christopher Nesbitt lowered his head, and his shoulders shook so hard that Jenna slipped her arm over them.

There wasn't a dry eye in the house. The music, the message, the awards, they were all beyond what she had thought Jason was working on. His imagination lifted them from the present and took them through each era in pictures, storyboards, rough hatch lines, and squiggles, a play of light and imagery that was absolutely breathtaking as it culminated in fifteen-foot oil panels. Deborah blotted her face and then gasped with the audience as gospels played and the panels came out with awards presenters in that category.

Clapping hands in his sketches danced across the curtains, along with preachers grimacing, fans going wild, and ushers running down aisles as people got their praise on, and then a wild-haired woman in the front, with shopping bags, in clear despair, dropped to her knees and threw up her hand, her tissue becoming a dove of peace, white-coated nurses lifting her as she screamed, old ladies nodding with deacons, tambourines shaking. Then the image became her in fifteen-foot relief, being helped down the aisle, only to grasp the lapels of an overwrought man, his Afro all over his head, dropping to his knees. Finally, the image became family all around a sickbed, doctors shaking their heads.

Charles Nesbitt wiped his face with both hands as the images played across the curtains; Deborah's father blinked up at the ceiling. Ms. Catherine was passing tissues around the table, to Jason's sisters and brother. Wil was rocking by the time the images of Jason and Deborah merged and they were holding each other up, helped by ushers, as a funeral director closed a casket.

The final piece that came out went with the Community Image Award, and it was a series in which his siblings were rolling and tumbling in the yard as children, but they had wings. And parents stood around them, Hastings, his mother, Nesbitt, his grandmother, and the rings became more rings, and the children became more children, until they all became dots all over a dot-covered globe, and then the dots began to disappear as they dropped a large disco ball, which transformed the dots into light beams, and pastel-colored lights put layers on the curtains as angels moved about, tending to the dots that had floated away from the globe. His grandmother and mother and all the females morphed into a fifteen-foot angel with her eyes closed, white wings spread . . . an angel with the face of Deborah Lee Jackson.

The capacity crowd thundered, stomped, cheered, and lost their minds as the awards presenters called for the artist to come up and receive his due. Hands pushed Jason up to his feet, and his father, her father and his brother nudged him along, calling out in support, with wet faces. Deborah's father kept looking between her and Jason's back, shaking his head as Ms. Catherine fanned her face.

"That boy loves you, girl. Hot damn!" her father said, his applause the loudest.

Nesbitt was whistling through his teeth, not caring that it was a thousand-dollar-a-plate event. But then, what did it matter? After all, Jared and Wil were barking, recreating a dog-pound outburst. Sheer pandemonium had eclipsed anything Jason might say as he held on to the lectern and looked out into the bright lights, squinting.

Finally, bit by bit, the crowd settled down, and he smiled. He laughed self-consciously, and people yelled out for him to take his time, like he was in church. But his gaze kept searching until it landed on her.

"I was honored to be selected for this project . . . to provide visuals for the music legends who have brought depth, color, and dimension to our textured lives for generations. What I do is just the backdrop. What they've done is immortal. My father and my mother gave me this gift," he said, pausing. "Dad, stand up. Toronto-based artist and genius Christopher Nesbitt, ladies and gentlemen."

Shocked but deeply proud, his father stood and bowed toward his son, and his son bowed toward him. Thunderous applause erupted again, and then Jason took the microphone.

"Family inspired this. My sisters and brothers, Jared, Wil, Jenna, and Jackie, and their children. Family, please stand. I'm nothing without you." He drew a deep, shuddering breath, and the audience members sat forward, expectant. "But I have to bring someone up here who is in every sketch, in my every waking thought, who penetrated my dreams, who is my blue and my orange. She's wearing a *vicious* copper gown. She blew my mind from the moment I saw her . . . I couldn't have even envisioned the project without my future wife, Deborah Lee Jackson, my angel."

Deborah stood slowly, and hands urged her forward. She didn't do big public anything, much less go up on a stage. Thoroughly panicked, she shook her head no, and her father walked over, stuck out his elbow, threw his shoulders back, and smoothed down his tuxedo lapels.

"Practice," Major Jackson shouted, making nearby tables laugh. "The bride is always shy. C'mon. Don't keep that man waiting."

She clung to her father's bicep and negotiated tables until her dad let her go, with a peck on the cheek, and Jason came to the stage steps to help her up them. With one hand shaking in his and the other clasping her gown so she wouldn't trip, she smiled nervously and looked down, her heart slamming into her chest. The murmur of approval that rippled through the crowd was audible. Then Jason traced her cheek and made her look up.

"Thank you, baby," he said, which put people on their feet again as his kiss claimed her and made her gently fly away.

The after party was insane. All he wanted to do was collapse at home, alone, with his gorgeous woman in the spaghetti-strap, dark copper gown with the deep, plunging cleavage. But he was jostled, hustled, interviewed, courted, bum-rushed. Business cards slapped his hand when he merely reached for a drink. Deborah was being pulled away by media mavens, who were no doubt asking questions that were making her blush. Yeah, he had to admit that he'd never thought about her father seeing some of the images. He had just been working on fire. But at least he'd put a ring on her finger.

Wil was in heaven as women aggressively sought him, becoming instant groupies once they realized how far back he and Jason went and that they lived in the same house. Jason's father was on a bar stool, telling old stories from the glory days and the civil rights era. Jared was discussing opening contract negotiations and offers for lunch with Jenna. Jackie was hemmed in by a very interested suitor. His nieces and nephews were in music celebrity overload, and Deborah's father stood with Ms. Catherine, both smiling hard and giggling like little kids as they watched it all.

Jason moved through the crowd in search of his fiancée, and his father caught his eye, excusing himself from the group. The two met on the steps leading to the third floor of Toronto on South.

"I just had to say this, son," Christopher Nesbitt said, clasping Jason's arm. Then he pulled him into an embrace. "Your mother is so proud. As am I." He let Jason go and nodded. "When I gave Nana Warren this old house, I was a broken man and had a broken spirit. And you breathed life back into it. Your work is going to the next level, taking this gallery to the next level, with new technology, all of that. Be happy."

"Your coming meant . . . ," Jason said. He couldn't finish. He didn't trust his voice.

"I know." Nesbitt squeezed Jason's arm. "Art is about emotion, right?"

Jason nodded. "Change . . . A lot has changed. A lot of emotion behind that."

"I almost let emotion keep me from coming," Jason's father admitted, holding Jason's gaze. "I didn't know if I could walk down these streets again . . . didn't know how Hastings's children would react, but I got a call from an angel."

Jason knit his brows, not understanding.

"I called one day to cancel and then hung up . . . I was just gonna let it go by, hoping you'd understand," Nes-

bitt said, not looking away, but courageously holding
Jason's hurt gaze. "But an angel called me back. Caught
me on the caller ID and began telling me how hard you
were working, how you'd renovated the house after
coming home from Toronto, and then gave me the play
by play on what happened at that dinner . . . how Wil
saved your mother's oil. I had to see it again, see what
you'd done."

Christopher Nesbitt released a sigh of gratitude.
"You got a helluva woman, mon. She took me through
the house while you were holed up. She wouldn't
break your trance even for me, which I could dig, if
anyone could, and I saw where you hung Janet. Yeah,
art is about emotion," he whispered. "Deborah poured
me a glass of wine in one of Janet's glasses and then
took me up to Wil's so I could go in the attic and sit a
while by myself. Now that's love, Jason . . . when you
want everyone around your partner to be healed, too,
for them, for themselves. The woman is profound."

"But I was in the house. She didn't . . . How long
were you in Philly?" Incredulous, Jason ran his palms
down his face.

"A week early. I needed to go visit all my old ghosts
and haunts so I could stand there for my son,
unashamed of myself." The older man lifted his chin.
"I needed that. Thank you. Go find Deborah. I've
found my old stool, the spot it used to be in when I
was talking my most serious rhetoric." He smiled a sad
half smile. "Come to Toronto soon." He shook his
head as he went back down the steps. "You even
named the place like you did," he called.

Jason watched his father go down the stairs and disappear into the throng, and then he bounded up the
steps before he got waylaid again. He found Deborah
in a small group of reporters.

"Can I steal her?" he asked.

The reporters' attention shifted to him, and Jason

held up his hand. "I'm about to drop, and I need to just kick back for a little while."

"Is it true that you holed up in the studio for weeks, not eating?" one relentless reporter asked.

"Uh-huh," Jason said, staring at Deborah until she blushed.

"Just one more, Jason," another reporter said. "Is this collective an outgrowth of your father's work here in Philly? We heard that this used to be his gallery and that you updated it."

Jason nodded, tracing Deborah's cheek. "Uh-huh."

"How does it feel to have him at your big debut, which was such a success?" asked another reporter.

"Uh-huh," Jason murmured. The reporter gave him a quizzical look.

Deborah smiled. "No further questions."

Epilogue

Deborah bent over the toilet and dry-heaved, and then shoved another mint in her mouth when nothing came up. She ran her hands across the seed pearls at her bodice and blotted her face with a tissue.

"You okay?" Jenna asked, hanging on the outside of the stall, in a midnight blue maid of honor dress, clutching both her bouquet and Deborah's huge spray of white roses. "I don't think I can keep your father out of this ladies' room much longer. The man is ready to go and *insists* that this wedding go off at the top of the hour, as planned."

"I know, I know," Deborah wheezed. "Time is one of his hot buttons. I just need a second to make sure I don't upchuck during the ceremony."

"Whooo, girl, you got it bad!" Jenna teased. "But you are marrying my brother."

Jackie burst into the ladies' room. "The major sent me in. The girls are lined up, and my brother is about to faint at the front of the church. Wil is holding him up by both arms. Please tell me you didn't change your mind?"

Deborah sighed. "No, I'm just—"

"Darryl, *please*. This is a ladies' room in a *church*,"

Ms. Catherine said, rushing around him and trying to push him out of the women's bathroom.

"I'm not going in the john part," Major Jackson fussed. "Everybody decent?"

"Yes, Dad," Deborah called out, trying to stave off another wave of nausea.

"Then lets get a move on. You're already beautiful enough," he said and turned to the women in the room. "Y'all help my baby out of the stall. What's the hold up?"

Deborah staggered out of the stall and pressed a wet compress to her throat, trying to keep from staining her satin, strapless gown, then dabbed her shoulders, wetting her long gloves as water dribbled down her arms.

"That child looks like she's got the flu," her father said, turning to Ms. Catherine. "She's all flushed. Aw, baby . . ."

"Yes, Darryl, the flu, so go stand in your place and don't move till I get her feeling a little better. One of you all go hit the soda machine and bring her a ginger ale," Ms. Catherine ordered, taking charge.

Jackie fled.

Her father stood in the bathroom, with his shoulders slumped. "Guess that sorta negates the possibility of a honeymoon grand slam," he muttered.

"Darryl! What did you say?" Ms. Catherine fussed, clucking her tongue.

"Grandkids. Aw, never mind. They got time," he murmured.

"Man, go stand outside," Ms. Catherine fussed, fixing Deborah's gown and veil.

"That's messed up, girl," Jenna said. "Didn't you get a flu shot, knowing you were getting married?"

"Shoo, Jenna. Let me work on the bride," Ms. Catherine commanded, pointing to the door. "She's a nervous wreck, which isn't helping matters."

Jenna blew Deborah a kiss and then fled the ladies' room. Ms. Catherine smiled as the door shut.

"Jackie's slipping." She hugged Deborah. "How many weeks?"

"Six," Deborah said, sipping air.

"You were scared you wouldn't fit into your dress, weren't you?"

Deborah laughed, and then Ms. Catherine burst out in ringing giggles. Jackie slipped into the bathroom, brandishing ginger ale.

"Here, honey. Drink this. How are you feeling? By this afternoon, you'll be all right," Jackie said, offering the soda with a cup of crushed ice.

"I take it back, Nurse Hastings," Ms. Catherine said.

"Nurse Johnson, you know I'm from Philadelphia, and we don't miss much here."

Both women high-fived each other and then squealed, hugged, and did a little dance.

"I'ma be an auntie," Jackie whispered.

"I'ma be a grandma," Ms. Catherine gushed in a conspiratorial whisper. "Oh, when Darryl finds out, we're gonna have to move to Philadelphia!"

Deborah's eyes got wide. "I haven't said anything to Jason yet. He was bugging me so hard about the wedding, making preparations, and fielding all the interviews and projects. I wanted to surprise him when he could enjoy it. Plus, I just got into Drexel, and I know he'd flip and want me to get an electric cart or something. You know him."

"Oh, chile, drink that ginger ale so we can have us a wedding!" Jackie squeaked, breezing out of the bathroom.

He stood waiting, watching the door, watching the white runner. Then music hit his nervous system and made him swallow hard, put sweat on his palms. Finally, an image that blocked out any other he'd ever had in his head walked toward him . . . seed pearls catching prisms of light, wisps of incandescent veil shimmering over brown satin skin, thick ropes of ebony hair twisted into a regal crown of braids . . . pearl teardrops encrusted with crystals swaying, and gloves gracefully covering sleek arms to her bustline. He almost closed his eyes to paint it in his mind, then felt Wil's firm grip on his shoulder.

But he couldn't even acknowledge the support as he beheld a mouth glistening with a sheer berry wash . . . midnight-blue velvet bridesmaids like the curtains at the gala . . . demanding sketches, life, erotic images playing across the drapes. Then her father left her, and she came to him. *Him.* She was so nervous, her bouquet was bouncing.

The minister said something, and Jason said, "Uh-huh," and everybody laughed.

They left their family and friends partying at Toronto on South, knowing that Wil would be the pied piper who lead the unending party back to their house. But they weren't worried. Jared and Jackie and Jenna would be on point, with the major, Ms. Catherine, and Sir Nesbitt as security detail. The Ritz-Carlton had a sanctuary of privacy awaiting them, a bridal suite; then, in the morning, they'd see Toronto in the spring.

Jason drew his bride against him in the back of the stretch limousine and finally kissed her the way he'd wanted to. "What do you want to do when you get to Toronto?" he murmured against her mouth, wishing that they were already in the bridal suite. "Take the underground PATH; enjoy miles of shopping, or go to the galleries . . . or . . ."

She laughed against his mouth. "Or . . ."

"Yeah, I like that option, too." He kissed her slowly again. "You happy, baby?"

"Yes," she whispered into the next kiss, touching his face.

"You had me worried for a minute . . . thought you might have changed your mind."

"We should have had an afternoon wedding, that's all," she murmured, pulling his bottom lip between her teeth, then releasing it. "Should have booked an afternoon flight, too."

"Uh-huh," he murmured, running his hand the length of her thigh. "What were we thinking?"

"Not about morning sickness," she said, kissing the underside of his chin.

"Uh-huh . . . I know," he said, taking her mouth slowly.

She pulled back. "This just proves you don't listen to me when you get like this."

"What?" he said, his eyelids heavy, as he nuzzled her neck. "I'm listening."

"You heard what I said?" she asked, chuckling.

"Uh-huh, baby."

"You heard me say I couldn't get out of the ladies' room, because I had morning sickness."

"Uh-huh," he whispered, caressing her arms and leaning in for another kiss. Then, as if some gear turned, fell into place, and locked in his mind, he sat back quickly. "Wha . . . whatduyou mean? Now? You know? You're—"

"Six weeks. You were working, and I wanted to be sure not to freak you out in the middle of—"

"Yes! Hot damn! Where's my cell phone?" He hugged her, making her laugh, and then jumped up, bumped his head, and banged on the window divider, laughing even harder. When the driver peered over his shoulder and opened his mouth, Jason barked at him, making the driver laugh. "How you work the limo phone?"

"Jason, who are you calling? Man, you are crazy!" Deborah said.

"I'm calling the major," he said, laughing. "I gotta tell him, 'Grand slam!'"

She snatched the phone, laughing. "You are *not* telling my father *that*. Oh no, you are not!"

Jason reached for the telephone, and she held it away from him.

"Then lemme tell my pop!"

"Not no grand-slam mess," she said, cautiously handing him the phone. She watched him, with a scowl, and then couldn't help smiling wide.

He scrambled far away from her and pressed his shoulder against the divider, laughing.

Caught up in yards of fabric, she couldn't get to Jason fast enough and could only squeal, "No," as he connected with Wil's speaker phone and started making barking noises.

"Put it on speaker, man. Make sure the major, my Pop, and Jared hear. Grand slam, six weeks in. I'ma be a dad!" He threw his head back and laughed at something ribald that Wil had said, something he'd never tell Deborah. "Yeah, custom made in the studio!"

It was a double blessing, something she'd prayed for so hard each and every day: that her daughter be born while her father was still alive, and that she and the baby make it, too.

Jason brushed the damp hair away from her forehead and kissed her gently.

A new lifestyle had prolonged Darryl Lee Jackson's life and spared him the health problems of the past, putting tears of gratitude in his weary eyes. "Can I hold her?" he asked, so quietly that Jason touched his shoulder. "She looks like a little papoose all wrapped up in pink. Hard to believe."

Deborah nodded and handed the small pink bundle to her dad and smiled, pure contentment washing over her, despite her exhaustion.

"Oh, she's *beautiful*," Ms. Catherine crooned as he took the small, fussing bundle and held the child like she would break.

"She's so tiny," Deborah's father whispered. "Look at her. She's gorgeous, just like her mom, and she came out just the same way, with all that hair." He handed the baby back to Deborah quickly, as though afraid to hold her too long.

"I can't wait for Nesbitt to get here and see her," Jason said quietly, mesmerized by the miracle of his wife and child. "I had to force my sisters and brother and all their kids to go down to the lobby to give you a pass. Wil got offended," Jason added, laughing. "I'm not sure if he's speaking to me yet."

"We would have fought," Major Jackson said, chuckling. "Either them or the hospital, but Pop Pop was coming to see his daughter and granddaughter without delay."

"Yes, sir, I told them," Jason said, with a wide smile, stroking Deborah's hair. "I told them all."

"Oh, you're gonna be spoiled rotten, little girl," Ms. Catherine said, touching the baby's silky curls with one finger. "A couple of outrageous Pop Pops and aunties and uncles and cousins . . . You are so blessed, sweetie."

Too emotional to speak, Deborah nodded and smiled and simply reached out to hold Jason's hand, cradling their daughter in the crook of her arm, looking up at him, allowing her shimmering gaze to tell him that he was indeed better than all the rest.